18.75

PETER

OWEN

A PETER OWEN PAPERBACK

Diamond Nebula

By the same author
(published by Peter Owen)

Fiction
Inhabiting Shadows
Isidore (Lautréamont)
When the Whip Comes Down (Marquis de Sade)

Non-fiction
Madness – The Price of Poetry
Lipstick, Sex and Poetry (autobiography)
Delirium: An Interpretation of Arthur Rimbaud

Poetry
Black Sugar:
   Gay, Lesbian and Heterosexual Love Poems

JEREMY REED

Diamond Nebula

a novel

PETER OWEN
London & Chester Springs PA

PETER OWEN PUBLISHERS
73 Kenway Road London SW5 0RE
Peter Owen books are distributed in the USA by
Dufour Editions Inc. Chester Springs PA 19425−0449

First published in Great Britain 1994
© Jeremy Reed 1994

ISBN 0−7206−0891−0

A catalogue record for this book is available from
the British Library

Printed in Great Britain by
Biddles of Guildford & King's Lynn

For Hanna

Blue, blue, electric blue,
that's the colour of my room,
where I will live.

David Bowie, 'Sound and Vision'

It was room number 35 in which I might have
awakened next morning mad or a whore.

Anaïs Nin, *House of Incest*

Preface

In certain kinds of fiction the external world provides a backdrop to the exploration of inner space, a vanishing-point rather than a structure for continuous reference. The poetry and fiction I like best are those that take me to places which exist on no map other than the geography of the unconscious. I want to be surprised by unfamiliarity, and the power of the imagination to create new worlds.

This novel is about mutation on psychic and physical levels. My three subjects are the obsessive preoccupation of a film director, who, together with a number of other survivors, has lived through a change-over that has transformed both the landscape and the sensory data through which they experience the world. And if David Bowie, conceived through the imagination, uses a thought processor by which to communicate, then Warhol exists on a different dimension, and Ballard as the chief proponent of the futuristic novel is seen as the person most receptive to occupying a colony that looks towards the arrival of mutants from the galaxy.

I have drawn on the factual, in terms of biography, to serve as a connecting thread between the real and the imagined. The work is a fiction.

Jeremy Reed

Chapter 1

It was neither night nor day. Zap lay back on an area of sand that had once formed a tidal beach, looking up at the violet sky. The landscape was deserted. The few beach-huts and the white, rectilinear building of the old Grand Hotel with its mock Regency façade were all that survived of a resort that had come to resemble a stage-set. The idea of the sea was a blue mirage. It had receded so far that he would have to cross a savannah to reach it, a plain littered with the anfractuous reefs and angular boulders that had once formed part of the sea-bed. Now it was a coral forest – a stone terrain waiting for a tide that would never reclaim it.

The sky too had altered. Its receding curve was visible now as a mauve polygon framed to fit the horizon. To Zap it resembled a series of props which had been incorporated into an imaginary landscape. He might have expected the camera crew to be elsewhere, busy inside the hotel's vacuous interior, a blonde girl naked except for a spotted face-net, lying face down on a divan, while the camera angled in on a cobra draping its folds around her legs.

So far he had met four of the people who had come to adopt this region as an improvised home. Johnny, who had been a singer in the old blacked-out Zero Club and who still wore his tight leather clothes, was adjusting from a drug habit. His slow, deliberate movements recollected the contortionist's gestures he had adopted on-stage. After the switch in which most of the landscape had disappeared he had raided a pharmacy and hoarded a supply of heroin. In time he had come to eject smack out of his body and to believe that the mauve light really did have transformative chemical properties.

And there was Cindy, a make-up artist who had drafted an initial biography of Warhol in a language so minimal it implied semiotics. She knew something the others didn't. The change was still in her nerve cells; you could see it in the way her thought turned inward at a tangent that precluded inquiry. She kept her secret and lived with it like a viral strain distinguishing her from the others. Cindy gave the impression that she had been dropped on the floor of a deep lake and was still reading surprise into her altered state of consciousness. Dressed in a gold microskirt and a red T-shirt inscribed with a logo proclaiming the twenty-third century, she cut an incongruous figure picking her way through the black laval stones lodged in the sand.

And there were the couple. The transvestite and the transsexual who had married under a red sky in a fisherman's chapel on the night previous to the change-over. Arc's clothes had been augmented by the discovery of a stage wardrobe at the hotel. They had probably belonged to a visiting pop star who had disappeared. Marilyn's silicone boost and the expertise of surgery had created with minor exceptions a flawless woman. After the initial shock, they had welcomed the desert in order to be alone with their revised vision of the world. They had established themselves in rooms at the Grand Hotel, and had soon succeeded in creating their own personalized studio and film unit.

Zap came out alone every day and tried to adjust. At first

he had translated the new into the old, and in place of the violet sky had seen a familiar blue crossed by fighter jets, and in place of the stone desert a sea pushing its measured surf inshore. For a long time his mind had gone on projecting what his visual memory imposed. He had grown so accustomed to the preconceived image that he continued to hallucinate it. And the real established itself only when knowledge of the old world had bleached out like a sepia photograph in which the scene depicted is no longer visible. It had been reduced to a pentimento that showed through only in blinding flashbacks. And finally as an implant in memory.

And with his acclimatization to the new, Zap had come to experience an awareness of loss. His visual imagination had set about retrieving his lost paintings. His life had been one of devotion to his art. His studio with its north-facing, floor-to-ceiling window-panel had been stacked with his predominantly blue canvases. He remembered his last months there and how the intensity of his creative drive had led him to identify so closely with his creations that he had taken to lashing his face and body with blue, yellow and red brush-strokes. He had painted naked in a shamanistic frenzy, re-laying colour to his body as a means of identifying with his medium. His cobalt lips and the random vertical and horizontal slashes applied to his legs and torso had resulted in a weird diagrammatic body-map.

At the time he had been obsessed with painting a series called *Planet Relays*. He had conceived the idea of a cinema screen sunk into the sky-face. Across this surface the events of the future showed. And by the use of stereoscopic photography he had discovered a means of identifying a 3D model of the Côte d'Azure with a fractal crater on Mars. The image of a crystal that had preoccupied as the luminous centre to his vision had been projected on the screen as a near planet. He had called the painting *Jumping Dimensions*. Windowed into the planetary crystal were car-parks, glass high-rise buildings and a mutant species. A man with gold skin, articulated breasts and leather suspenders that supported fishnet stockings vanishing into thigh-boots was seen confronting a woman whose silver miniskirt corresponded to the colour of her skin. Her star-shaped hand fitted round his erect gold penis which emitted a trail of nebulae. Zap used his time, lying on the beach, to recompose his lost works. One by one they returned to him, and stood around the walls of the imaginary gallery he had constructed in his mind. In time he would re-create the work of a decade. The approximate and the variable would disappear, leaving in their place the concrete, the particularized creation as he had painted it.

There had been so much to take in. The horizon appeared to be squared like one side of a rectangle, and Zap believed that if he walked out far enough he would find a tangible end to the world. He would run up square against a mauve partition in the way that fish nosed against an aquarium wall. And once there he might find himself magnified so hugely that he became a universal shadow, a man contesting his weight against final boundaries.

Zap's vertical vision searched out what he took to be a hole in the sky. He looked for it as a jeweller might a flaw in a diamond. Illusory or real it preoccupied him as an obsessive punctum.

Zap knew if he sat up and looked around he would find Cindy crouched down about a hundred metres to the left of him. She would be hunched into herself, drawing figures in the sand which she would later meticulously erase. Zap assumed that she had developed this habit to compensate for the internalized crisis about which she never spoke. She sat with her legs arched, long legs with delineated curves, and if she got up it was to walk down to what she remembered as the former tideline.

So far the five of them had avoided discussing the issue of abandoning their present location and going off in search of the eventual sea. Distances were impossible to calculate. What frightened Zap was the possibility that his vision of the world could be at variance with that of the others. What if each of them were projecting self-generated universes; square mauve, oval red, triangular blue? The possibilities were inexhaustible.

Johnny spent most of the time going into the old town that stretched behind the deserted waterfront and its hotels, returning with hi-fi equipment and cartons of records and CDs that he appeared to be hearing for the first time, rather than recollecting.

Zap had woken from a trance one night to hear Bowie's histrionic voice issuing across the sands. Right out in the middle of the magenta desert he had heard the androgynous singer theatrically declaim

'Motor sensational
Paris or maybe hell, I'm waiting
Clutches of sad remains
Waits for Aladdin Sane, you'll make it'

relayed through speakers with the urgency of an urban apocalypse.

Flashbacks, hallucinated reminders, everything required a delayed connection. Zap still wasn't sure whether he should be attempting to reorder the past or live in the immediate with a mind to the future. It was Cindy with whom he felt a genuine empathy. He knew that if he could persuade her to talk of what she had seen and known, some sort of realization might be achieved. As for Marilyn and Arc, they were outsiders intent on creating a new species. Marilyn spoke only of wanting to conceive a transsexual child, one who would be born with inherited rather than acquired genes. In that way the parental autonomy she had established in becoming her own creation would be repeated in the child.

The two of them had already succeeded in establishing a sense of territorial possession. Their hotel suites pointed to how they had begun again to establish an association between things and security. Arc had looted the downtown stores. He was to be seen in sheer dancer's tights, vinyl halters and red high heels. Marilyn's tight silk skirts and overcompensatory make-up seemed directed towards an inner need as much as her partner's sexual orientation. Zap felt cut off from them, disconnected by the estrangement of the world in which he found himself. And now in visiting them under a mauve sky in which the light was uniformly consistent, Zap experienced a pervasive sense of paranoia. He was struck by how little he knew of what was expected from him in such radically altered circumstances. He had still to formulate a code of behaviour that brought his past into alignment with the present.

The couple's existence served only to magnify Zap's sense of isolation. Arc had come to this resort with a video team to film an incomplete script left by Luis Buñuel. When the old surrealist had gone south in search of rejuvenation, there were rumours that he had taken with him a proposed film of David Bowie reconstructed from footage of the early Ziggy concerts. Arc and his colleagues had set about restructuring the apocryphal film which had come to them through equally ambiguous sources. Marilyn had been part of the make-up team, and the two had found a unifying bond in their emphasis on gender mutation.

As Zap walked over the sands towards the Grand Hotel, he tried to remember the last time he had known this beach before the change. He had come here regularly in the intervals between painting. The sea had been a mirror in which to test his moods. Was it the day when he had picked up cuttlefish from the shore and incorporated them into an imaginary portrait of the poet Eugenio Montale – *Ossi di Seppia*? The chalk strokes made to resemble cuttlefish were angular, rugged, like the images thrown up by the poet's tidal rhythm. He remembered the day for the lunch he had had with his agent and the demure Japanese prostitute he had visited in the late afternoon. He had counted the steps on the way up to her room and on the way down. The sunlight was trapped in the landing window.

He felt reassured by the sequence he had pieced together, as though he had chipped a tiny fragment from the cubic block he had come to associate with amnesia. Other images were returning. The first came as a row of double buttons and moved upwards to a blank face. And then it was Xenia he was recollecting. It was she who had been an integral part of his life. The black streamers of her Latin curls; her face smiling up through cigarette smoke at a café on the Lido: and yet dispossessed of her he experienced no real sense of loss, only a renewed feeling of estrangement, as though he had stared at a painting too long and thought himself into the imaginary landscape.

When Zap reached the Grand Hotel he looked back over the beach. He was convinced he heard music, that pure music engendered by geometric abstraction.

Marilyn was on her hands and knees searching for rhinestones that had spilt from her necklace. Arc was following her around the room, rubbing his erect penis against her black silk panties visible beneath a rucked-up black skirt. When Zap entered, they tumbled together laughing, knocking over an open wine bottle. Neither expressed any embarrassment at Zap's presence. They were too unified for that. They had the others stand on the edge of the desert and look in.

What disquieted Zap was the evident power that the couple manifested. They didn't need him. They appeared to occupy their own immediate space so fully that they short-circuited anything that didn't belong to their shared perception of the world.

'Scrunch those balls, lover,' Marilyn drawled, pushing her lipsticked mouth to an exaggerated pout. Drink had made her dangerously lucid. Zap had the feeling that her eyes were inside his head. 'We're just kitten-smooching,' she continued. 'Drag-tagging through the martini hour.'

Zap sat down near the window and looked out on the beach. He could see Cindy still sitting there tracing cryptograms in the sand. Johnny was watching her from a vantage-point that she couldn't see. He had adopted the mean pose of a singer on-stage, one hand projected from his left hip, the other offered palm out to an imaginary audience.

'Do you wanna come clubbing with us tonight, Zap?' Arc said in a quasi-derisive sneer.

Zap let the question ride, and pulled nervously at one of the wine bottles that stood open on a lacquered art-deco table. For a moment he thought he heard the low-flying reconnaissance of a helicopter; but there was nothing. There couldn't be anything, he reasoned, not within the radius of the bay. There was a large blow-up print of David Bowie on-stage with the Spiders from Mars on the wall facing Zap. The singer was dressed as a bisexual android, his blown-back, poppy-red hair offsetting a blue glitter leotard.

Zap sleep-walked his way back into the picture. Marilyn and Arc were watching a video. A helicopter circled parallel blocks of white skyscrapers. It went down so close to a landing-deck that the couple standing in a roof garden were blasted by its tornadoing fan. Her blonde hair and floating skirt stood up vertical. The man could be seen raising a machine pistol, his mouth stretched to the ovoid of Munch's *Scream*, before the camera shifted and the helicopter lost altitude, dipping down into the canyon. A speeded-up film showed the interior of twenty or thirty apartments; a face looking out from each in an elongated strip, so that eyes and mouths synchronized in a blinding flash. When the helicopter stood off immobile, the scene opened up to disclose a man standing central to a leather room. His ghost-writer sat naked in an emerald floor-pool. The man was rehearsing a speech, and in a sort of *mise-en-abîme* effect he kept diminishing inside himself like a Russian doll, so that when the co-pilot's round blasted through his skull it was the tiny figure of a child with an adult's head who crashed backwards into the green pool. As he did so he was buried by flags representing all the nations of the world.

Marilyn and Arc were fondling each other as the film shifted to a montage of Spanish Civil War excerpts superimposed on New York street scenes. Lorca was seen riding through Manhattan in an open car, his white, blood-stained suit saluted by the crowds simultaneous with David Bowie's coming on-stage as the Thin White Duke in Madison Square Garden in 1976. The helicopter was still circling the roof-tops, depositing streamers of red and white carnations raining on to glossy car-tops.

Automatically Zap found himself connecting the dissociated images with their possible inclusion in his art. Through the window he could see Cindy sitting with her head hanging between her knees. When his focus intersected with the screen again, it was to realize that it was Xenia's face who was addressing him from a silent black and white film. Her face searched the screen with the passive containment of a silent victim.

'Can't you see she wants you?' said Arc, turning on Zap with peremptory malice.

'This is your film, honeybunch, the one we've been waiting to show you,' said Marilyn, disengaging herself from Arc, and making dumb eyes through cobalt mascara.

Zap watched the film-frames isolate interiors which had once formed the privacy of his home. Each arrived simultaneous with his instant recall. The studio he had been at such pains to memorize, its clutter of brushes and tubes as pronounced as Henri Michaux's work desk in Brassai's celebrated photograph. The bathroom with its Yves Klein prints, the bedroom with a pair of Xenia's black stockings floating provocatively over a white chair, the open-plan ground floor in which his sculptures depicting the stages of an erotic-visionary journey were still incomplete; he was shown these things in the manner of exhibits, the still-life evidence assembled for a trial.

He was compelled to watch in order to retrieve his memory. He saw the streets around his house which he had come to know by long familiarity. The white houses walled in by protective gardens. Chestnut and plane trees screened their tall, narrow façades.

The camera angled into an alley which joined two parallel streets. Zap had been there. He recognized the Virginia creeper arrowing a brick wall, and the graffiti hieroglyphed across back doors – a vocabulary translating a Klee painting into fragmented Sanskrit. Xenia was standing up against a wall. She appeared to be laughing. She was wearing nothing but a halter top and black suspenders and stockings. A man crouching from behind so as to be hidden by her body had placed his hands over her breasts. By a synchronized rhythm

Zap could see that the man was making love to her from behind, lifting her by the urgency of his strokes. The camera isolated the ecstatic geometry of facial planes depicting orgasm.

The fractional fade-out presented a blank wall. It was a wash of blood; Zap could see that from the detonative impacting splashes. Someone had been shot there. He could hear a woman running before the camera picked up on her discarded high-heel shoes. Then the screen went dead; blank as a snowfield turning blue under moonlight.

Chapter 2

Zap got back to the beach, needing the quiet in which to piece together the fragments of a shattered mosaic. Cindy was still crouched down on the sand, head arched like a swan. He supposed she had fallen asleep in that position. Johnny had disappeared. He would be sleeping somewhere in the town which Zap was reluctant to visit. He felt separated by a screen from the events that had shaped his present. Was it a psychopath or a deviant film-maker who had orchestrated the sequential shots surrounding Xenia's escape and the implied death of her anonymous lover? The film had faded out to the sound of Bowie singing 'Scary Monsters Super Creeps': the vocals strung out across dissonance.

Zap replayed the film in his mind. His memory cells were coming alive again after their prolonged dormancy. It was like the crackle of a bee each time a cell was alerted. On the day before he, Cindy and Johnny had experienced what in time they had come to recognize as the change-over, he had come down from long hours of absorption in his studio to find a brief note from Xenia saying that she was out with a friend on a prospective film project. Zap remembered how he had felt disquieted by her clandestine assignation. Xenia had featured in several advertising videos for lingerie, her long, sheer-stockinged legs frictionalizing silk as she sat on a white chair adjusting a suspender strap. But these were minimal virtuoso pieces that had terminated when a new model had been employed to maintain interest in the firm's escalating sales. She had mentioned nothing of her intended plans; and he, had he been too solipsistically absorbed in his work? There had been weeks when he had hardly spoken. In his obsession to find a new juxtaposed relationship between objects in the mesocosm, he had felt himself testing the frontiers of perception. Strange, tense days in which he had burnt up nerve. And as though to precipitate the crisis that would have occurred, Zap had accelerated it by swallowing two tabs of acid.

He had found himself orientating towards a purple sun that stood at the end of the desert road on which he was marooned. On either side of him black snakes with red pyramids mounted on their backs pushed forward towards this huge concentric sun. In comparison he was immobilized, and at the same time aware of a threatening pressure building behind him. He was terrified and wanted to get up and run but remained belly down on the road. It was at this point that a man had stepped out of the sun and placed a red pyramid on his back. With the acquisition of this gift came instant mobility. He joined the black snakes in their convergent arrowhead, while a whirlwind of vultures whistled overhead.

During the weeks of isolation, his painting had grown more frenetic as he realized that three-dimensional space is a preconceived and not immediate experience. He had grown to question the input from our eyes and skin and the whole question of real space as it is written into the nerves. What he had been searching for was access to the non-geometric dimensions of consciousness, its observables existing in an unquantifiable location.

When the creative process had proved intolerable he had

walked to the Zero Club and blanked out on live music. It was there that he had first seen Johnny, a single red spotlight focused on his mean, posturing body, his naked torso covered with a slashed leather jacket. A spiky red-haired guitarist, a cigarette angled from his mouth, followed the vocalist around on-stage. The bass-player was catatonic, ramrod stiff. Johnny went down low on a syringe with a crucifix for a plunger, stood upright into the stage, and prayed. Feedback screamed over his intoned lyrics:

> 'And when you drive me insane
> I drink the golden rain
> That falls from a statue's eyes
> And when you twist your knife
> I resurrect my life
> I'm atomized inside my brain.'

The guitarist described a circle around Johnny's convulsive body and pointedly stubbed out a cigarette on his arm before retrieving the song's maniacal leitmotiv.

Zap had stood mesmerized in the tightly packed cellar. The club's polysexual atmosphere, its mutants delighting in obscuring gender, had fired him with a new response to sexuality. He wanted to be initiated into sensory experience in the same manner as he had explored an inner world that existed independent of physical space. The sensory too had its unlocatable map – its ecstatic regions that were often the result of surprise. A threesome or the unexpected discovery of unzipping a girl's jeans to find an erect penis throbbing on release from constriction.

It was there too that he had seen the first of the cut-up graffiti proclaiming David Bowie as the prototype of a new species. The cryptograms were signed *Major Tom*, as though the fictional protagonist of 'Space Oddity' had turned up on earth after all the years of being lost in space. Zap half expected to discover the astronaut, still impaired by partial amnesia, drinking up against the bar.

Cindy remained sitting on the beach. She must have fallen

asleep there. Zap headed towards her. He would take her back to the shelter of the beach-hut in which he lived. It was adequately furnished, and it was with a deep sense of relief that he was able to draw curtains on the unremitting violet light. Only then could he find the dark he associated with self-containment.

He walked across to Cindy and lifted her. She was light like a bird, a figure of increasingly anorexic proportions. He took her into his cabin and wondered where her mind was now. Was she dreaming forwards or backwards, anticipating a world or recollecting one that had vanished?

Despite the drawn curtains, light filtered into the room. Zap recorded this as an expansion of consciousness. Now that his memory cells were coming alive, and establishing a tenuous bridge between the past and present, he could realize the light emitted by relative thought.

He sat, knees drawn up on the floor, and watched Cindy turn over in her sleep. Instinctively she lifted the blanket over her body. Zap knew the colour of her dreams: they would be violet like the sky.

With renewed powers of concentration Zap examined the books that had been left in the converted hut. They were nearly all novels by J.G. Ballard, whose hallucinated imagery anticipated a continuous future. One that was contemporaneous with the ballistics of inner space. Zap turned up *Crash* and recalled the incredible acid implosion that came at the book's climax. There would come a time, he realized, when hallucination and reality intersected. When Ballard's protagonist, Vaughan, would drive a battered Cadillac decorated with rhinestones across this beach.

He prepared himself for the false night. Usually he sat up in a chair, periodically lapsing into disturbed pockets of sleep. It was then that he would hear the evocative loneliness of Bowie's 'A New Career in a New Town' come searching across the beach spaces. It was like an elegy to a deleted species. He hadn't accustomed himself to a world that dispensed with the cycle of day and night. His paranoia told him that Cindy had, or that she inhabited her own imaginary state; one that had no correspondence with his own.

Zap was too restless to sit still and allow his mind to range over the desert. His impulse, building as he hooked on the idea, was to go into the town and rediscover those fragments of his past that had survived the change. He felt compelled to search for the house and street in which he had lived and to relocate the alley which had been frozen into his consciousness by the video exposures. Could he walk there or was it a planetary journey from the beach to the town?

When he set out he could hear laughter ringing from an open window in the Grand Hotel. Marilyn and Arc would remain haloed by a drug-blaze until they sped into a blank wall of consciousness. A mannequin with a white Warhol wig stood guard on their balcony.

Zap kept thinking that there must be others. Five seemed too small a number to have survived. His fear was that he might encounter other groups established within territorial zones in the town. As he came up off the sands, glass shards scrunched beneath his boots. He must have been unconscious at the time the explosion occurred, locked into his dimension.

Zap found himself marginally off-balance. He felt uncoordinated, jet-lagged without having flown. The road was dusted with sand; coarse marram grass grew in the gutters. At some stage he encountered a child's toy missile nose-down in a sand-drift. Its silver casing gave no clue as to its identity. For no reason at all Zap found himself thinking of Major Tom. Was there a link between Bowie's mythic astronaut and this scale-reduced pointer to his dead orbit? He found himself studying its streamlined proportions before releasing it into the open doorway of a department store.

And how in Arc's theory had the ageing Buñuel gone to the Ziggy concerts unobserved? In a crowd of young, mutant clones, he would have appeared conspicuous and misplaced. Zap let the drift of thought overtake him. What would Buñuel have found, other than what was presented at Radio City, that giant auditorium filled with Walter Carlos's recorded cybernetic music from *Clockwork Orange*, as Bowie dressed in a zoot suit was lowered on to the stage from a

23

concentrically shaped model planet? Was there something connected with these performances or Bowie's futuristic *Zeitgeist* that had eluded the audiences intent on rock animation?

Zap stared at a roofless boutique. Thistles invaded a truncated mannequin wearing a black suspender belt. He was becoming more attentive to his surroundings. On either side of him, the buildings were staggered, lopsided, the gradient running from left to right as though a part was attempting to detach itself from the whole. Every ten metres his foot turned up one of the missiles that lay half concealed by sand. And in order to convince himself that he wasn't hallucinating, he ran his finger over the block capitaled blue paint on a wall: MAJOR TOM HAS FINALLY TOUCHED DOWN.

Zap felt overexposed, as though each of his actions was being recorded by a video lens. His movements were unconsciously timed, deliberate and seemed to be accompanied by an audio-hum. Great shocks of nettles clumped against the house walls. Their viridian arrowheads seemed electric in the tense air. Giant thistles had cracked open into mauve craters. And there were sunflowers, their yellow heads inclining by heliocentric impulse towards a hidden sun.

He moved on with the stiff gestures of a somnambulist, occasionally stopping to turn round and review the backdrop. He knew he was being followed. A flurry of small pebbles loosening informed on his pursuer. Or was it only the light vibrating in its atomistic dance? When Zap looked back from the High Street, the shore seemed to have receded. It was like the land-mass had gone off to join another, and the Grand Hotel was perceptible only as a retinal blur on the horizon.

Zap listened to the dialogues established by his unconscious. The silence was unnerving. No wind and no punctuation by the elements. It felt as though he were making the first tentative exploration into a country created by the mind. He kept to the one street, afraid he might lose contact with the beach. He was obsessed with the need to refind the alley in which a murder had taken place. And was Xenia somewhere in the town – a blood-stained revenant in hiding from a killer? From somewhere he could hear the persistent minimal chords of a guitar build to an amplified stridency. It was Johnny's voice that cut in above the volume. Zap listened to the anarchic, elliptical words dilate to a lacerating urgency. He traced the noise to a complex of buildings grouped in a former shopping precinct. These had survived intact with only minor wall fissures. Again there was the incongruous massing of giant sunflowers. They were everywhere; periscoping from cracks in the parking-lot, big yellow rag-doll faces inclined towards the sky.

Relocating his memory diagram, Zap realized that it was here in the Peppermint Suite that Johnny had first attained a cult following. He must have returned to the place and, finding it still standing, taken up residence there. The scrambled guitar-break and attempt to retune told Zap that it was Johnny he was hearing and not a record.

Zap picked his way through the exuberant nettles washing the rectangle, and looked in at the shop displays that had so incongruously survived the change-over. The shop models were robotic simulations of Bowie's face awaiting the hour to come alive. In one window he could see bleached-out bookjackets with indecipherable titles; anonymous rectangles, they faced the analphabetic future as remains of an outmoded system of communication.

Zap stood and listened at the entrance to the cellar. A needling red strobe-light fragmented on the bottom step and repeated itself with blinding monotony. He realized he had been so long alone that he needed to encounter someone, anyone; a simulacrum or a drugged vocalist winding himself like a vine around the microphone.

In the past Zap had used this place as an alternative to the Zero Club. He had stood behind the seething crush and emptied his mind. And at other times he had gone back to his studio and painted under the impulse of an inspired delirium. Bowie tracks like 'Jean Genie', 'Cracked Actor' and 'Fashion' had crashed across the dance area, and remained as an invigorating stimulus to his art.

From where Zap crouched at the bottom of the stair, he could see Johnny kneeling on-stage, acting out his number to

25

an imaginary audience. He had monitored the stage-lights and red, white and purple streamers whiplashed his leather body. The guitar was stood upright between his legs; the chords viciously snarling in response to a primitive sexual urgency.

Zap stood with his back flat to the wall, conscious of this act of intrusive voyeurism. He would be found out when the tension broke and Johnny's convulsive circular movement involved him in its arc. He stood waiting for the protective half-circle to break on an eye-beam. Johnny was dragging his knees round the pivotal guitar. He was intoning without chords. A mantra to the purple god.

Johnny must have made this place his own. Zap looked at the costume models that Johnny had placed in the audience. One wore a Nazi leather-peaked cap; the other was dressed in a shoulder-length, black-ringleted wig. Male and female, their arms were linked in a weird symbiosis. One side of the stage was screened by mirrors on which someone had postered facial shots of Jim Morrison, Jimi Hendrix and the novelist William S. Burroughs, amongst a montage of futurist sculpture.

The blank was filling in for Zap with faces, names, the decades through which he had lived. The world of obsessive modern image, artists, film stars, pop stars, all hyped under the same persuasively subliminal logos, the rush of information scattered across the nerves. He was shocked into a state of recall, uncertain still whether a century may not have passed in the time that he had been mentally away.

Zap was forced into breaking the circle. He moved in on Johnny, fixated, wanting to shout out that he knew, knew everything. He saw the singer's eyes unfilm from trance. Johnny was a figure suddenly receding, lashing out the left and right while he retained hold of the hand-mike. He was a priest liturgically imprecating, insane with panic. Zap could sense the drug overload wiring the singer's chemistry to mania.

When Johnny dropped the mike it spat voltage. He was leading Zap backstage, shouting, 'Meet the leaders of the new species, the ones who have given birth to us.'

Backstage, the mirrors were confettied with photographs of the stars with whom Johnny empathized. Zap recognized

Arc's obsessions in the pictures of Warhol outside the Factory, snow-haired, soft-focused, and blow-ups of him being carried into an ambulance after having been shot by Valerie Solanas. There were photographs of the youthful Mick Jagger, electrifying balletics launching him into the air, his leotard studded with rhinestones. Zap recognized Madonna's bee-stung pout, her scarlet lips signposting the way to erotic fantasy.

Johnny crashed into a chair, jolting a chaotic glitter of tequila bottles. His eyes were two black storms.

'You're with the stars,' he shrieked. 'Get out of here, you don't belong in this place.'

Zap was backing away, burnt by the singer's mania. He found himself retreating to the wired stage. Johnny's obsessions were superimposed on Arc's obsessively repeated triumvirate. Zap tried to connect with the idea of Bowie still enthralling stadiums, of Warhol relaying his endless self-taped conversations through a simulacrum at a New York party, the glitterati forgetting that he had died, and straining towards his casual, aphoristic delivery. And from the excessive evidence of photographs in Arc's suite at the Grand Hotel, Zap recognized Ballard's features. Arc had spoken of how the novelist would be forever navigating new frontiers, pushing the novel further towards interplanetary reception, and how he alone would transmit fiction to the near planets. Johnny had aerosoled graffiti cryptograms across mirrors and walls. A photograph of Keith Richards was juxtaposed against the image of a city burning. Apocalyptic statements were everywhere in Johnny's stage-set and dressing-room.

Zap got out. He could hear Johnny shrieking backstage, a tone half-way between demented prayer and delirium. He imagined the singer returning to the stage, his drugged monomania unleashed to silent appraisal.

He got back to the complex and heard the music taken up again. The reverberations demanded urban immanence. Johnny was creating thunder, his lyric imprecations lost to the manic primitivism of his guitar frenzy.

As Zap picked his way through the street, he felt compelled to go in search of others who may have been hiding in the town. He recognized the town centre, its courtyards, alley mazes, zigzag mosaics leading to geometric deformations, honeycombed infrastructures existing as illusory storeys in air. There was a fire-escape supported by nothing – just a rusty vine declining to fall from a vanished hotel wing.

Zap stumbled across a series of circular, white café tables placed amongst a litter of chairs. On one of them a pair of red-framed sun-glasses was mounted on top of a copy of Ballard's *The Atrocity Exhibition*. Opposite this exhibit, as though positioned in a surreal montage, was a suicide note weighted by two pebbles. In purple ink someone had written: I LIVED FOR YOU. IN DEATH I WILL CLAIM YOU.

Zap recognized the scarlet Dior frames as Xenia's, so too the paperback book that had once occupied a place on her bookshelves. In his mind he was trying to piece together a plausibly cohesive narrative. Had the man featured in the video shot himself as a post-climactic expression to orgasm? Zap was only too knowledgeable of Xenia's bizarre sexual exhibitionism. She had sprung sex on Zap in public places; on beaches in the middle of the afternoon, in parks, public gardens, leading with such provocative initiative that he could not refuse her insatiable demands.

Sex in an alley leading to the house in which Zap had most probably been painting, would have been characteristic of Xenia at her most perverse. But Zap found himself aspiring to no emotion for her; neither that of jealousy nor hurt at her behavioural confusion. What returned to him were visual memories. Xenia ostentatiously slipping from her skirt on a crowded beach, revealing not a bikini bottom but transparent panties.

Much more of the town had survived in this quarter. Posters advertising *The Man Who Fell to Earth* had peeled off a stucco wall. Sunflowers had grown up over Bowie's poppy-red, hennaed hair. Zap walked across the turquoise tiles of what must have been a private swimming-pool, and on a white wall that formed a T shape with a blue right-angled support, the other two walls having gone missing, he came across more Bowie posters. White shirt, black waistcoat, a thirties' cabaret artist with gelled hair and blacked-out eyes, his mouth was open on silence.

On the same wall someone had made a photomontage of Bowie, Ballard and Warhol driving in an open car. A black cross had been painted over Warhol's face. Behind them on the New York skyline a mounted camera was left running to record an airliner's imminent collision with the Empire State Building.

Zap couldn't figure out how long he had been alone, only that he was beginning to establish a relationship with a double. A figure, composed of light, a molecular form, moved to right and left of his focus. It was how he imagined himself: a luminous sketch broken up into the dimensional planes of a diver's body.

Zap was moving forward with a purpose now, as though the film in which he was acting had been speeded up. Debris littered a side-street. Blow-ups of Warhol's mid-eighties' self-portraits were splashed in hectic yellows, violets and pinks across an entire house-front. Zap struggled with this recurring, obsessive culture, and hoped by confronting it to discover topological connections with his past. Written up on a wall of the same postered house, was Warhol's desire to become an automaton: *The reason I'm painting this way is because I want to be a machine. Whatever I do, and do machine-like, is because it is what I want to do. I think it would be terrific if everybody was alike.*

Zap found himself meeting an echo that fitted his mouth and knew that he had been calling Xenia's name. She was somewhere in this maze. He could smell her presence. She was apprehensible if only he stepped out of his dimension and met up with her in her time. He was beginning to run, to step up his pace in panic. In front of him an empty delicatessen remained shadowy like a wall aquarium. It was untouched; an exhibit frozen in a time-still.

Zap went where the impulse decided; a way in here, a way out there. He visited houses and shops with the inquisitiveness of someone returning to a reality they and everyone else had forgotten. A black silk stocking lay like a transpicuous snake bunched into folds over three sunflower heads. He thought of Xenia. Stockings were a mark of her seductive femininity. He balanced its weightlessness on a finger and placed the stocking in his pocket. Zap's sense of caution increased as he sniffed out the place. There was a volatile ruck of sunflowers screening the entrance to a narrow passage. The staged theatricals were disarming. It was the novel again: Ballard's *The Atrocity Exhibition*. Someone had pasted a shop-front with dust-jackets, the blood-red lettering showing above a reproduction of Dali's *City of Drawers* in which a deformed, bicephalic creature, raised slightly off the ground, struggled against an inhibiting inertia. A second black stocking had been thumbtacked on to a poster of Warhol's *Monroe*.

Zap brushed through the sunflowers and found himself in an alley that opened out at a right angle to the left. He had been here so often before that he looked for the arabesques of graffiti. Beer cans glinted against the walls. He kept turning round thinking he was being followed. Marilyn and Arc and their weird grafting of sex on to mania moved around in his head as fluid threat. He was certain they were watching him now on the same screen as he had seen Xenia straining towards an orgasmic crescendo.

Zap dropped down to one knee. He found himself cradling a pair of snakeskin stilettos in his hands. He had known these before and had mapped out the erogenous zones in the stockinged feet that had slipped into and out of them. He was already taking them for Xenia's.

He stayed down, only half connecting with the sequence of events that had brought him here. He found himself staring straight ahead at the words *Major Tom*. And was it a trick of the light, a flashback perhaps to the Bowie video for 'Ashes to Ashes' or a jump in consciousness had him conceive of the man as standing in a doorway, dark glasses shading his eyes, a flying jacket draped over a silver space-suit? The man was looking at him through brain-fade. Two survivors of amnesic journeys through inner space, each was searching for a clue to identity in the other. It was a pilgrimage now to go on to his house if it still existed. Zap moved quickly. He could hear someone rapidly making a get-away down a side-street. He stifled his instinct to shout out, Major Tom.

Chapter 3

When Cindy woke in the beach-hut her mind tilted with expectancy and then froze. It was the same purple day outside, only she could feel something was going to happen. The presentiment was in her like a sun obscured by a cloud ruck. She was recalling colour: a red sun, green sea.

She could hear the music again. It was carrying across from giant speakers placed near an open window on the top floor of the Grand Hotel. Cindy recognized the music as Bowie's 'Ashes to Ashes', the song in which Major Tom is resurrected from his burn-out in 'Space Oddity', and is revived as an astronaut high on his own altered chemistry.

She remembered Zap bringing her back here. She experienced the present like floating in a dream. There was no gravity, so you couldn't drop over the cliff-edge, only experience the idea of doing so. And it had been like that for her when the change-over occurred. She had entered it partially and then been thrown back by the wave. And in turn she had resisted remembering what she knew.

Cindy stood at the window in a gold leotard. She expected to find Zap sitting contemplatively on the near shore, but he was nowhere to be seen. She hurried into her clothes and ran out on the beach in black leggings and a scarlet top. Zap's footprints were everywhere. They formed an equivocatory graph – a diversely converging arrowhead. Cindy looked for a direction but there was only a conflicting maze. She feared that Zap would be sucked to the centre of events. And Johnny? He would orchestrate an electronic death-trap.

Cindy sat down with her head between her knees and let the flashbacks arrive. She had been coming to the beach on the day it happened. It had been oppressive; a molten white furnace of thunder-heat. She had been doing research on her Warhol book; taking notes on his satirically disarming reductionism.

Half-way to the beach and within sight of the indigo horizon she had experienced the sensation of thinking she had too much light in her head. It was like the dazzle preceding migraine. She couldn't account for the state. The magnitude had increased. Cindy thought she was going to black out, but she had already got through that stage. She had heard people running back from the shore. And as they fled, so they dematerialized. She was looking at a stream of men who were blown into light.

Cindy remembered how the buildings had started to shift and variegate: some were tilting at a gradient as though dislodged by a seismic flaw. Up on a roof-top she had identified the two figures she had come to know as Marilyn and Arc. She recalled not only their imperturbable cool but how they appeared to be filming the events, tripodding a video camera at the retreating beach crowds.

She had gone forward in opposition to the flow. The mauve dazzle had begun to be a part of it. The ground ran in the opposite direction. And there was music. She had realized that someone must have amplified Bowie's 'Cracked Actor' to stadium proportions. It was like being trapped inside a film and running across an imaginary landscape to improvised stage-props. Behind her 'Panic in Detroit' had begun to build to a delirious falsetto, as though the singer were performing it live on a roof-top.

Cindy had come to on the beach not far from where she was sitting. She remembered her improbable apprehension that the sea had disappeared. She had felt disconnected, as though the stone landscape was compacted into her head and prevented her from seeing externals. She had thought that if she could rid herself of the visual block, the landscape would rectify. The displacements were unnerving. Giant, helium-balloon models of David Bowie silvered the air.

And now as she prepared to go in search of Zap, Cindy was aware that she was being watched. Arc had taken to monitoring the beach from their fourth-floor balcony. A tele-photo video camera was left running from an inconspicuous vantage-point. Linked up to a closed-circuit television, Cindy imagined Arc watching with concentrated vigilance for a break in the rectangular blank. There would be nothing, then someone; a figure relieving a lunar desert.

Cindy walked parallel to Zap's footprints, as though as-similating an electromagnetic charge from their indented regularity. She imagined herself through Arc's or Marilyn's eyes as they fished the screen, and in this way avoided the self-conscious gestures that might have betrayed her knowl-edge of being filmed. She was wired to a pocket Walkman and her distracted air gave the impression that she was too preoccupied to dictate consciously her steps. She moon-walked across the beach towards the Grand Hotel and then went off diagonally to the edge of the stone forest left by the tide. It appeared that she was following a drift of thought to its inconclusive patterns. Reorientating her path, she made to go back to the beach-huts, only she kept on walking and joined up with the road leading to town.

Cindy had grown to magnify the place so internally that now, in returning to it, it was like she was discovering the location for the first time. She got off the same road down which the massed current of people had blown, and slipped through a blank window in a house-front to her right. She encountered riotously overblown gardens. Sunflowers formed an impenetrable stockade, so too did red hibiscus, sinuous lianas and a panoply of tropical orchids.

33

Cindy looked across at the houses to her left. It was on a roof-top over there that she had seen Marilyn and Arc orchestrating the catastrophe. They had stood there shooting film and watching the contrived become a reality. She strafed through dense foliage, her hair scalloped with red blossom. She made for a narrow cinder path that had run behind the gardens adjacent to a canal. It was still there; gritty, sharded, skirting a waterway which had disappeared, leaving in its place a deposit of holograms, giving the illusion of depth to a mauve sky falling through water.

The path was less strangled by roots, allowing Cindy to hurry through a dense emerald arch. She might have been travelling through an air pocket in green water, so massed were the sunflower stems to either side of the path.

Cindy trusted to instinct. The distance from the beach to the town centre was written into her mind. Something told her that Zap would be locked into the illusion of his former home. She imagined him obsessed with thinking things back into place, creating an external reality for what was internalized.

A number of ruby and emerald humming-birds were suspended in flight, sipping nectar from lilies. Cindy wondered how they had adjusted to the unrelieved violet light. They were the first birds she had seen since the change-over; and if they were here, there must be others.

Cindy pushed forward, holding on to her shoulder-bag. She found herself in a garden interior, as though drawn into a deeper dimension. It was darker here. She struggled for breath at the shock, as if she were swimming. Cindy couldn't account for the sense of sudden displacement. It was the reverse of being a child again: what she had imagined then as far away was in fact very close. There were white chairs and a white table, an uncapped bottle of Pimm's and two glasses placed on the table-top.

Cindy listened. She could hear music. She was hurrying forward now, overtaken by the fear and expectation of encountering a survivor, someone who lived on her dimension. She knew the words of the song: 'Blue blue electric blue / That's the colour of my room / Where I will live. . . .' The voice connected with her as David Bowie's 'Sound and Vision', one of the elliptical montage-effect lyrics from his mid-seventies' Berlin period. The music no sooner phased out than it began again. The same song played monotonously over and over, as though its elegiac tone accorded with a vanished community.

Cindy couldn't locate the source of the music. There was no indication of a human presence. She followed in the direction of a renovated outhouse; a flight of steps led into a nuclear dug-out, an insulated space erected against the insuperable heat-flash. For a moment she thought she saw someone dressed in silver, but the image dematerialized.

Inside, her eye was arrested by an open photograph album. There was a pile of press clippings and photographs that had not yet found their way into the book. The photographic dates were mounted in computer type beneath each exhibit. David Bowie at the Rainbow Theatre, 1972; at the LA Forum in 1976; Hiroshima, 1973; LA Amphitheatre, 1974; Wembley, 1976: the images seeming to have been chosen for their visual diversity and metamorphoses. Over the page were weirdly angled shots of Ballard getting into his car at Shepperton after the publication of *Crash*; and then the publicity photographs of him that had appeared on the jackets of *High-Rise* and *Myths of the Near Future*, together with a series of solarized images in the manner of Man Ray, in which the writer's head was superimposed on Brancusi sculptures. Cindy flicked through the obsessive preoccupations: Warhol screened by black glasses on a couch at the Factory, and then seen filming Edie Sedgwick and Gino Persicho in *Beauty 2*; and a few pages on, isolated, filming *Chelsea Girls*. After her biographical efforts to make an ingress into his cryptonomous life, Cindy was fascinated by the range of portraits. She could establish no real person in his photographs, rather a series of personae with an adopted mask. She closed the album afraid she might discover the real man minus his make-up and platinum wig.

Cindy thought of staying here and living amongst the personable items accumulated by its owner. She felt reassured by its composition, the selective criterion that governed its obsessive taste. These things had a historical connection, she told herself; the signed copy of Bowie's 'Young Americans' mounted on a wall, the bootleg double 'The Thin White Duke' from the Nassau Coliseum in 1976. Warhol had autographed his banana sleeve for the Velvet Underground's seminal 1966 album. Albums were stacked against the walls; an alphabetical chronology of Bowie's commercial and bootleg recordings were prepared as an archive for future musicologists.

And there were posters advertising exhibitions by Matisse, Miró, Klee, Kitaj, Bacon. She would come back here and share the previous occupant's propensity for art and avant-garde popism. As Cindy left, the triptych were watching her – Bowie, Ballard and Warhol, each of them seeming to strain forward from the isolation of a photograph.

Cindy took up with the road further on. Made up and dressed in skin-tight black leggings, she might have been a model posing for Helmut Newton.

Her calculations had taken her wide of the town centre, and she found herself at a point where the long, vectored road branched off into parallel filters leading to a sports arena. Its walls were aerosoled with a weird acronymania.

Cindy was beginning to pick up on the subdued reverbera-tion of a guitar played underground. Its throbbing resonance reached her as an interference with her nerves. It was as though she were registering its decibels in the manner of the green and red flicker indicating volume on a cassette deck.

She started to go wide, menaced suddenly by a distorted close-up of Warhol. The picture showed a face sagging be-neath its make-up. She stumbled across ephemera. A white high-heel shoe, an ashtray, the patterned mosaic on a maroon Persian carpet, a *Playboy* cover disclosing a topless pin-up. The pieces were like fragments of an insoluble puzzle. Cindy found herself rediscovering things that she had once accepted as an integral part of her life. They seemed without rep-resentation now; scattered, insignificant objects begging appeal. A vase, an earring, a telephone directory.

Most of the windows had been blown out of the properties in this precinct. Cindy called out at the threshold of a property she recognized. For a moment she anticipated finding someone upstairs. She slipped in through a window and almost mistook the life-size portrait of Warhol, cleverly mounted on a closed door, for a person. Everything was there as it had been left or abandoned. The table was laid for three people. Cindy picked up a book. It was Ballard again. A paperback copy of *The Day of Forever*, open on 'Tomorrow Is a Million Years'. It was the atmospherics disturbed her. There was a frequency, a charge in the air like hidden speech. It was as though Warhol were addressing her, instating an audio-hallucinated speech pattern that came on in her mind involuntarily.

Cindy climbed back out of the window and made towards the quarter in which she knew Zap had lived. She had seen him in this area in the past, sketching at a café table or staring at the immediate as though time were momentarily arrested in a glass of water.

Cindy pushed the door to of a Euro supermarket and collected tinned asparagus, caviare, mineral water and whatever items of preserved food appealed to her diminished appetite. Instinct had her head towards the cash check-out, where she recoiled from the officiating presence of three mannequins. The one nearest her was made up in a platinum wig and white foundation to resemble Warhol. A shirt, tie and tailored jacket were worn over jeans and sneakers. The central image was recognizably that of David Bowie, a cigarette drooping from red crayoned lips, the dummy's eyes coloured one blue and one green, the bleached hair blown back. The third figure was less easily identifiable, but Cindy was certain from the book photographs she had seen that it was J.G. Ballard. His face had been sprayed silver. Cindy recollected the line of his novels in the beach-hut. The pages had been underscored with ink. Someone had read them with minute care and imposed annotations in the text.

Cindy found herself heading towards a group of houses constellated beyond the ruined polygon. A small oval fish-pond had turned violet from the reflection of the sky. A transistor had been left behind it. The kids who used to hang out here were gone.

Cindy startled at what appeared to be footsteps behind her, their intrusion amplified by the unconditional silence. She stopped and waited. It was nothing. There was a pause before it started again. Three steps forward and a can dislodged into a sequence of tin reverberations. She was being spooked. And then the music again. 'My mother said to get things done / You better not mess with Major Tom.'

The thought hit Cindy in a light-flash that there was nowhere to run to and no one to help. It was like being exposed in a dream, when you wanted to shout back to yourself to come to the rescue, only it's all spun out of control. Cindy modulated her panic. Orchids and scarlet geraniums had rioted through a roofless greenhouse and projected a tropical verticality. Everything was reaching in a blaze of colour for the purple sky.

Cindy found herself in a narrow alley branching out to the left. Her eye found the conglomerate of posters pronouncing *The Atrocity Exhibition* – book-jackets blown up to accentuate the typography and front cover illustration. A cocooned black stocking floated from a Monroe poster. Cindy found herself reacting without surprise to a code of visuals that seemed to embody clues to a pictorial cryptogram.

She moved forward suspended in her own dimension of inner space rather than realizing the energy demands that propelled a body between two given points. A rapid, sequinned flurry spiralled from a prostrate position on the ground into the figure of a human making lightning speed across the sky. She watched it go; a cosmonaut tracing a luminous parabola above the town.

Cindy turned round, and the music started up again. 'The shrieking of nothing is killing me / Just pictures of Jap girls in synthesis.' It was a trick of light that someone was standing there. A man with blood pouring down a white shirt-front? An alien who resisted time notation? On the right-hand wall children had chalked up coloured graffiti on a brick surface. Pink and white love-hearts and drifting capitals – SPACE-MEN LIVE IN THE TV, JANE SUCKS COCK – lived on the wall as exclamatory reminders of a vanished neighbourhood.

Cindy connected with the captions. MAJOR TOM LIVES. They appeared to belong to dead time, to the hiatus between the past and future. Her flamingo-pink hair was like a sunrise in the constricted alley. She was light, sinuous, a hologrammic body defying gravity.

Her mind refocused as she was startled back into awareness by pursuit. The interval between her and her pursuer remained equidistant. Three steps were answered by three, four by four. Injected stimulus by injected stimulus.

She wanted to shout, it wanted to shout. The big build-up, the big build-up. Get outta here, get outta here. It's Andy, it's Bowie, maybe it's Ballard, it's Andy, it's Bowie, maybe it's Ballard.

Cindy took the left-hand turning out of the alley. She recognized the place as Zap's neighbourhood. And her pursuer? She questioned the silence. Was he watching, or was it someone gone off into space? Who and what was this Major Tom?

Cindy stopped in front of the crescent that the alley gave on to. There was a studio conversion built on the top floor of one of the opposite houses. She stared at the footprints mapped out in the dust coating the house stairs. Her thoughts banged at her to go forward. She placed her sneakers in the contoured treads by way of a companionable exchange. There was the possibility that Zap might be here, inside.

Cindy locked the door behind her with instinctive caution. The fixed pattern of light and dark as a consequence of the sky's immobility pulled her up short. A skylight looked down through a stairwell. It seemed impossible to conceive that this had once comprised a living space – floors and stairs leading to floors across which people had moved.

Cindy sensed that there was somebody upstairs. She stood in the hall like someone who had just died waiting at the entrance to the underworld. The circular mirror on the wall showed how thin she had grown. Her make-up accentuated her hollow cheeks, steeply angled eyes and high cheekbones. Whenever Cindy looked in the mirror, she felt possessed by the need to outrage, to strip and adopt erotic poses. She resisted the temptation and moved towards the stairs. There were paintings on the walls which she understood to be Zap's: a naked man sitting chained to a black sun, a red rose in the place of his penis being watched by an eye in a pyramid. The powerful image embedded itself in her consciousness, before she took in others: a woman's curvy, glass-stockinged legs were parted to admit the sinuous blue folds of a snake; a young boy with purple hair looked on as a voyeur partly concealed by a chair. Colour imploded in her mind. Cindy moved through a galaxy of fetishes and bizarrely juxtaposed imagery.

The first flight gave on to a landing filled with what she recognized as prints from Picasso's blue period. She stood there and listened. There was no sound of her pursuer. Perhaps, she thought, he was inside her mind, his movements programmed to hers – his frequency becoming audible only when she grew frightened.

She took the stairs quietly in her sneakers. The house was like a private museum preserved against the great absence of the future. Masks, collages, woodcuts, psychedelia, a black chest on which coloured shoes with ultra-stiletto heels were balanced. There were shoes the pink of her lipstick, snakeskin ones, patent, scarlet, gold and silver. She was momentarily fascinated. She pulled herself away and climbed towards the third storey. A skylight admitted a purple filter from outside. She could hear him now, up above, shifting his weight slightly on muffled boards. She thought he must be painting, for it was always within the same constricted radius that the person shifted position. She wasn't afraid of Zap; she had seen in him affinities that might have brought them together under different conditions. She knew that what had drawn her here was the feeling that somewhere they intersected on an oblique line running through the graph of possibilities.

When she got up a flight and looked into the room he didn't see her, so intense was his concentration. He was standing there absorbed to the point of falling through a hole in his vision. Cindy saw the bleached highlights almost outgrown by the black hair beneath, the blue denim jacket open on a bare chest, the stonewashed jeans, the intense concentration written into the lines of his face.

It was his absorption that fascinated. Cindy could hear the hum of his nerves; their discharge appeared to crackle in his brushstrokes. Even if he knew she was there, he didn't look up, so powerfully concentrated was his subjective focus. Cindy wondered for a moment if she were invisible. She was frightened she might have drifted wide of Zap's dimension and become lost in her orbit like space debris floating up above the world. She was there to herself, but so much else had disappeared.

Zap was painting with a mauve north window behind him. She didn't hear herself move, rather she was there staring unobtrusively at his creation. Now that she could see his visual target, connect with the physicality of his work, she entered his flow.

Cindy's eye travelled through the decked geometric planes of a sky graduating towards a central vortex. Grouped in the foreground, she recognized the three faces so lividly portrayed in the supermarket check-out and in posters pronounced on walls all over town. She repeated their names to herself like a ritual chant: Bowie / Ballard / Warhol. They had somehow come closer. They wanted to impart a way of life she resisted. Bowie's mouth delineated by a perfect Garbo red lipstick-bow was open on something that would never be articulated. Ballard's was frozen into the speech mimetics of someone being interviewed with the sound off. And Warhol seemed to know he was dead. He wanted to say, 'It's really me, only I'm offstage now.'

Zap casually took in Cindy's presence. She could sense the indifference in him, the separation from speech that had come to characterize the change. She felt as though she had entered the architectonics of a dream and couldn't find a way out of the maze. She kept thinking there had to be an alternative state to this one, a parallel world whose function she would rejoin in a transitional flash. Her mind ran back to the nuclear dug-out, the assembled possessions to which she could relate. Was it an astronaut who had set up home there? She imagined his orbit-dazed mind, his precaution of extracting his eyes in the manner that Bowie had instinctively adopted in *The Man Who Fell to Earth*, the intravenous shot by which he fed protein into his metabolism.

Zap stood back from the board and let his brush fly. He was empty for the moment of the creative *élan* that had dictated his ungovernable impulse to paint. He looked at Cindy with the detached expression of someone who believes nothing to be real. If the vision empties out, he thought, perhaps we'll die with it. He remained with his imaginative vision. He had succeeded in making an external reality of what he feared to be a paralysing inner state. And who were they, the figures who had unconsciously introduced themselves into the empty seascape? They were there like pilgrims who had come this far across the sands to find a world in ruin. The receding coral forests were affirmative: they were permanent fixtures; they gave the impression they wanted you to think it had always been like this. They were a beginning to an end. And a continuity.

Cindy sat down on a black floor cushion. It was starting up again, the weird interpretative beat of someone or something in pursuit. She could map out her progress here by following a spiral rhythm, an equivocatory zigzag approach that had her reach for breath and tighten as the decision was made to stop or go on.

Zap went over and stood at the window. The asymmetrical skyline was dominated by an insurance emporium, the block standing upright as a cubic reference to the twenty-third century. A green balloon fastened to a safety-rail on the flat roof hung there, weightless, a gesture left over from a drunken office party.

Cindy tried to swallow on her panic. She could track the footsteps by their increased volume through the narrow alley. They hit her auditory awareness as though she were listening to music through headphones. She anticipated their approach with the involvement of someone expecting to see herself arrive through the door; the real Cindy and not this dissociated identity.

As the crisis built up, so it was interpolated by music. She could hear guitar riffs punctuating confused vocals. She recognized snatches of Bowie's 'All the Madmen' phased in and out of Mick Ronson's psychotic chords. Voices were engaged in a studio dialogue in which Warhol's name was thrown in the air. 'Andy Warhol' was given the intonation of a Cockney accent. She could hear the voice rehearsing: 'Andy walking. Andy tired, Andy takes a little snooze. / Tie him up when he's fast asleep, send him on a pleasant cruise.' The voice cut out in a rush. Zap had swung round from the window, and someone was standing dead centre to the room. The drug-wasted features from which all gender had receded, the silver leather jacket open on a skeletal torso, the outline of genitalia tucked into a pubis, Cindy registered these things before her eye shot to the empty window and connected with the tiny green balloon anchored from the high-rise opposite. Then she was plummeting head over heels into the drop.

Chapter 4

Marilyn watched the blank screen register an empty beach. It was more like a lunar landscape, black rocks standing out in a silent, unrelieved immobility of time and place. And who was he, the unidentifiable alien they had observed patrolling the beach? Two or three times they had isolated him in the lens. A man dressed in silver, or was it an android, his stars-and-stripes zipper-jacket worn with tight blue jeans and silver boots. He had eluded the lens, marginally dipping out of its magnified radius as though he knew he was being watched, as though the transmitted beam offended his skin.

Marilyn searched the beach. It was only when she began to look for the fixtures she assumed were there that she realized the figures had disappeared from the shore. They were no longer in the places she had taken on visual trust. She had grown accustomed to Zap's sitting there, his head resting on his knees, or else reclining, hands placed behind his back, face tilted at an angle to the sky. His meditative passivity had suggested someone too displaced to adjust. And Cindy? Arc had felt instinctively uneasy about her change-over. There was a restlessness in her, a self-questioning that they had viewed with suspicion on the screen.

Marilyn adjusted the plane of the wide aperture lens and watched the beach travel across an aluminized surface. The high-quality input obtained from the display system had the sanded areas show up ivory. She adjusted the tone from black and white to colour, and granite blocks of the old sea-wall showed their yellow encrustations of lichen.

Periodically the sky vibrated with music. They would hear it at night standing on the balcony of the Grand Hotel:

> 'This is ground control to Major Tom
> Commencing countdown, engines on
> This is ground control to Major Tom
> Take your protein pills and put your helmet on.'

The voice sounded like it came from the back of the sky. It reverberated and cut out.

Black tree stumps from a carbonized forest had poked through an area of sand adjacent to the old slipway. Marilyn zoomed in on the derelict huddle of villas that had once formed part of a fishing village, roofless, windowless, maintained here and there by an upright wall. She anticipated Cindy and Zap exploring these ruins, showing up in the camera as inert, disorientated survivors. There were spars, timbers, fishing-nets and lobster-pots strewn across thistled interiors. An incongruous arch gave on to the receding stone forest, an orange marker-float hung up on a hook against the purple sky as though the arrangement belonged to an abstract expressionist painting.

Marilyn could hear Arc editing film in a suite next door. Buñuel claimed to have filmed the ultimate Bowie concert, performed under high security for astronaut trainees and astrophysicists at Cape Kennedy in early 1973. Dropping from the flies on a prop decorated with moons, Bowie, who went through twelve costume changes, had painted a gold circle in the centre of his forehead. In between numbers he had spoken of UFOs, extraterrestrials, his alien genealogy which extended to Mars. Dry ice machines had emitted cumuli through which Bowie would stroll, his scarlet and silver leotard sequins compact over his protuberant crotch. Or else he would appear metamorphosed into a zoot suit, while an animated film of the cosmos rushed at light-speed towards the viewers. On bleachers at the rear of the stage a mime troupe performed expository gestures of fellatio. What Buñuel had been in search of and partly depicted was the metamorphosis that had actually occurred on-stage. In an act of visible terror Bowie had reputedly been transformed into his persona, Major Tom. What looked to the audience like a theatrical mutation devised for stage histrionics had seen the singer exit in a confused, dissociated way. A green-haired Mick Ronson and his associates from the Spiders from Mars had continued with a stomping entry into 'Jean Genie' before the curtain had come down.

Was it Bowie or Major Tom whom they had seen making solitary excursions across the beach? And the perfectly scaled missiles they had discovered along the coast? Marilyn let the idea float disquietingly and went in to join Arc. As she moved, her gold-sequinned miniskirt flashed with the brilliance of a tropical fish. She balanced on gold heels which created in her the constricted walk of a strip-artist. She pushed her blonde hair back over one shoulder.

As Marilyn entered, Arc was screening an edited text. In the crazy days preceding the change-over she had stood with Arc on the opera-house roof-top shooting scenes of crowd panic, while a red helicopter had added to the apocalyptic urgency by continuously circling and standing off above a backdrop of cubic business emporia. From their vantage-point they had recorded images that they now spoke of in terms of the old world. No one had questioned what they were filming or even asked who they were.

Marilyn stood back and watched a building's vertical spine twist into a banana shape. The loud prop revolution of the helicopter grew voluble as it angled in above a high-rise, a locust tilting for the roof before it dematerialized in a white flash. Marilyn stuck her tongue in Arc's ear and cupped her hands over his cock. Their bodies seemed to have adopted the missing links that stood out in the architecture.

Arc let Marilyn coax him erect with a single red finger-nail. He liked the throbbing constriction that his tight vinyl jeans created, and even more he luxuriated in the delay. Marilyn would perform this little conjuring trick twenty or thirty times a day until the uncontrollable suspense had him cradle her head to his zip, her lips engorging his swollen cock.

Arc twisted free as the camera zoomed in again and picked out a giant-sized poster of David Bowie wearing a black eyepatch. Warhol was there too on this opposite roof-top, his blown-up poster showing him with a camera strap slipped over a leather shoulder, his platinum hair austerely parted. And Ballard dressed unostentatiously in a herring-bone jacket and green polka-dot tie completed the visual triptych. These posters had formed the foreground to much of their shooting.

When the sequence resumed, Marilyn found herself watching what looked like a disbanded business congress straggle up to the roof. A party of white-shirted men stood shading their eyes and looking towards the sun. They were standing there, a group of urban penguins, curious, apprehensive, and then there was nothing. Just a blank space giving on to a backdrop.

Arc adjusted the control track and corrected the sound spectrum. A sonic wind-tunnel created the atmospherics to a roof-top scenario. Marilyn reflected on how Arc had climbed back through a skylight and fixed the camera inclining up-wards, out of the wind, cradled in an anchored tripod. There was a lag before the sensitivity of the tube was automatically raised to cope with dark images. A helicopter slipped out of control, a violent tail wind breaking it up, was seen detonating on impact with a high-rise wall. People were viewed running away in a migratory exodus. Music accompanied the film relay.

Arc remained absorbed in cutting and replaying. 'Your face is starting to sag,' he told Marilyn. 'You're going to lose that precious surgery, baby. Who out here can repair your face-lift?'

Marilyn instinctively raised her hands to her face, her long, pointed red nails acting as protectives to further scrutiny. She could see herself as a geisha, the white foundation increasing to the texture of pasto as she walked across the beach in search of Major Tom. And if they never got back, if they remained frozen in a hallucinatory vista, then they might flip like two astronauts grown hysterical in space. Already Marilyn had begun to feel that she was drifting into a timeless mental orbit. Her dreams were full of statuary, alhambras, scarabs, pyramids, processions turning to dust. And Arc was turning too, towards whatever fixed monomaniacal obsession he had come to worship. She could envisage a time when they wouldn't even recognize each other, both would have travelled so far in their imaginary journeys. She was worried too that Arc's obsessions had created the alien who had come increasingly to be seen on the beach. Arc's preoccupation with the David Bowie transvestite persona from the early seventies had reached a degree of fetishism whereby he appeared to have embarked on a mental voyage towards his fiction.

Arc was shooting directly from the replay machine. A crowd emerging from a cinema could be seen frozen, looking up at the sun behind the camera, and then running away with the panic of people watching themselves take flight into a dream. They must have known they were running to nowhere; and that nothing would ever be the same again. When they could no longer stick together, they fractured into split-offs dematerializing in the sun's ray, suspended for all time within inner space.

Arc zoomed in on the conflagrations of burning cars. Marilyn watched him freeze into a figure who had adopted the impersonal objectivity of a lens. In watching his absorption Marilyn realized that Arc was still living out that dimension. He had become fixated by the liberating moment of his power. He had learnt to assume the detached role of Ballard's solitary protagonist Vaughan in the techno-eroticism of *Crash*.

Marilyn picked up her shoes and went back to the bedroom. For the first time she realized that she was coming down. Neither she nor Arc had ever contemplated the disunity of their vision. Who was he, she asked? In his mind he had come to identify so closely with Bowie's chameleonic mutations, Warhol's sophisticated naïvety, Ballard's creation of futuristic myths, that he was someone intent on splitting himself in three.

Marilyn returned to the blank rectangle monitoring the beach. There was still no trace of Zap or Cindy, but in her mind she was hoping to surprise the alien – the silver booted, red-haired figure walking away provocatively with his back to the camera, the music of 'Space Oddity' accompanying his filmic gestures.

When she grew restless she would prowl the hotel corridors, let herself into rooms and ransack the wardrobes. At first her looting had been random, but later on she had developed a strategy of raiding one room at a time, a scheme she undertook with the incisive caution of a trained hotel thief. What she discovered were passports, jewellery, clothes, condoms, bedside books, letters received and ones half written; boxes of chocolates, black suspender belts, splays of credit cards which would never again be used; a copy of Ballard's *High-Rise* open at page 53.

Marilyn kept remembering the incidentals attendant on Warhol's funeral. How he had been buried in a black cashmere suit, a loud Paisley tie splashed from a white buttondown, his dark glasses continuing to shade his eyes, his make-up done perfectly, a red rose placed in one hand, a prayer-book in the other. It was the sort of style she would have accompany her into death. But had they already made the jump into deathlessness? she asked herself. Andy had gone too soon. Or perhaps he was playing tricks? He might still be selecting jewellery in an imaginary Bloomingdale's, or raising a Belgian chocolate to his anticipative palate.

Instinct compelled Marilyn to take out the key to Room 213 from the wallet she had prepared at reception. Something told her this room had been lived in since the changeover. On the inside she found the bed littered with papers. Champagne and cognac bottles were everywhere. A bedside reading-lamp had been left on.

Marilyn knew without looking that this was Arc's work.

Video cartridges teetered in columns on the floor. Arc must have been creating a secret film archive. Out-takes, unedited film, vertical pan shots awaiting a more coherent image, narrative, atrocities. He had labelled each with a scarlet felt-tip.

When Marilyn opened the wardrobe in search of clothes left behind by the previous occupants, she encountered a mannequin made up to resemble David Bowie. Modelling it on Nicholas Roeg's film-stills from *The Man Who Fell to Earth*, Arc had sprayed the head silver and created the vertical pupils in oval eyes that had so evoked the presence of an alien. On the forehead he had written the word AUMGN, Aleister Crowley's bastardized version of the Buddhist mantra OM. He had drawn pentagrams on the arms, and had blocked in the words MAJOR TOM above the navel.

Marilyn backed off. The time-trap that she and Arc had devised in its initial stages was growing into an obsessive maze dominated by the latter. She was no longer clear about events. The excitement generated by the prospect of mastering and editing Buñuel's secret film of the Bowie Cape Kennedy concert and the footage prepared by the old film-maker to accompany his death, had served as a mutual stimulus to keep the two together. Standing there, Marilyn felt the rift widen between them. Her eyes ran like insects across a page of boldly written notes that Arc had prepared. She continued to search the room, but the clue which she couldn't outwardly locate was satelliting her mind. Somewhere else in the hotel she could hear Arc dubbing Bowie's 'Five Years' on to a shoot that took in a low-diving helicopter. The apocalyptically urban lyrics explored the perverse life-style they had come to share in a relationship calculated to outrage. And now with the absence of social comment, the lidding of a voyeuristic eye, the ostentation in their relationship had diminished.

Marilyn was beginning to crave attention. Her psychology depended on being wanted for her anomalies. She had established the erotic panache, the sense of daring and overcompensation which is the product of created rather than natural gender. With Arc withdrawn into a psychotic vision of reality, she had come to feel like a superannuated movie star, a

Monroe consigned to the part of an extra.

Marilyn froze. A shiver that congealed to a stalactite ran down her spine. The mutant she had seen at intervals crossing the beach was standing watching her from inside the door. And this time the face was consistent with Arc's mannequin, the vertically slit pupils standing out as black apertures in silver. The figure wore a stars-and-stripes zipper-jacket open to the waist, tight blue jeans and silver boots. Red hair was gelled back above features that portrayed no immediate identification with the human species. It looked as though a second skin had been superimposed on the face beneath. Snake-hipped, wasted, the body transmitted sexual urgency, erotic curiosity.

Compelled to respond, and turned on by the prospect of contactless sex, Marilyn felt directed by a mental beam to act. She created a red carnation on the mirror with her lips, wriggled out of her sequinned skirt and raised her stockinged feet in the air. By degrees she extended her legs vertically so that the silk was brought into frictional contact with the mirror. Unclasping her black bra she began rhythmically to undulate her hips, rotating, pelvically thrusting, fixing the mutant figure in her mind, so that it was his android image that had her mouth arch, the imaginary contact with his enigmatic pubis that had her climax correspondingly delayed and then urgently convulsive. Again and again she alerted herself to orgasmic frenzy. And after it was over her mind buzzed with images. The figure was still standing in her head. He wanted to lead her somewhere, and in time she knew she would follow.

She lay there pacified by the satisfaction of her desire and savoured the perverse delight of having had sex in Arc's private studio. The music that came out of the sky to surprise her by its apparently issuing from nowhere, had returned again.

> For here am I
> Sitting in a tin can
> Far above the world
> The planet earth is blue
> And there's nothing I can do.

And the music had become inseparable in her mind from the figure she had just encountered; the solitary android who showed up on the beach and never stayed.

Marilyn pinned her hair up in front of the mirror. She was obsessed with the over-emphasis of make-up, the heavy lipstick and eye colours that Warhol had given his images of Monroe and Liz Taylor representing for her the depiction of a trans-species – women whose excessive feminity transformed them into drag artists.

She would have left Arc, but she lacked the knowledge of how to escape from the film-trap. All preconceived notions of reality had disappeared. The community that lived in and around the Grand Hotel were imprisoned within the context of a delayed or speeded-up film.

Marilyn knew she would come back to this room and search Arc's film archives. It seemed like a long journey from one floor to another, as though she had crossed a complex geography and retrieved a portion of her memory in the process. The shortest distance had assumed magnified proportions. She wanted to leave, but there was nowhere to go, only the transformed ruin of a town on one side, and on the other the forbidding maze of an exposed sea-bed. She checked the screen again to confirm her suspicions. Cindy and Zap must have gone off into the town. But they couldn't get anywhere, she assured herself, they would run continually into the dimensions of a film-screen.

When Arc came through he had tied his hair back in a pony-tail, like the pilot in Ballard's short story 'Low-Flying Aircraft'. He had persistently read Ballard's fiction aloud to Marilyn in the weeks preceding the change-over. Arc was obsessed with Vaughan, the protagonist of *Crash*, in the same way as he appeared trichotomized between the variable personae belonging to Bowie, Ballard and Warhol. The mock interviews he staged between himself and the latter, working at the dialogue for hours on a word processor, filled wadded folders.

Marilyn wondered how and when Arc had compiled this work. Their slip out of time was marked by a lack of chronological memory. Was it a day, ten hours or ten years ago that they had participated in the change-over?

Arc busied himself in putting on the compilation tape he had assembled from Bowie's acclaimed trilogy: 'Low', 'Heroes' and 'Lodger'. His mania had cooled to a disconcerting lucidity. He wanted to push Marilyn to the edge and still reclaim her. The prospect of facing the unpeopled desert alone was too much for him. What frightened him was not that she knew too much, but that she might break. But the perverse within him, the emotionally mutilative, needed to hurt her, as though by lacerating her anomalies he was vindicating his own.

He crossed the room and manoeuvred his way into an exposed area of her neck. His teeth picked up on her black bra strap and worked it laterally to the edge of her shoulder. 'We're misfits,' he kept whispering. 'We've created this world because we couldn't live in the other. Don't you remember how we conceived of creating mutants? We wanted a new species. We believed that one day we would do it. A transsexual would give birth to the first of a superior race.'

Marilyn recoiled and fought free of Arc's hands, which were tightly kneading her shoulders. The twist in Arc's mood had unnerved her. She righted her strap by the window and took in the mauve horizon. He must be out there somewhere, she thought, the red-haired android with the stars-and-stripes jacket. Or was he too an actor who wouldn't fade from the screen, someone caught walking away as the credits took precedence over the timelessness of their journey to nowhere?

She could hear Arc's voice still jabbing at her vulnerability. 'And what are we?' he was questioning. 'The effects or the reality? We don't know because we haven't gone far enough. You used to be crazy, but now you're pulling out.'

Marilyn withdrew into herself. She was a student again, sunning on the bank by the Pont Mirabeau. Someone's radio was on in the still July afternoon. She had lain there reading Genet's *Journal du voleur*, speaking the words out loud with the gesture of blowing smoke-rings.

Arc was turning a circle in his thoughts. 'You're going under, sugar cube,' he taunted. 'There's no help for you out here. Paris, Rome, New York, they've all disappeared. Your surgery will fall apart.'

Marilyn let his voice go. The flashbacks were beginning again. The horizon appeared to be a bank of giant TV screens. On each of them Bowie, Ballard and Warhol were engaged in a silent dialogue. A red screen, a blue screen, a green one. A film-maker's mounted triptych.

Marilyn heard herself banging doors as she rushed for the corridor. Arc didn't give chase. He was too out of it. She let herself into a room on the third floor, lay back and listened to the silence solidify. The last occupant had left a bottle of Chanel No. 5 on the dressing-table. She released the stopper and settled into the fantasy that she was Monroe. She knew in her mind that the red-haired android would reclaim her. He was out there, only on another dimension. She would resign herself to waiting for the music, the chords from 'Space Oddity' that anticipated his arrival.

Chapter 5

He sat with his interplanetary Walkman buzzing in his ears. The same little green balloon flopped from a roof-top on the skyline. Always the same punctum which found the eye; the same landscape, imaginary or real.

He looked at the two bodies he had sprayed with novo-caine. He had stripped Cindy of her top and leggings. The red powder dusted on her blue lids co-ordinated with her red see-through panties. Even drugged she appeared to be actively following a dream narrative, pursuing its transitional tangents to the black strip between two film-frames.

He had placed Zap alongside her so that their bodies were parallel. Using Cindy's make-up bag he had given Zap a red lipstick bow, and shaped and tailed his eyes with a green crayon. He stared at them with the objective detachment of someone who dissociates from emotion. The two figures were mannequins in a perverse psychodrama. He could hear a voice transmitted through his personal sound system: 'You are the only one. Your music will realize the android race. We are here and waiting for you on Diamond Nebula. Remember your own words. "I must be only one in a million."'

He disconnected the earphones and looked around Zap's studio. His earth memory associated with flashbacks from the tours. The wild costume changes that had characterized the Ziggy Stardust and Aladdin Sane tours, the emaciated extraterrestrial who had crossed America under the sci-fi dramatics of his apocalyptic 'Diamond Dogs' set, the cocaine-stimulated rock cabaret figure who had personified his 'White Light' concerts, the sailor-capped Berlin survivor who had taken to the stage in 1978, then the long interlude broken by his celebratory 'Serious Moonlight' itinerary in 1983, the return to extravagant histrionics for his 'Glass Spider' stagings in 1987, and then his retirement tour three years later when he had renounced any intention to perform his solo repertoire ever again.

Dressing-room scenes, make-up artists, pre-concert adrenalin, the endless limousines, hotels, excessive earnings and expenditure, the whole unreal, chameleonic life he had known reinstated itself through visual recall. Faces jumped at him out of a memory blank, Marc Bolan's blacked-out eyes, Iggy Pop's muscular torso, Brian Eno's sedate presence in Berlin *circa* 1977, his assistant Coco Schwab holding a yellow chrysanthemum as they departed to Europe in 1976, his long-term producer Tony Visconti, and finally it was his one-time wife Angie who came into his mind, as though her face were suddenly isolated on a television screen. It was Angie as he had known her in the early seventies, dressed and made up to look like his female counterpart.

He let the images rush his mind and slow. Concert halls in New York, Paris, London, Rome, Milan, Melbourne. He had always been the special one, his one brown eye and one blue accentuating his alien physical characteristics. He searched his features. It was his eyes they had changed. He had lost the colour differentiation, and his pupils had been altered to vertical slits. He moved back from the mirror to the paintings in the studio. He saw each as a door into imaginary space. His heightened faculties allowed him to apprehend the

56

artist's struggle between the image and the form it borrowed. It was transparent to him how in the space of a microsecond the concept translated itself into visual embodiment, but how in the very act of doing so it was transformed into a foreign body. It became a variant, one in a thousand possibilities. What allowed the right perception to come through in place of the many determined the quality of a painting.

He looked at a painting in which a white gondola carrying a black coffin was entering a woman's wide-open scarlet lips. In another, a pair of fishnet stockinged legs were arched over a grave. The inscription read: *This is the true grave of Marilyn Monroe.*

What time was it? The mention of Monroe recalled lyrics from an old song 'The Jean Genie': 'Talking 'bout Monroe, walking on Snow White / New York's a go-go and everything tastes nice.' He remembered having written the song on his first Ziggy Stardust tour of America.

He replaced his earphones. A voice was connecting. 'Transmission: Review your past. Go back to the dug-out and acquaint yourself with your achievements. Allow your past roles to create a synergistic future.'

The voice went dead. He searched for an old cocaine habit, looking for a bowl snowed with powder he remembered having stood in his room. But the need was a shadow reaction. He found himself high on an implosive blaze that registered holistic vision. He drifted right into the next painting. A blond-haired man with an erect penis was lying on a roof-top terrace. A man and a woman looked down at him from the sky. They were identically made up: red lips, gold frosted eyes. Their long, prehensile tongues flickered over the tip of his cock.

Cindy and Zap lay stiffly side by side. When he checked their pulses it came to him that he had done this for a purpose and then lost it again, like a ball thrown too high, which he would catch years later, spontaneously on the beach. And Johnny? He had recognized the latter's rehash of Hendrix's 'Purple Haze', the discordant riffs whiplashed from a maniacal guitar. In his mind he visualized placing giant amplifiers on the high-rise roof-top and performing there above the town's geometric anomalies. He would perform to his own people and send back the master tapes when the next shuttle arrived.

He knew he would have to contest his rights here with Arc. He imagined the chase from one deserted building to another; the dead telephones in offices and apartments, the blue globe thistles cracking through upholstery, lianas strangulating the cool silks in a wardrobe. They would never intersect in the timeless maze; their lives would go wide of each other in divergent parallels.

He realized now that it was curiosity, the need to recover knowledge of the human anatomy which had led him to strip Zap and Cindy. And correspondingly he felt the need to explore the house. He found himself in a pink and black bathroom, randomly spilling colognes and perfumes over his body. Things wouldn't stabilize in his hands and seemed to be endless in their falling. A bottle fell like a Pacific splashdown indefinitely suspended by the camera. When his face came back off the mirror it was a stranger's. It was someone's he had known and forgotten. It had once stared back at him from billboards, posters, megastores, displays.

Something within him wanted to retrieve that fame. He unprized his face from the mirror and followed through into the bedroom. An oval bed dominated the space, rose-pink cushions heaped on black. There were paintings here too, one that resembled the ordered chaos of a Pollock, another with the individual mythology of a Picabia. A sequinned dress was thrown across the bed, a pair of discarded black silk panties. A half-open drawer revealed the silks and chiffons of lingerie. The transparent panelled wisps settled in his hands like exotic butterflies. Black and scarlet and white and pink, the immaterial triangles evoked in his mind a string of white, black and Asian models. And the woman who had lived here? He pictured her with her back to him, facing a mirror. Her bottom was caught tightly in a transparent black mesh. She was fixing a jade necklace, feeling for the clasp. For a moment he thought she really was there, pulling a straight seam towards a red suspender strap.

He found himself curious about everything. The way in

which a white pearl necklace warmed on contact with his skin, the bottle of Volvic mineral water on a bedside table, the green numeraled clock that had stopped at three o'clock, how many days, months, years, centuries ago? He would take away whatever afforded clues to his mutant identity.

He wired himself once again to the interplanetary Walkman. He listened to the big silence of space before a voice transmitted instructions. 'Reacquaint yourself with Ziggy Stardust. Your earth memory is intact. The music will assist you.' He listened to the vocal delivery needle his cells: 'Ziggy played for time, jiving us that we were voodoo / The kids were just crass, he was the nazz / With God given ass / He took it all too far, but boy, could he play guitar.'

The vocal cut out, as though the alert was deliberately minimal. But something within his mind made the jump, the quantum connection with memory. The lines he had sung so often were coming back to him. The words that succeeded the snatch he had been given, were suddenly alive and on his lips.

And he had done just that. His Ziggy persona had acquired an autonomous existence. His image had attracted clones, trans-people who dyed their hair shades of orange and pink, wore satin thigh-boots, drop earrings, and drew bright circles on their foreheads. Ziggy's concerts had grown to be sacrificial rites. The audience hysteria had effectively assassinated the mask behind which he had lived and performed. And something had broken within him, releasing a spiral series of identities. He had gone too far and been jettisoned into inner space.

Inquisitive, he made his way from the bedroom to Zap's sculpture room. The deformation that characterized the sculptures was consistent throughout, suggesting an obsess-ive concern with bizarre or incongruous sexual unions. Mick Jagger, James Dean, Jayne Mansfield – he recalled their faces – were all portrayed as entertaining new forms of erotic expression. Jagger faced Jayne Mansfield with his penis in his ear; James Dean was portrayed with one eye, the other one having inserted itself into an aperture in a woman's upraised foot. All the sculptures were disunited in their attempts to form a cohesive sexual geometry.

59

He edged his way between sculptures, alerted by his findings to the time-lapse. The work showed evidence of the schematic images he had employed in stage-sets, right up to the theatricality of his 'Glass Spider' tour. He placed the palms of his hands flat against the wall and let his thoughts go blank. Bits of his earth life continued to reactivate memory cells. He saw himself as he had been in LA in 1974, reclusively holed up in hotel suites, his cocaine habit demanding dark; a photophobic sensibility freaked out on lines. He relocated himself depressed in Berlin, at odds with the commercial pressures of his contract, attempting to realign himself with the avant-garde. For the better part of the seventies he had achieved the wasted image of a rock star free to pursue his fantasies without intrusion from the public. Now he waited for his people to gather at the desert's edge. They would find him in the ruins. They would follow him and take up their places in the audience. It would all begin again.

His mind was buzzing with images. He could see nothing but a vision of crystal buildings. Helicopters were sitting in the glideways above heliports. Gold-suited pilots relaxed on balconies listening to pop. Each of them kept in their cockpits copies of Ballard's *Low-Flying Aircraft* and *The Unlimited Dream Company*. He stared out of the window at his future city. If Arc or Marilyn were looking for him, they'd never get through the light. He was somewhere else. They'd never find him as he retreated into his vision of packed stadiums.

When he returned to Zap's studio, he knew she would be there. She was sitting in a microskirt and boots facing the two bodies on the couch. He knew without asking her that she was Xenia. She seemed to be trying to remember who the two people on the couch were. She was straining to find access to their lives.

He stood in the doorway and looked at the long, curving lines of her legs, her black hair shaken out in a contained storm. Something had brought them together, although she gave no indication of knowing him. He knew he would have to take her to the interior of his vision, have her live on his dimension, and participate in the awakening of a new consciousness. At one time he would have expected her to wriggle out of her constricted skirt and come searching for him across the floor, her teeth unzipping his fly, her lips imparting moist stings to his body. He knew that if he wanted to, he could fly. He could slip out of the window and hang motionless above the street before circling the building and returning.

When he looked again, Xenia was gone. It was as though she too had developed the faculty to dematerialize, come and go in the light and register only where she sensed a corresponding facility.

He uncapped the bottle of Jim Beam he had discovered on a bedside table. The full-throated shots he took from the bottle-neck exploded in his nerves. The more he acquainted himself with the architectural skyline extending beneath a mauve sky to the sands, the more convinced he grew that the town and its few remaining survivors were features of a weird time-flaw, its diagrammatic props fixed in his mind like recurring film-frames. His vision of reality had crystallized into a set involving people and an articulated dream city. It was as though the transitional inhabitants of this landscape had become trapped in his mind. He alone as the invincible one had escaped domination. Zap, Cindy, Marilyn and Johnny were minds lost inside Arc's choreographed drug-trip. And there would be others. They might search him out through the crazed labyrinth, daring to show only if they were odd enough or beautiful enough to fix his attention. The posters had informed him that Arc's world government comprised a triumvirate: Bowie, Ballard and Warhol.

Much more of his past was returning. He remembered how the schizoid split had occurred during that private concert at Cape Kennedy. There were trainee astronauts in the audience, astrophysicists, a small audience intent on finding in him the qualities of the extraterrestrial. Something had happened on-stage. Instead of inventing the characters he sung about, he had been completely taken over by the figure of Major Tom. Was it cocaine, his hallucinated belief that he was a demigod, or an actual psychic transference within his brain chemistry that had allowed the character invasion to appear so real? They had rushed him back to the privacy of his hotel suite. Tony Defries, Angie, members of his band the Spiders from Mars, had all filed into his room. A Cape Kennedy psychologist had been enlisted to speak informally about stress and the alienated environment that had contributed to his mental state. It all came back to him. And how he had trained as a space-suited Biospherian in a glass terrarium in the Arizonian mountains. Here, artificially cut off from the earth's atmosphere, he had listened to his song 'Life on Mars' reverberate through speakers in the way it might be heard on the red planet: 'It's on America's tortured brow / That Mickey Mouse has grown up a cow.' He had been one of the initiates who explored ecosystems within an air-sealed microclimate. A rain forest, bamboo groves, tropical reefs skirting a lagoon, African grasslands generating a valuable source of oxygen, he had lived within a colony that fused earth sciences and space technology. Tanks of tilapia fish had lined the walls. Computer banks, sensors and monitors flashed into consciousness. He remembered the two gymnasium-sized lungs, each attached to a giant rubber diaphragm that had expanded and contracted in response to the temperature. The whole thing could have been one of the elaborate stage-sets he had contrived to launch his American Ziggy Stardust concerts.

He remembered the esoteric initiation into this sect. And how he had sworn secrecy as to its discoveries and aspirations. He had worn a red space-suit and taken up with the belief that life on earth was dead and that the colonization of Mars was the only tolerable future for a select number of adepts. And there were drugs involved, pharmaceutical experiments that allowed inner space to expand, specific planets to be isolated in the brain cells. And the principal one was Mars. When the mind was capable of realizing that dimension, so the way was prepared for inner flight. He had never become a member of the core group, but members had introduced him to the writings of Aleister Crowley. He had grown obsessed with black magic, occultation. He had consulted the *Thesaurus Exorcisonorum* and attempted to exorcise himself. He had stored his urine in the refrigerator, he had sat inside a huge pentagram drawn on the floor, he had believed that he was a walk-in, an alien who would instigate dramatic changes in the universe.

He was in the process of relearning his life, but in a detached way, as though it had happened to someone else in whom he was still interested. He had still to reconnect with that person and assimilate his past.

He found himself returning again and again to the window. He was searching the mauve skyline, the decks of blank windows, the exotic vegetation usurping technology, but more than anything he was looking for someone or something that would convince him he wasn't entirely alone. There was Xenia, the microskirted model who had found her way on to his dimension. He would meet her out on the sands. She would be sitting on the roof of a buried car, dark glasses accentuating her enigmatic beauty, her leopard-spotted shoes and violet skirt giving her the air of someone stepped out of Paris *Vogue* into a dream. The possibilities for erotic and psychic permutations were inexhaustible.

His nerve impulses were feeling towards new experience. In the past he had known a frustrated sense of delay between what he wished to achieve and what he could actually do. That awareness of separation between thought and action had disappeared. The human need translated into sugar and metabolites was something that belonged to the past. Sensation was now immediate and not attached to toxic stimulus. The goldfish bowls full of white powder that he had snorted belonged to a phase of his life in which his vision of himself as a plutocratic leader of a generation had lagged behind the reality. He had confused Hollywood with reality, and as a consequence he had flipped. During the shooting of *The Man Who Fell to Earth* he had lived in a cocaine daze punctuated by the realization that he had somehow to maintain the momentum out of which his fame had grown. Long months of touring, the extravagant panache associated with his mystique, the identities he had adopted and rejected, the nagging emotional contradictions surrounding his failed marriage, all of these pressures had contrived to break him, dehumanize his relation to the world.

He was high on reacquainting himself with the past. At the height of his fame Xenia would have been one of the more sophisticated groupies hoping to find admission to his entourage. They had waited outside hotels, the entrance to recording studios. He had been under constant watch. His limousines were followed, people broke into his hotel suites to grab clothes, Marlborough cigarette packets, make-up, whatever possessions they could find. And their persistence was unremitting. He had grown isolated, thrown in on the few who protected his privacy from the masses, the paparazzi with their endless penchant for scandal.

His confession to being gay and overtly bisexual had invited universal speculation as to his erotic orientation. He had been photographed kissing a transvestite in a Paris nightclub, and also in Hitler's bunker. His name had become associated with fascism, Crowley, the Nietzschean drive towards the superhuman. And he had renounced nothing. Notoriety had enforced the legend. Hadn't he given a presumed Hitlerian salute to the crowds at Victoria Station? Standing in the back of an open car looking like a German cabaret artist from the thirties, he had appeared to side with political extremism. The certifiable media celebrity had once again risked his image for a spontaneous act of controversy. He had spoken in support of a fascist government, he had hinted that he was the leader who would revolutionize politics. He saw himself, remembered himself. He had hung around cafés in Berlin, worn a worker's cap and overalls with inimitable style, he had lived above a shop that sold motor parts within view of the Wall. He had spent the nights at fuck-clubs, he had survived his own fragmentation by decommercializing his image. He had returned to the avant-garde at a time when it was underground.

And suddenly it was all there again. The Hansa studios in West Berlin, finding his name written up on the Wall in hashed graffiti, a love-heart enclosing the words DAVID BOWIE, his emotional vacuum finding its counterpart in the city. He had wanted to experience the danger of living on the edge, stimulate his art by borrowing from a foreign place. He saw himself again in a herring-bone overcoat and lace-up boots, sipping nervously at a familiar Gaulois. And there he had refound the past. He had communicated with David Jones, the person he had abandoned for years in order to live out the characters he had created for the stage. He had reclaimed an inner identity. He had cooked and washed for himself, and kept away from the house he had bought over-looking Lake Geneva. He had spent his time in Berlin with the cabaret artist Romy Haag, and his friend Iggy Pop. And there was Coco Schwab his assistant, she had known his life intimately, the seismic character splits he had undergone in the search for identity. He saw his fingers buttoning a check shirt, feeling the cold confiscated from his back and chest, and in that moment sensing the person come alive in him, trusting to his new stripped-down image to represent the music in which he believed.

He found himself questioning whether they had ever re-alized the change that had occurred to him on an inner dimen-sion. His astral visitants, the planets that sometimes showed in his eye pupils, his lapses into trance when he communi-cated through nerve impulses, he had lived with these things, compensating for periods of dissociation by immersing him-self in work. The entertainer had persisted despite his belong-ing to another species. And the very transience of his earth life, and knowing that he would be instructed to leave, some day, any day had accelerated his adoption of images. The door in his consciousness was a fixture that would open, allowing him to pass through.

And there had been signs. His videos had been demonstra-tive of his imminent change-over. He recalled how he had made up as three different persons in drag for his *Boys Keep Swinging* video, and how in the promotional shots for *Scary Monsters* he had externalized the alien within him. Wearing a silver off-the-shoulder dress and silver shoes, his face whitened by powder, a cigarette drooping from scarlet lips, he had made Major Tom's whereabouts very clear. The junkie astronaut was strung out in space. The singer was to follow, but through different means. His trajectory would be more disarming, for it would pursue an arc to a timeless interior.

He saw himself waiting, apprehensive, chain-smoking in hotel rooms, preparing to go on-stage, knowing that at any moment he might be called. The transition would be sudden, and as the reverse of death it would take the form of instant rebirth. For a long time they had thought he was faking the appearance of an android. He had been driven across the desert and had sat in the rear of the car huddled into a mink coat, Aretha Franklin's music jumping from the stereo, his figure so wasted that it appeared he was being driven towards a secret burial-site to be cremated. His ashes would be discovered in a missile-shaped pyramid.

He had believed this. The idea of a death cult. Silver men appearing in the American deserts, his posthumous records released autonomously and recorded in space. They had expected this of his influence. And he had gone on knowing the myth was a reality, preparing himself for the change-over, the freedom from gravity.

Rapid pictures filled in like a jigsaw. His thirtieth birthday, with Romy Haag and Iggy Pop present. Brian Eno mastering the studio, translating his knowledge of cybernetics into the cool, impersonal synthesizers that dominated his late seventies' music. He had stabilized by provoking musical accidents. He saw himself sitting in his room at the Dorchester, giving interviews, saying of Hollywood that it was 'like being trapped on the set of a movie you didn't want to see in the first place'.

And the people who had come to know him best were random associates. He had felt compelled to travel, to search for inspiration in all corners of the world. He had gone to Israel, Africa, Japan, China, Russia, Australia. He had been trying to find in the external world a momentum that he lacked in his inner life. He had walked clean through the plastic celebrities who had attempted to engage him in their life-styles. Elizabeth Taylor had tried to rejuvenate her image through inviting him to her mansion. He had noted her reconstituted features, her obsession with baroque kitsch. Her entourage wore sequins. They were pink, blue, orange, yellow clone fish flickering through an aquarium. And then there was Marlene Dietrich, the mother of the sexually androgynous image, who had come out of retirement to co-star with him in *Just a Gigolo*. He remembered the impasto texture of her make-up. Age had transformed her from a cabaret star to a Germanic geisha. Not a facial line escaped the crust of her foundation. So many faces reached out of the past. The diminutive Marc Bolan, eyes blacked out, the glitter coruscating on his jacket, his musical expression lost in the rage of conflicting fashions, the alcohol level in his body soaring like mercury in response to a fever. Mick Jagger, with his indefatigable energy and love of clothes, was suddenly in the room, one floating pink sleeve, one diaphanous red, his top open over a black T-shirt embroidered with a *diamanté* crescent moon. Bette Midler, Andy Warhol, John Lennon singing the high-pitched vocals on 'Fame', they were names and faces that belonged to his past. He thought of Warhol's silver helium balloons, and how the man's presence was intimate with this place, this frozen movie-set; and how he expected to see him standing on a roof-top, a camera strap slung over one shoulder, his black shades cancelling the glare. There would be a box of Swiss chocolates open in his hotel room, the strawberry centres lifted first, the cherry brandy second, then the almond swirl, the various hard centres from nut to caramel to toffee.

What a long journey it had been, but at the same time it was less than a pin scratch on consciousness. He had become the ultimate star, the man whose visual metamorphoses had influenced the modern world. People had carried the idea of him inside their heads. And each time they had tried to isolate him, he had changed.

As he sat back in a floating chair giving on to the skyline through a window, he realized his body had undergone the ultimate transformation. The biochemical data necessary to his earth-life was no longer relevant. What he experienced was a sense of fluency. Instead of projecting his image on the universe, he had achieved autonomy. He could make things happen without an audience as an accomplice. The days of stage nerves, adrenalin overdrive, make-up artists, hairdressers, parties after the show were over. If he needed to recreate this attention it would be by way of a different species. Humans had proved unfulfilling. He had always been aware of their limitations. He had never accepted death, and it was in part the mental schemas he had evolved to transcend the idea of his end that had opened the door for the change that had occurred within him. His private reflections had always been meditations on the suprahuman. Sitting cradled in the back of a limousine driven through Hollywood at night, and out to the beach, he had realized visions that had confirmed his belief in extraterrestrials. He had watched saucers stand off above the Pacific surf. He had got the driver to park the Cadillac on the beach, switch the lights off, and he had lain back insulated by the metallic shell and listened to the breakers interpret the universal rhythm. They were waiting for him. Extraterrestrials had been in the audience during his concerts at the Los Angeles Amphitheatre. People had mistaken them for the Bowie clones he attracted. The silver pentagrams marked on their foreheads had been interpreted as attempts to imitate his own facial decoration. But he had distinguished his own. They were there and their eyes never left him. He had counted twenty. He was terrified they would come backstage. The time wasn't right. His act had still to be perfected, enhanced, taken to ultimate extremes. He had become an automatized mutant, a rock android. People paid to see him with the expectation he would die on-stage.

And he had got out of that. He had gone back to Europe in the belief he wouldn't be followed. Performing and then going anonymous had instilled in him the belief that he could go on living independent of his higher realization. But they hadn't gone away. He had come down to breakfast in a Berlin café, glanced around the room taking in the workers engaged in political discussion, and thought that the jittery present was no more than that. There was a man with his back to him dressed in a dark-blue overcoat. Nothing special.

A person come in out of the cold to drink steaming coffee. Someone who seemed to be rooted to his chair, local gossip. And without reason the man had floated his head round, fixed him momentarily with eyes that changed from red to silver. The flash of recognition was blindingly immediate. He knew then that he could never be free. He had been singled out. They would be there whenever he performed. He would be pursued from one stage to another until he made his true identity known.

He placed the interplanetary Walkman in his pocket and continued his exploration of the house. Zap and Cindy were breathing regularly. He would be gone before they awoke, but he remained fascinated by their bodies and the difference in their genitalia. As an android his sex was perfectly integrated. Now he could experience both male and female orgasms through sensitizing thought. The impulse could be directed through whatever zone of his body on which he wished to concentrate.

He continued to pick up objects and regroup them. A kaleidoscope, the black cardboard tube sprinkled with stars, an address book, blue ceramics, whatever seemed familiar to his eye. It was like playing a game with the past. The cars parked out in the street were metallic carapaces, exhibits obsoleted in the waiting, they would never now be driven away. A pink Cadillac with a blown-out windshield had been invaded by giant thistles. They projected into the driver's seat, prehensile feelers searching across the mink-lined steering-wheel.

He kept returning to the skyline, avoiding planetary contact through his Walkman, and taking in the immediate. The silence that walled him in was suddenly slashed by guitar lines cracking the still air. He knew immediately that it was Johnny. He was using a fuzzbox pedal to recrank 'Purple Haze'. Without Hendrix's virtuoso expertise, the sound was overloaded, manic, it spiralled back on itself, then lit into a wall of decibels. The overload hung like an electric storm in the air, thunder trapped in an underpass. Someone was courting him through music. The solitary guitarist was playing through an open window in the opposite house. Or was it further back in the complex distribution of ruins? The vocals weren't added. There was just the caterwauling howl of a guitar elegizing a lost world. He imagined Johnny, knees bent, back arched, standing in the slipstream of a directed hurricane. He would be smoking a DC, a cigarette cut with heroin, his eyes fixed on the image of a TV studio in the desert.

For a moment he wanted to go out and locate Johnny, have him strip his excess to the weird riffs created by his own guitar extremists, Mick Ronson, Heydon Stacey, Earl Slick. Each had in his own way devised a sound that had interpreted an audial psychosis. But it was a music generated by his lyrics, a volume that exploded around images. Johnny's connection was with his drug. He was an apocalyptic Keith Richards, mainlining inspiration, shuffling in suede knee-boots from one side of an imaginary stage to the other. He was performing for the frozen ones. An audience that had dematerialized into a hallucinated cosmos. The dimensions explored by Ballard in his pushing sci-fi frontiers into a psychic reality.

He waited at the window, half expectant that Johnny would show on a roof-top or boot the glass out of a door and perform on a narrow balcony above the street. He would be dressed in a military coat loaded with gold braid. The archetypal rock star differentiating by his appearance. The sound waves continued to ricochet off the surrounding walls. Ululating medleys that were translated into a ferocious assault on Johnny's imaginary audience. It came back to him how as a teenager he too had performed in the solitude of a Beckenham sitting-room. He was conscious then of the power he would come to assert over the masses. The young were looking for an androgynous leader. A red-haired, rock-messiah, a dude posturing as a Martian, his lipstick pout so huge it was like Man Ray's depiction of giant red lips floating in a blue sky. That had grown to be his ideal. And it had been realized. His face had become one of the most recognizable of his times, its cosmetic mutations never detracting from the alien characteristics that distinguished it.

At another stage of his life he would have tensed at the idea of confronting Johnny. Now, he experienced a sense of detachment. He could dematerialize at will. His people saw to that. He was clear of Johnny's vulnerability.

His eye fell on the outline of a cigarette packet. Cigarettes had formed a part of his life, they were an inexorable habit. Now he found himself disinterested. His body was no longer metabolized by need.

When the glass blew, it was a detonation. Johnny had come out on to an adjacent balcony. He was laser thin in the unreal light, his guitar wired to a long lead, his leather jeans and red velvet jacket affording him the looks of someone stuck in the era of seventies' glam rock. He retuned hurriedly, letting the three individual chords resonate, then savagely smashed into a ruptured version of 'The Midnight Rambler'. He recalled the menace of the Jagger/Richards original; the song lines punched out with cadenced, knife-throwing authority.

Johnny's music seemed like a frantic attempt to establish a bridge between the old and new world. He heard it as the art of someone who had failed to make the transition. A part of him wanted to re-earth and take up with the guitarist's invitation to instate rock as the futuristic credo. He went back into the room, checked the two bodies for consistent breathing, relocated the bathroom and shut the door on Johnny's overdrive. He stared at himself for a long time in the mirror. He was looking for the familiar dissimilarity in his eyes. This had been rectified in a face that remained true to his original. He sat on the floor, back to the wall, and recontacted Diamond Nebula. The voice came in immediately: 'Return to the dugout. We have plans for you. Your fame will be greater this time round. Our planet will send helpers when the time is right. You are not alone. Not alone.'

He stayed in the silence. He would meet up with Johnny later. Another time. Another place. He had arrived to stay. Lyrics were teeming across his mind. He could control the flow with a portable thought-scan. He froze the individual lines and edited a new song on the miniscreen. The music to be recorded on Diamond Nebula would follow. Cybernetics would be carried to their ultimate. He would go back to the dug-out, prepare himself all over again for his final mission.

Chapter 6

Marilyn kicked off her heels and sat inside the driver's seat of an old bronze Citroën parked face up to a Lamborghini on the ground floor of a high-rise car-park that had disappeared from the second storey up. After her flight from the hotel she needed to rest. She felt vulnerable in a town to which she had lost the index to security. All her life she had suffered from the contradictory impulse to outrage by her dress and at the same time remain invulnerable to the enmity her appearance aroused. She was dressed like the last hooker in a post-nuclear landscape.

Marilyn cradled her head into the leather support. She would use the car as an emergency refuge, and on the back seat she had placed a bag containing medicines, make-up, the stashes of credit cards she hoarded in the belief that they were still currency. She felt dissociated. She needed to contract into herself and shut out the landscape. Arc and their life together at the Grand Hotel was something she wanted to put behind her. All those crazy days of lifting the roof on the world, seeing people and buildings radically alter, hearing the silence move in as the trap asserted itself. She wanted to disown Arc's notion of turning life into a film-set on a universal screen.

Something told her she had to find Johnny. Drugs had afforded him an extrasensory clairvoyance, a transparency of perception that allowed him to read an aura, a situation with obliquely disarming truth. And there was a connection between him and the android who inhabited the beach, the mutant who had surprised her at the hotel.

On the other side of the car-park the remains of a rescue helicopter littered the thistled concrete. The amphibious hull and tail pylons had split free of the foreward fuselage. Humming-birds darted in and out of the cockpit; a green lizard seemed crystallized to one of the sponson support struts. Marilyn could still make out the embossed word RESCUE on a crumpled sliding door. There was no sign of the pilot. He had probably dematerialized while flying, or else had escaped into the ruins. In her imagination she pictured him slumped, catatonic in one of the existing Euro-supermarkets, an uncapped bottle of vodka cradled between his legs, his mind unable to take in the changes. Fixed in his consciousness was his last split-second record of the world before he crashed. Nothing now would dislodge it.

Marilyn thought of the hidden caches of dresses and the contents of the hotel safe she had hidden in a concrete bunker a little further round the coast. She meant to reclaim them. They were an investment for a possible future. And for once she didn't fear Arc's recriminations. Now that he had assumed a self-appointed omnipotence, she knew he would never leave the hotel. It had become a retreat, hermetic as Graceland, air- and light-sealed like Michael Jackson's Hollywood mansion. He would work at editing films; cutting, panning, modulating speed and focal length. Only when he had perfected a self-realized apocalypse would he come in pursuit of the survivors who lived in his dream landscape.

Marilyn checked the car mirror. She was increasingly anxious about her face. In time the lift would drop. After years of avoiding UV rays and maximizing on photo-regulating creams, she feared a structural collapse.

She moved on, picking her way from one obstruction to the next. The further she gained on the interior, the more involved were the constructs. St Laurent autumn fashions stood in a window display without the accompanying building. Further on an arranged tetrahedron of Ballard's novels had as its background Warhol's *Monroe* and the splintered debris of one of the crashed rescue helicopters. An alligator dislodged from the mosaic of a nearby antiques shop had been positioned on a car bonnet. Bizarre visual information littered the precinct.

Marilyn found herself entering a maze. She imagined the time would come when Arc would transform reality into a massive display system. Television banks would relay his cinematic obsessions; a red-haired David Bowie would remain immutably young, his image and music superimposed on the future. The selective ads would introduce the books that Ballard had continued to write on the near planets. Warhol would be seen supervising the mass silk-screening of his Elizabeth Taylor print. Arc's fetishes would be perpetuated on violet screens.

Marilyn experienced the idea that she was creating the future autonomously. It was as though someone were thinking for her, she was seeing by projecting – the film-frames released spontaneously by her stream of consciousness. She imagined Arc's film world speeded up and out of control. Shots of Jean Genet at the microphone, speaking on behalf of the Black Panther movement, would devolve into captions of astronauts attempting to catch cherries in their mouths in the capsule's gravity-free pressure. And they would all crash through. Warhol with Liza Minnelli, Bowie with Marlene Dietrich, Ballard with Monroe, Lou Reed with Rachel, Cocteau with Coco Chanel, Yves St Laurent with Pierre Bergé.

Marilyn knew she would find Johnny in whatever area of town reminded him of the past. He would be drugged or drunk, searching out the remains of pharmacies, bathroom cabinets, dashboard pockets, any conceivable stash-place from which he could get high. Johnny could never live at his own level; he had to go beyond himself, come at the world from the invulnerability of a drug screen.

Marilyn listened to the atmospherics; she was half expecting the red-haired android to materialize, the collar of a silver leather jacket turned up, his back towards her showing the logo of a single shooting star pursuing a meteoric trajectory. She would encounter him in a corridor leading from one street to another under the vitrified river. She kept moving where the music followed. Bowie's 'Golden Years' slipped in and out of the silence. Buildings appeared to have been shifted like stage-props; a cinema front gave on to the proportions of a botanical garden, its other three walls arranged as a horizontal triptych scored with posters. A wardrobe screen open on a swathe of dark suits stood in the middle of an area overrun by opium poppies. Shocking-pink graffiti was slashed across most uprights – ciphers, numerals, overtly gay propaganda. And star-treks written up in indecipherable script. Marilyn skirted an oval swimming-pool with the caution of a Hollywood star emerging from the reclusion of a Beverley Hills mansion. Sunflowers massed across the enclosed area of a municipal park. White chairs were grouped loosely outside a café. She picked up a glass of mint julep. Pink lipstick fibres were visible around the rim. The place was sufficiently unaltered for her to recognize she was in the vicinity of the Peppermint Suite, the packed student dive in which Johnny had won a cult following. It was here that the leather people had congregated to see his suicidal stage act, his drugged body testing the ultimate frontiers of advance. Johnny had tried so hard to be the archetypal rock star that he had grown to be parodic in his excesses.

Marilyn checked on the surrounding buildings. A Body Shop, a newsagent, a pharmacy with its Chanel and Guerlain products in the window. She pushed through the complex towards the basement stairs. Her associations with time and place were returning. She had come to this square so often in the past. Her brain fade was lightening, the amnesiac cells unfreezing to address the present. A giant screen television set was on in one corner of the rectangle. She stood back and saw the familiar figure of Arc standing on the balcony of the

Grand Hotel. The isolated frame remained exposed for a long time before the picture jumped to show Arc amongst his triptych of world leaders. The lens zoomed in to isolate the three arriving in the coastal desert, and then a montage of isolated images. Bowie's interviewer in a hotel room was Ballard; Warhol leant casually against a white wall filming the proceedings.

Marilyn fixed her eyes on the ground. She half expected to hear a Sten gun open up from a low-flying helicopter. She was anticipating the opening bars of 'Space Oddity', and the mutant slipping in and out of view, his hologrammic body asking that she follow into the eroticized dimensions of inner space.

She stopped at the entrance to the basement stairs. She had come so far in her journey; events that would have occupied a car ride of ten minutes seemed to have extended across decades. She anticipated the red cloakroom door with its skull logo where vamps had made up in front of wall-panelled mirrors. Microskirted, wearing pink or black fun-wigs, they had rechecked lips and eye points with an obsession for fetishistic detail. People had lost orientation in this club, they had appeared to levitate or have the drug lift them off the floor.

Marilyn kicked off her shoes. She was beginning to form a recognizable map from Arc's deliberately repetitive symbols. The town was taking on the construction of his mind. If she kept on exploring it she would end up in the labyrinth inside his head.

The club evoked for her an ersatz death cult with its attendant exhibitionism and ambivalent sex rites. Names and numbers had been picked into the black walls – a cryptic serialization of contacts. Where were they now, Boogie Sue and Black Rosie, Skinflick Three and Jimmy Dean's Revival?

She sat down on the edge of the stage and waited. She sensed Johnny's presence. He was somewhere in the building, putting on a red-sequinned jacket in the dressing-room, spooking himself in the mirror or lying low like a leather snake in an aisle. She knew he would break on her suddenly, dramatically, his hand-mike shrieking with dissonance. Thin as a pasta strand, resembling Nick Cave when he occupied the lights like a vertical laser beam, Johnny would launch himself from madness into reality.

Marilyn had spent her life on the fringes of the famous. She had worked on making her body the expression that others achieved through performance. And now, with the adrenalin jump of someone going on to applause, she manoeuvred into centre stage. For a moment she was the acclaimed one; the band's intro had diffused itself into the specific chords of the opening song. In her mind she was Lou Reed coming on-stage in 1973, hands on his head, his butch, skeletal figure moulded to leather, his spiked wristbands raised triumphantly towards a pink affirmative flicker of gay rights, a man revolutionizing pop with a bull-whip and leather elbow gloves. She wondered if Lou would have let her paint his eyelids. This was what she knew best. Or would he have been too far out, brutally untouchable, slugging whisky from a three-quarters empty bottle?

Johnny didn't make any noise. He could see right into Marilyn's head as though he were looking into a kaleidoscope, revolving the lens so that the patterns fragmented and re-formed. Drugs had given him this clarity. And it was terrifying, watching images, obsessions recur. It was like being crouched in front of a human television screen. The blanks between interpretable thoughts were no colour at all. Just a trance condition through which nothing showed.

Johnny kept to the side of the stage. His world excluded anything and anyone who didn't contribute to his self-acclaimed apotheosis. In time he would play to the gathered nations. The Indians waiting patiently on horseback in the shade, Middle East terrorists embracing tight-jeaned American girls, the Europeans forming a giant metallic beetle's back of cars, couples sitting on the roofs, straining into a red sun setting behind an elevated stage lit by blue spotlights. And as a support act the chained figure of Charles Manson would kneel in confrontation with a python.

It was all a matter of spontaneous projection. Marilyn was so transparent he could walk through her, take out her interior and fit whatever was useful in her chemistry to his own.

He delayed his approach; his voyeuristic powers afforded him the advantage that no scientific exploration had been able to achieve. Johnny wanted to break free of Arc's tyranny and coerce the mutant whom he knew to be David Bowie into joining him in creating a music that would prepare the way for a new species. And he would find the others. All over town in deserted high-rise apartments, basements, defunct car-parks there would be people. Those who had survived the change. His guitar noise would chase them out into the open. They would gather one day beneath the balcony of the house in which he had taken refuge. He would stare out and encounter eyes, hundreds of silver eyes pinpointing his movements. He would pull on an old slashed leather jacket scored with badges, lift his hair back, maintain the suspension and then rip that silence to shreds with his guitar chops and fuzzbox.

He hung on to the suspension dots following each breath. Marilyn had created her own spotlight; her thought forms were variants of herself, magnifications of her imagined potential. He had learnt from tracking the mutant that to spray someone was the quickest way to have them out. After that, he would hold Marilyn captive and extract from her mind the information necessary to him for cracking the android's secret of exchanging one body for another.

He savoured the waiting. In his mind the cheering had begun. Bowie was there to welcome him on-stage. Advertising balloons drifted across the stadium. He was black on black, leaning into himself, determined not to part with even a shadow. If he raised a dusted eyelid, it was too generous a concession.

When he sprang, it was with the ferocity of a big cat on amphetamines. His menace stood her upside-down. There wasn't anything to hold on to as the blackness exploded inside her head. Marilyn felt her thoughts uprooted like hairs.

Johnny carried her backstage, a transsexual exhibit for his experimentation, her microskirt up above her waist, and laid her out on the dressing-room table. He lit a joint and riffled through the fat scrapbooks of cuttings he kept as an emulative mirror to his own imagined achievements. He flicked the pages, turning up cuttings of Jagger on-stage in the Hyde Park free concert, his short white dress and long curtained hair creating the ultimate in androgynous chic, and there was Johnny Rotten on-stage at the Winter Gardens in LA, his mouth spitting venom, gobbing at the audience, turning his body into a Dadaist expression of anti-pop, a punk assault on every living institution. He leafed through his favourites. Iggy Pop's muscular torso bared on-stage, a leather peaked cap on his head, chains wrapped around his body, a man who would crawl across the stage barking like a dog to the accompaniment of Beethoven's Ninth. And Siouxsie was there in black vinyl hotpants, her hair blown back in purple and red spikes standing up vertical like a porcupine's erect quills. Her dance contortionism was molecular, the Banshee guitars created the current to which she moved like a pot in the spiral of being created by animated hands. He flicked the pages, getting high on the iconic revelations that fuelled his adrenalin. A cigarette drooped from the lip corner of an emaciated Nick Cave, and there was Keith Richards out of it on smack, his eyes blacked with kohl, a beret pulled over one eye. A man living five miles back on the peripheries of consciousness.

Johnny was fixated by his pantheon of stars. There was a picture of Freddie Mercury taking off from the stage in a high balletic kick. His long hair and moustache were in contradistinction to the artificial breasts under his top. And there was the man six or eight years later, his torso built up by weights to a muscular elasticity, his hair cut square and short, his clipped moustache conforming to the image of gay rights.

Johnny continued to draw on his museum of stars. He dragged on acrid smoke as his eyes shot into Madonna's gold crotch. Dressed by Gaultier in a pointed bra, metallic basque and fishnet tights, the blonde hedonist was caught with the red pout of a full carnation. One hand between her thighs, the other supporting the back of her head, her outrage and vivacity had stormed the world in her Blonde Ambition tour. And her counterparts, Michael Jackson and Prince, were depicted in corresponding variations of erotic provocation. Jackson's silicone features and white skin had created in him the looks of an alien. Dressed in military jackets loaded with gold braid, and leather jeans, his profile had been shaped to resemble that of his sister La Toyah's. And Prince, wearing high-heeled boots, a white frilled shirt and purple velvet jacket, looked like a nineties' version of Jimi Hendrix. Armed with a custom-built yellow guitar, his ego pounded off mirrors, came back to him magnified by a telescopic hall of mirrors reaching all the way to Jupiter.

Johnny was getting higher. He found himself fixated by cuttings of the diminutive Marc Bolan, the guru of early seventies' glam rock, the man whose 'Jeepster', 'Ride a White Swan' and 'Get It On' had created the necessary precedents for Bowie's career. Bolan stood posturing in velvets and sequins, his heavy eye make-up adding to the meringue puffiness of his cheeks. His body represented a microcontinent of stimulants. It was a state with which Johnny found an immediate empathy. The wasted hero, the man kept alive by toxins.

Johnny jumped at random from one decade to another. Pictures of the acid-demented Syd Barrett fronting the early Pink Floyd were counterbalanced by his modern equivalent in the likes of Julian Cope. The latter had lacerated his body on-stage at the Hammersmith Palais in 1985, attempting the same sort of effortless self-mutilation once achieved by Iggy Pop. It was incidents like Cope's that Johnny had emulated. He wanted rock to reacquire the shocking stage antics of Hugo Ball's original Cabaret Voltaire performances. Only the punks had picked up on their Dadaist progenitors. Johnny needed to go beyond that, and to take his music into the deepest recesses of psychotic inner space. He wanted to undergo metamorphoses on-stage, become a dog, a leopard, a woman, an astronaut, any one of a thousand variants, and then revert to himself. And he would embody each transformation as a reality. He would leave the stage as a red-eyed wolf in a top hat and tuxedo.

He could feel his mind spin into orbit. He was the pansexual amalgam of all the stars who had ever been. From Presley to Jagger to Prince, Johnny had assimilated the total rock 'n roll sensibility. He was still awaiting his moment. Excesses had prepared him for the ultimate act, the dismemberment and reintegration of the singer on-stage. The sacrificial ritual would find its affirmative properties in rebirth. He was indestructible. His intended liaison with Bowie would prove that. Drugs had afforded him immortality. Heroin had eliminated all potential of cancer from his cells; his immune system was resistant to every form of viral invasion.

Johnny stabbed his finger at a shot of John Lennon, *circa* 1970, his messianic beard, long parted hair and white kaftan lending him the aura of a desert prophet. There was no mistaking the man's universal mission. He was dispensing his presence to his adulators. His vibes buzzed like a string of karmic bees. And he, Johnny, was greater than all of them. He picked up his guitar and got off on the reverb. His mind hummed at the centre of an electronic hive. He could feel each overcharged cell disengage and come alive. His head had interiorized Hendrix's fuzzbox. Songs like 'Hey Joe', 'Purple Haze' and 'Voodoo Child' were no more than faded blueprints for the songs he had conceived.

Marilyn was still out cold. When Johnny had discovered Zap and Cindy, he had attempted to reconstruct the alien's moves. He had assessed Bowie's primary motive as that of curiosity. Both people were unharmed, their bodies lying parallel, their breathing regular. It was as though the third party had wanted to emphasize the separation of the sexes and the possibilities inherent in this arrangement for the creation of a new species. Cindy's being stripped to her panties was not an enticement so much as a warning. It was a gesture devoid of all provocation. And Zap too had never appeared so asexual, his body seeming to exist independent of his contracted cock. The two might have been laid out on different planets, one on Jupiter and one prostrate on Mars. There was no sense of a shared body time. Both appeared to have entered independent orbits in inner space. Each was a brain-bleeped satellite monitoring intrinsic planets. Cindy might have been diving to retrieve a book buried on the ocean floor, and Zap involved on a journey to the interior of a building realized in dream, each corridor narrowing to another, a leopard sitting at the library desk in central office archives. And he had arranged Marilyn with a similar detachment. He had opened her legs in a coital position, her made-up face resembling a doll's head sloping at an angle from the neck. But his wish was to dehumanize further this surgically reconstructed body. Marilyn represented someone in need of adoption by extraterrestrials. Whatever race she had belonged to was used up, burnt out, the *disjecta membra* of dead sexual fantasies. They wouldn't return again as erotic symbols, Monroe, Loren, Bardot, Madonna. They would go begging attention through dream auditoriums, recurring with cyclic monotony, unable to arouse interest in the curvature of their bodies.

Johnny knew he was anticipating the future. The millennial transition would bring about a re-evaluation of body functions. The advanced would have dispensed already with their physical motivation and have concentrated on molecular ballistics. They would be going inwards, pursuing trajectories that traced individual arcs towards the great uninhabited cities. Johnny had visited so many of these places. He had taken to marking them on a chart. The alhambra situated in a black desert in which a woman with gold hair guarded the secret to the elimination of all disease. He had seen her pink Cadillac kick up a dust-storm of black sand. And there was a river come out of nowhere and flowing through nowhere. It carried on its surface all the poets who had ever lived. They floated on the current's spine like sleep-walkers. Johnny had entered a port where Jacques Brel was still composing, recording in a giant warehouse. Brel's frustration was that dead, his voice was untransferable to tape. He kept on devising lyrics and melodies that could never be heard.

There were so many locations Johnny had visited. With Bowie's help he might get back to each. He wanted to plug in on Mars and let the power rip. He felt his potential would be realized on the near planets. The pink birds whose wings completely covered a lake were in some way related to the empty, blue-tiled swimming-pool he had discovered in the middle of a cypress forest. Both were presided over by an ovoid-shaped couple. Each had a conical breast situated centrally on the torso, each communicated through a series of numerals that flashed up in their eyes. And he had really been to these places. He had seen Madonna squatting, her urine jet creating a hologram. There wasn't any reason to think that places visited mentally couldn't be revisited. It's just that no one ever tries, he thought, no one ever seems to think it possible to reconnect with a sequence of images.

He dragged at the smoke. He was conscious of living out the role of the archetypal rock star, a scarlet guitar propped up against his left leg, his leather trousers creased from consecutive one-night stands, his fingers knuckled with rhinestones. And he would be the one who would dismantle minds, extract from individual chemistries, build up a process of deathlessness by his invasion of the human psyche. He saw himself in the manner of an analyst examining obsessions, fixations, neuroses, as though they comprised the microscopic fauna of pond life. Whatever was most transparent in a person, he would take for himself. Drugs had given him this insight. He could add to his talent, experiment with other thought processes, reject what proved to be of no value to his advancement.

'Maybe the person doesn't need to be awake,' he told himself. Up on a mental high his senses penetrated every barrier. He knew he had access to anything and everything, even Arc's psychotic fantasies. He had watched thought shapes stream from the latter's mind like big mauve clouds.

Johnny squatted on the floor and lifted back the lid of one of Marilyn's eyes, then the other. Two green twists of colour showed in the surrounding whites. He sat there coaxing himself into the belief that he was a magician, a mind invader. He laughed out loud at the sense of his indomitable power. He could turn it on, increase the current like volume control. It was like using a psi laser. He could see that Marilyn was dreaming. Colour flashes buzzed across his vision. In her dream, Marilyn was walking down a long pink road lined by regularly spaced poplars. The road sloped downhill towards a city on a lake. Johnny had the advantage of interpreting what for Marilyn was an autonomous sequence of images. When she came to the lake, she was confronted by Arc riding on a black swan. The surprise generated by this meeting at the water's edge had her unconsciously terminate the narrative. What took its place was transferred to Johnny as a blank. There wasn't anything there but primal fog, grey spaces punctuated by occasional tremors. Johnny lived with the fog, waiting for another dream journey to show, the constellations of a mythologem to burn in a blazing meteoric cluster. There was a pulsation of yellow light, then a red pulsar signalling in the blank as Johnny watched another unconscious fiction unfold.

Marilyn had situated herself in a tropical forest. Arc was walking away from her through a clearing. Big red birds with gold tails clapped into the air, wings beating furiously as they raucously sat in tree-tops. Positioned between her and the rapidly disappearing Arc was an open suitcase. Marilyn ran in pursuit of the vanishing figure and disturbed a snake uncoiling from a wad of letters that spilled out of the blue leather repository. And the more she rummaged into the pile, the greater was the increase of paper. And each time she used both hands on the density of envelopes, so they flew up over her head into the air. They were like paper birds that resisted the least contact, and soon the sky was full of them. And suddenly aware the chequered snake had gone missing, she realized that it had become her spine. Its spiral loops ran up and down her back. It twisted her round according to its convolutions.

Johnny noted everything. He appropriated whatever images could feed his mind, augment his psychic input. He confiscated the snake, felt it coldly settle in the base of his skull. And he took one of the envelopes, opened it and inside found the number 666, the numerical designation of the Great Beast. His brief readings of Crowley told him that this was no accident. His mission was being defined. Power had been given him to subjugate those who encroached on his self-appointed task. What he wanted from Marilyn was a symbol, a key that he could use in his aspiration towards longevity. What he stole from others would fortify his cells. He would grow to be multidimensional, the indestructible migrant who moved on from one planetary station to the next.

84

Johnny left Marilyn asleep and headed out into the ruins. His red velvet jacket seemed even louder against the mobbed invasion of yellow sunflowers. He wanted to locate Bowie and search out the other occupants of this millennial time-warp. He imagined them huddled around fires in the back-yards of tenements, in the husks of hotels and apartment blocks. Some would be intoning mantras, others conferring about the change, guarding the secret of their food hoards. They would have formed reconnaissance groups, and in time internal warfare would ensue. Breakaway groups would seek to dislodge those who wished to remain at the interior. Johnny imagined the shots ringing out, and fires jumping up as orange banners in a gutted quarter. His music would accompany this apocalyptic crescendo. He would lead the extremists towards an escape route out of time.

Johnny forced his way through the precinct and out into Bridge Street. Someone other than himself had smashed holes in car windows in order to snatch valuables from dashboard lockers. A line of vehicles parked along one side of the street had all been raided in this fashion. Chips of glass sparkled underfoot, shards that seemed to spell out a diagrammatic message, the fragmented mosaic of a disordered mind. The level of damage to each car had increased in a descending line, suggesting that the assailant unable to find anything of value had addressed his mania to random forays on body-work as well as glass.

Johnny kicked his way through glass studs. Store-fronts were in most cases caved in. To Johnny it was like reclaiming a place he had visited in a dream or experienced in another incarnation. He kept telling himself that he had jumped a life without transitional warning. It was like going to a movie to discover that he had stepped direct into a film-frame. There would never be a way back to the High Street, the late afternoon to which the crowds would return. People would be shopping, buying a Paris *Vogue*, pointing to oranges in a fruiterer's display, disengaging from the dream state induced by the film, while he would have gone off down the poplar-lined avenue, the atmospherics accompanying the narrative as a young boy raced down a dry earth slope to meet him.

Johnny got into the entrance of a pinball arcade. An empty Beck's beer bottle had been left on top of one of the machines. The back of the building was missing. He found himself looking at the inquiring faces of huge tropical cactus flowers, orange corollas exploding from blue cartwheels. His eye encountered the by now familiar graffiti: MAJOR TOM'S A JUNKIE. BOWIE'S BACK ON PLANET EARTH. The stuffed panther mounted as a prop in one of the aisles was a reminder that someone other than Arc was loose in the precinct. He was sure he heard somebody laugh, slowly, articulately, a tone suppressed before it ascended an excited scale. But when he looked round, no one was there, just an empty street scene, a cobalt Volvo parked nose up to a maroon Range-Rover. Everything stalled as though the entire world had gone away.

He got back to the street, cautiously looking up at a top floor opposite. A window was open on a sloped roof. A line of coloured shirts hung like pennants above the street. He heard the laughter again. It might have been a bird, a video prop that had come to life, all gold plumage and big garnet eyes. The sort of exhibit placed in a rocking-chair opposite a seated woman wearing nothing but a monocle and a pair of red spike heels.

Johnny took the stairs up, his mind going ahead of him, projecting itself into an imaginary meeting with a monkey-bird or a spaced-out survivor huddled against a wall, slugging Scotch from the bottle-neck. He had heard Arc speak of the mad ones, those whose fuses had blown, and who had gone off in packs before dispersing to solitary nomads who lived by looting.

Johnny listened for a long time on the stairs. He could smell smoke, as though the occupant had reverted to the primitive instinct of lighting fires as a protection. A white-painted door was open on what must have been a top-floor flat. The air was loaded. He expected that at any moment someone would jump him, that an eye was watching, searching his face, line by line. He heard his own pulse coming back at him as a drumbeat. An uprush of adrenalin took him into the room. What he saw was himself, his reflection crashing obliquely off a mirror, a red spiral fish lunging at the surface. The room was empty. The remains of a fire still snuffled in the open chimney-place. A chair had been broken up for fuel. Whoever had lived here originally, had done so minimally. A white table occupied the space in front of the street window. A portable television sat on it. A Hockney poster had been blu-tacked on the opposite wall. The slanted verticals of a line of paperbacks had partly collapsed on a shelf. Nothing else. A CD unit. The uniform mauve sky framed by the window.

Johnny went into the bedroom. Its furniture was correspondingly minimal: a waterbed was the dominant feature. Monroe's face looked across the wall at Madonna's. Red lips opposed by red lips. The pill popper and the macrobiotic plutocrat. Johnny went over and kissed each as though it were a reality. He was in love with stars, the Warholian ethos in which the desire for fame became the thing itself. The open wardrobe unit suggested a designer, an architect, someone who expressed himself through bright colours. Floral shirts mixed with denim and leather, a white suit had a red Paisley tie draped over one shoulder.

Johnny searched through the bathroom cabinet for pills but could find nothing that would give him a buzz. Then something caught his eye. In his rush to try to find a supply that would increase his stash, he had neglected the sign in the bath. It had been executed crudely but with care. Someone had used a lipstick to draw a hexagram. The words MAJOR TOM had been written inside, and outside the symbol the warning WE'RE WATCHING YOU.

Johnny let the threat sink in. He went cold knowing he had still to encounter the ones out there in hiding. He wanted to get out of the place and run towards someone, anyone, and tell them the news. But there was no one to inform. The dead telephone, the empty streets, the madmen gone underground, the arena of a giant film-set in which he couldn't locate survivors. Johnny leapt the stairs in his leather thigh-boots and got back to the street. He thought he heard the whirr of a helicopter's props going over towards the coast, but assumed he was hallucinating the sound. The sky was vacant.

Johnny hugged the sides of buildings. He toyed with the idea of stunt driving a Lamborghini through the ruins. Heading out of town for the coast, the scarlet car hanging a dust-storm in its wake. Arc would hear the car reverberating round the coast, tailing off into impasses, then buzzing back into an audibly monitored trajectory. Johnny imagined himself on a crash course, jumping clear of the car before it exploded on impact with a wall.

He drifted towards the centre of town. The architecture he discovered was like a Gaudi extravaganza, baroque hallucinations implanted in high-rise escarpments. He might have been tripping, watching the visible world change into prismatic dimensions. He wanted to find the mutant. He knew that Bowie was somewhere in the complex maze of inner space, or he would sight him on the roof-top of a building he had taken over for its computer bank. He remembered the titles of Bowie's old bootlegs: 'Nazi Heroically', 'Immersed in Crowley's Uniform', 'Cocaine Adds Life', 'Resurrection on Bath Street'. His devotees had anticipated the singer's adoption of extreme roles. What they hadn't reckoned on was that their fictions had grown into a reality.

Johnny wondered if Zap and Cindy were out here in the concrete maze. Found out in Zap's studio, they may have chosen to migrate in search of the lost world, stopping off in any one of the abandoned buildings, consuming supplies and moving on.

Johnny smashed his way into an off-licence. He felt the give in the glass partition as it connected with his heel. He finished it off with the iron bar discarded by the car vandal, watching a star open round the reinforced mesh. Inside, he grabbed a bottle of Jack Daniels, uncapped it and felt appeased by the raw stimulus to his nerves, the way the heat concentrated itself in his abdomen. He knew the way back to the club. His guitars were standing in the dressing-room, his stage clothes

88

massed across a table and chairs. Sequinned jackets, boas, leather trousers, leopard-print ones, he had never made a distinction between his appearance on-stage and the one he adopted for the street.

He took off with the bottle in his hand. There was smoke rising in a black spiral column from a high-rise block behind him. Someone must have set fire to a top floor, a deserted open plan, the word processors still switched on, green and blue rectangles, each with a bottom line of white print pulsing to go forward.

Johnny was beginning to feel overexposed from lack of human contact. He needed to siphon images, ideas, energy, the input that comprised the individual's chemistry. His constant obsession was the need to assimilate others, translate them into his own sense data. His reserves were inexhaustible. All the thought impressions, alpha rhythms, dream implosions, DNA spirals, genes, chromosomes he had stolen constituted a pool that would place him among the deathless ones. He wanted to get back to the Peppermint Lounge and invade Marilyn. He would play his guitar over her prostrate body like a ritual. If she regained consciousness, he would subject her to dementia by his music. His guitar generated a current that could blow the back out of anything.

Other fires were starting up in the district where he had noticed the menacing plume of smoke. He could hear the flap and crack of flames as they licked high-rise constructions. He encountered tropical fauna. Orchids were belling through involuted lianas; mango and rubber trees had taken root in the scratchy area of the municipal park. The sparsely planted gardens were now a riot of sunflowers, tobacco plants, bougainvillaea, red hibiscus, glowering cacti.

Johnny had to pick his way through the extravagant foliage. It was like entering a tunnel of peacocks' feathers or walking direct into a Max Ernst. He had the idea that there was a big blue sun at the other end, but there wasn't. He might have been looking for the elevated stage at a free festival, the platform on which he was to perform to the ones come out of hiding. In the middle of the trees he found himself face to face with a cenotaph on which the figure of Andy Warhol was positioned like the Statue of Liberty holding a Coca-Cola bottle to the stars. There were cedars, Judas trees, palms, an avenue of monkey-puzzle trees, a bright pink Cadillac parked diagonally across the path. To Johnny, it was like cinema. He got through the park and out into a series of side-streets that connected with the way back to the centre. The old Doors song 'People Are Strange' flashed through his mind. He half expected to see a figure with a shaved head standing outside a building, his back to the wall, his eyes looking out for someone or something to move into his field of vision.

He might have encountered these streets before in a dream. The same houses shut to the light as in a mauve siesta hour. Graffiti Sanskrit scored across the lower walls, a back-brain flash from a previous life engaging him in the immediate. His involvement with drugs had made it increasingly hard for him to differentiate between the past and present.

He kept on going, making his way against a uniform backdrop of stucco façades, warehouse and shop-fronts. He was in a hurry to get back to his retreat. He wanted to lash the basement with his vehement guitar work, take his nerves out on an extension that connected with dead idols: Jim Morrison, Jimi Hendrix, Brian Jones, John Lennon. He would locate all the dead ones: Edith Piaf, Billie Holiday, Janis Joplin, Elvis Presley. They would resonate in his chord work. He would convert their astral vibrations into electricity, his guitar would be the weapon he directed at the world.

He was about to turn the corner into the precinct when Bowie materialized. There wasn't any warning. It began as a 3D hallucination which steadied and translated itself into the two dimensional. He was just standing there, red hair pushed back off the head, a black vinyl jacket open on a naked torso. He was in jeans and silver thigh-boots. The image lasted a matter of seconds. Johnny ran towards the disappearing figure. He could hear the music arrive, the plaintive chords to 'Space Oddity'. 'Ground control to Major Tom'. There wasn't anyone there. Johnny uncapped the bottle of Jack

90

Daniels and rocked backwards on the sustained impact of liquor. He stripped off his red jacket and got into the shopping precinct. He was hungry for sound. When he hit the basement steps it was two at a time, tripping over himself, and finally he landed head over heels at the bottom.

Chapter 7

Arc sat looking out from his studio balcony at the Grand Hotel. The ruins around the coast were in themselves the perfect film-set. He could imagine Helmut Newton photographing transvestite models against such a backdrop. Only this time the parts in the film were real. It wasn't like a series of extras disbanding after shooting and the director going off to the Train Bleu at the Gare de Lyon to talk about technical problems and the authentic kicks created by the hookers in *Belle de jour*. Arc had contrived to establish an altered cosmos with his camera.

Arc looked at the mauve sky for reassurance. His reclusive life at the Grand Hotel and the prospect of a stone desert receding to an imperceptible sea had grown to constitute a reality. He had become the last great director, superior to Buñuel, Cocteau, Fassbinder, Eisenstein, Herzog, Wenders. He would work on shooting his great masterpiece in which a select company would feature as the last survivors on earth.

In the last of his downtown raids Arc had looted a video store. Among his hardware discoveries he had salvaged an electronic still video camera with an advanced storage system. He had brought this back in an old red Chevrolet, with abundant fuel in the tank, together with a camcorder and sealed cartons of Metal Evaporated Tape. Arc was fascinated by video accessories; they corresponded to his desire to create a new fictional universe. Shooting film had become a substitute for ejaculation. If sex existed for him now, it was through the medium of film. The sight of a Warhol tumulus of smashed cars, selected passages from Ballard's *Crash* or the discovery in one of the hotel rooms of a black dildo concealed beneath lingerie in a suitcase, were sufficient to compensate for lack of erotic orientation. Arc had surprised himself in these perverse acts of consummation. When he found himself unzipping and working himself off against the cool bodywork of the Chevrolet, he had realized how far he had come towards adopting a new identity. And it had grown into a ritual, this contact between his sensitive glans and the Chevrolet's sprayed bodywork.

Arc's mind was big with his plans for filming. The environment, the incongruous juxtaposition of a car half buried in sand with a store mannequin seated on the roof, were only one example of the inexhaustible surreal connotations implied by the landscape. To look outside was to enter the world of Yves Tanguy, Max Ernst, Dali.

Arc turned on his own television station. Footage from Bowie's 1980 Floor Show, excerpts from Warhol's *Trash* were phased into the showing of a short documentary on Arc's life as a film director. He watched himself working in his fourth-floor studio. He might have been looking at the actions of a stranger on another planet. The room was stacked with video cartridges, cassettes, CDs, album covers, and behind him his blond mentor Warhol stared vacantly from a poster triptych. And in the same way as Warhol had grown obsessed with recording conversational trivia at Studio 54, so Arc had grown preoccupied with monitoring his own work in the studio. If anyone broke through his defences, he wanted documentaries to exist as the authentication of his genius.

Arc had filmed his bizarre sexual fetishes, using the camera as a voyeuristic aperture to auto-eroticism in the manner that Robert Mapplethorpe had come to photograph himself impaled on a dildo.

Arc had established an inventive archive of self-fetishes. Using a still video camera he had let his ejaculation snow into the lens. The constellated spermatozoa was his ultimate union with autobiographic film. That and his conjugation with the Chevrolet suggested a new vocabulary of sensory experience, one that convinced him he was migrating towards the new species.

And now that Marilyn had left, there was no one who could reach him. He imagined himself living for ever in the Grand Hotel, reappearing a thousand years later to watch the planetary shuttles leave earth for Mars.

He would work on his film until it was complete. The dematerializing crowds, the radical mutation of a landscape to a stone forest defined by actual tangible skylines, a town littered with his own poster and graffiti obsessions, the architectural anomalies, the interspersed Bowie, Ballard and Warhol footage, all of these factors would combine to create the film with which Arc hoped to end the existing universe.

Arc thought of all the dead cinephiles, the stoned television cameramen, the Hollywood archivists, the crews who followed the Rolling Stones across east to west American stadiums, and wished they could all assemble to view his work on a huge screen in the desert. It would be a form of cineastic euthanasia. A last momentary confrontation with the figure of Bowie seated, playing an acoustic guitar on Warhol's grave.

Arc put on a Billie Holiday cassette and listened to the lady swing from 'What a Little Moonlight Can Do' to 'I Cover the Waterfront'. The voice was perfect in its cadence, a blue ovoid framed by a mulberry lipstick bow. The live recording had the piano sound like it was being played underwater.

94

Arc felt cooly detached from Johnny's intentions. He knew that the latter would come in search of him, but that was when? In a week or another century? The bottles of Veuve Clicquot that he had removed from the hotel's cellars were a further aid to oblique perception. When he wasn't high on substance, he turned to liquor. The champagne had his head rush. He wanted to accelerate through a thousand years. In a new millennium he would make entire films out of individual chapters of Ballard's fiction, focusing for days on the perverse sexual detail established in *Crash* between metal, lesions and the orgasmic attraction to multiple injuries.

By magnifying the particular he hoped to create a still-focus film. The image would remain suspended for the duration of an hour, at the end of which the action would be relayed at incalculable speed. The accelerated flashes would be transmitted by a futuristic code of ESP. In the course of dreaming, the spectator would replay the film at normal speed. It would be like a movie capsule visualized for delayed internal release. Arc scanned his preparatory script; his draft had begun to map out the possibilities of a future world. He moved between cine-film cuts and video editing, transferring his original shots on the master tape to a blank tape on a slave machine. Film had created the hallucinatory cosmos in which he lived. Only screen ghosts or video aliens could intrude on his plans for an unlegislated genocide.

Exhausted from studio work Arc patrolled the hotel corridors. For several nights he had been awoken by what he thought was the generative hum of the now dormant elevator. He had come to create its transit between floors, its punctuated stop and start in the insulated shaft.

Arc was cut off. He half expected to find Johnny waiting for him at the end of the corridor, mean and posed and psychopathic in his intentions. He would be standing there as though his rehearsed action was a stage gesture. Or would he discover the android materializing suddenly at the end of a corridor, a hologrammic body gone as quickly as it registered?

Arc's recreation, rather like Marilyn's, was to loot the

guest rooms. And now that she had gone, his pleasure was increased by the prospect of hoarding the valuables he knew she would wish. He had taken to reading through diaries concealed in handbags and to empathizing with the sexual, speculative or commonplace entries recorded in those confessionals. He flicked open a red leather pocket-book and dipped in at random.

Monday 31 March: Drive from Toulouse to Biarritz. Windy pines, green skies. Billy says he can no longer deceive his wife. Oral sex in a clearing. Picked up a prescription for Secanol. Remember nothing of the night. Awoke from a dream in which someone had broken down the door. I saw only the feet and torso of the intruder. As I was about to meet his face I woke up.

Wednesday 2 April: Billy calls from Paris. His voice is furred from drink. Even down the telephone I can smell whisky. He wants a pair of my silk panties and the photographs. He hints that there will be chances to meet. 'Only wait,' he advises. 'Things must take their course.' Our desperate mutual insecurity.

Arc threw the pocket-book back on the blue counterpane with the other spilled contents from the capsized handbag – tortoise-shell glasses, a pink Dior lipstick, a snakeskin wallet and purse. He had also begun to accumulate shoes with the excruciating concentration on detail that obsesses the fetishist. He had made a cache in one room of a collection put together by a couple for whom it evidently provided the main sexual stimulus. Thigh-high black patent boots alternated with scarlet stilettos. There were shoes with chain and padlock fastenings, all of which must have been made to order, and a black leather mask silvered with studs. He handled the leather, vinyl and satin exhibits as though he were stroking a series of pets. Who and where was the woman who had worn these? He imagined the schizoid split in her life, how she buried her secret by day, working as a literary agent, and at night engaged in a ritual of algolagnia, bondage, a mutual sharing of pain that reduced her to a compliant Sadean woman.

Arc locked each room with the proprietorial instincts of one who has come to stay. In his mind the Grand Hotel had become the universal studio. It was the equivalent of Warhol's *Factory*. In time the disembodied Warhol would see this as the new locus; Bowie would record here and Ballard would occupy a suite on the seaward side, looking out over the coral forests, the rusted bodywork of cars improvised as a foreground, a 747 standing nose-up as an aeronautic sculpture.

Arc ransacked bedside drawers in order to add to his supply of cocaine. The American pilot's attaché case had been lined with sachets of white powder. His habit was kept alive by the clandestine supplies he had found in travelling-bags, in the linings of Armani suits. Arc had begun recruiting valuables and storing them in his room adjoining the improvised studio. In the top-floor suites he recognized traces of Marilyn having got there before him. He knew these signs by the magazines she invariably left open at a fashion page, the imprint of her lips as a signature on the mirror, the electric hum that lived in the air as though her absence transmitted cybernetic impulses. He would use an air-brush on mirrors he knew she had used, creating an untutored homicidal Pollock on the glass.

Arc's mind was shooting up eight million miles high. He returned to the notion of reoxygenating and reheating the surface of Mars. Creating at least a micro-environment within a spheroid space station. An idea that could be translated into the temporal emporium he had created on this coast.

He felt the inhaled crystals blow constellations across his mind. He was moon-walking, then suddenly manic about maintaining control of the hotel with its legendary potential. He checked the closed-circuit screen, looking for the alien, but there was only the uniform expanse of sand, the visual silence that translated itself into haunting. The whole landscape seemed to be coming inside. The forests were entering his head, all preconceptions were crowded out as his own creations displaced them. He and Marilyn had filmed the dematerialization of an entire coastal population. The flaw would widen. He imagined the sea withdrawing from the Mediterranean resorts, evacuating from the African coastline, receding so far from California that people camped on the beaches, intoning a mantra to a blue mirage. At intervals they would see the illusion of a car driven across the foreshore with someone recognizable as Bowie standing up saluting in the rear, a blonde transvestite screened by shades sitting back deep in the upholstery.

Arc checked and rechecked the twenty-five doors on the first floor. And having assured himself of the security, he returned to testing every other odd number on both sides of the corridor. There was always the nagging consciousness of having forgotten a door that didn't exist. And when he'd finished, he realized that what he was looking for had gone missing in his mind. It had entered a chemical orbit and wouldn't return until his thoughts slowed down.

He returned to his studio and armed himself with a Super 8 camera. It was his defence. As long as he was shooting film, he had a screen between himself and the world. Freeze-frames built into a multi-storey block were his vision of the new city. He would superimpose his dream on the stone forest. Monroe would be seen sunbathing on a roof-top, while Artaud declaimed from an adjoining fire-escape. The stars would inhabit his montage city, all the faces he loved would be represented: Ava Gardner, Louise Brooks, Riki de Montparnasse, Lee Miller, Sophia Loren, Brigitte Bardot, Catherine Deneuve, Jean Cocteau, André Breton, James Dean, Jean Genet, Mick Jagger. He would construct a universal montage, a futuristic New York fragmented into hallucinatory planes. He was the cine-god of a cult that had still to rise and proclaim him. His created universe invited the reign of his heroes. He imagined Bowie disembarking from a saucer, stepping out across the sands, a life-support system strapped to his grey Paul Smith suit.

Arc poured a generous dash of UV defence lotion on to cotton-wool pads and applied them to his face. He had come to cultivate an obsessive fear of skin cancer. Although his time was spent hermetically sealed inside the Grand Hotel, he feared radiation from ultraviolet rays. He had forgotten what century he was living in. He and Marilyn had so dislocated time in cleaning up an ethos that he no longer remembered whether they were living through a post-nuclear interregnum or if they were still anticipating the decisive heat-flash of World War 4. He imagined the dead cities extending beyond the horizon. Rubble from seismic fissures, scorched foundations, forests reduced to cinder beds, multi-storey car-parks buried under ash. And out of this would come a new world which he would oversee. The potential was endless.

He switched on Bowie's 'Time' with its lyric evocation of transience. The singer's histrionic falsetto could be retracked endlessly on the Aladdin Sane CD. But for Arc, time had ceased to exist. When he closed his eyes, the big planets whirled across inner space. He had the feeling that he was telescoping through billions of light-years, he had access to the inhomogeneities of galactic clusters. He was discovering in his DNA chains the whole spiral cosmos. It was as though an internal space probe were relaying data about the interaction between planets and molecular formation.

Arc was growing more aware of the absence of his triumvirate. He had created a world for their inclusion, an ethos that would allow Warhol to go on living as a psychically informed robot, one that would incorporate Ballard into the natural landscape of his novels, and accommodate Bowie's concern with extraterrestrial vocals. He wanted Bowie to paint and Ballard to direct films. He hoped the singer would depict the autonomy of his unconscious mind, and that the most visually atmospheric of novelists would become by extension a supremely innovative director.

Arc had already prepared an audio-questionnaire for his

subjects. He riffled through the notes he had transmitted to tape.

A to Ballard: You've carried the novel closer to the edge than anyone writing in the twentieth century. Your poetics of space appears to be a reading of parallel dimensions. How would you react to the idea of being read on other planets?

A to Warhol: Living as you do on a plane of altered consciousness, do you see your apocalyptic auto-crash screenings as visuals deleted by your apprehension of a new reality?

A to Bowie: Is there a place for soundless music? I'd like to see you perform at the Grand Hotel miming the lyrics which would be simultaneously, together with the atonal music, printed out on a screen.

A to Ballard: The solitary white-suited voyeur who first appears in your fiction in *The Atrocity Exhibition*, and recurs as the protagonist in so many of your subsequent novels, is to my mind the vision of the last man on earth. Is there a chance that we'll discover him in the desert? This cine-country is haunted. The white ghost on the screen could turn out to be Vaughan?

A to Warhol: What about a microscopic film of Bowie's left eye turned into a planet? A dislodged speck of iris blown up to the magnified impression of elevated terrain on Jupiter.

A to Bowie: If the inherited observables of consciousness have disappeared, so too our bodies may change. By a process of bionics we may evolve as a disembodied species. The inhabitants of this beach will never die. Can you adjust to the thought of living in the twenty-third century?

A to Ballard: All imaginative writing presupposes that conglomerate publishers need hallucinogens in order to have access to the subject. The Jonathan Cape's reader's report on *Crash* suggested that you were pathological and in need of help. Out here, things are reversed. What was odd is seen as the dimension in which we live. If we take that a step further, we as people will become sci-fi materializations. Will that lead to the deletion of language? Can we realize the novel as transmission on to a thought processor?

A to Warhol: Is the ultimate minimal film the camera recording the camera? A lens masturbating with a blank? We're waiting for you. How does it feel to be a series of electronic impulses?

A to Bowie: In the song 'Ashes to Ashes', Major Tom is conceived of as the first astronaut junkie. What do you think of blow-jobs in space? Do you think the future of music lies in recording studios on Mars?

Arc listened to his pre-recorded tape, anticipating a time when he would confront his interviewees. He envisaged driving out to them across the sands in his old pink Chevrolet. Within minutes of doing so the saucers would arrive. Warhol would appear with an entourage of astral minders. Bowie would be adjusting a red Paisley tie to a soft white collar. And Ballard awakening to the reality of sex between himself and the decapitated simulacrum of Jayne Mansfield.

Arc felt menaced by an unlocatable sound building in his head. He kept on rechecking the screen, to find the same menacing blank. Just an empty rectangle like a pane of sky. In his mind he was certain he was being hunted for the archives. His banked film contained the bridge between the old universe and the new.

When he took the lift back to the ground floor, he knew something was wrong even before the visuals registered.

There was a car outside parked on the rise above a sand-drift. Arc recognized it as a bronze Jaguar convertible. Someone had driven it here. There was a black oil leak being absorbed by the sand. Inside, he could see Marilyn's body propped up at the steering-wheel. Her legs were hooked up vertically over the windshield. Someone had stuck a poster of Warhol on the panelling of the bronze passenger door.

Chapter 8

He said to himself, 'My name is David Bowie. I've been away for a time, I've lost my identity. But now it's all very clear.'

He had been exploring the dug-out which seemed purpose built for the interior of one of his old songs. The kind of solitary space he had written about in 'Breaking Glass' and 'Sound and Vision', fragmentary lyrics which hinted that somewhere there was a refuge for his state of internal disintegration. At the time he might have imagined a place like this. The walls had been painted blue to suggest the idea of a sky contained within a brutal utility construct. For a moment he wondered if he had used this underground lair in the past, *circa* 1977, as a retreat from insupportable drug and identity crises. He might have been perverse enough at that period to situate himself in a dug-out, and to have sat day after day staring at the mosaic of photographs that portrayed the various personae he had adopted on-stage. There was even a blue packet of Gitanes cigarettes, like the one he had incorporated into a black waistcoat pocket on his 1976 tour. And the shots of Ballard? There were pictures of him typing at a small table, and others of him out and about against a distinctly suburban backdrop. And the copies of *The Atrocity Exhibition*, *Crash*, *Concrete Island* and *High-Rise*, these are books he remembered having read, together with others of their period, *The Naked Lunch* and *The Soft Machine* by William S. Burroughs, and Jean Genet's *Our Lady of the Flowers*. They lay around on a desk-top as an intended reminder or pointer to something to be revised for the future.

He had never liked Warhol, despite writing a song about him and visiting the Factory. He had admired him as the progenitor of popism, the proponent of a ruthlessly conducted self-promotional stardom, but had felt alienated from him as a person. The platinum-haired man conducting fellatio with pink bubblegum.

And there were old record sleeves, himself on the covers of 'Young Americans' and 'Station to Station.' There were bootleg albums from the same period, the sound-perfect 'The Thin White Duke', with its mauve cover depicting two exploding asteroids, and the more soberly presented 'The Wembley Wizard Touches the Dial'. It would take him a long time to read through the assembled files of press cuttings, systematically chronologized as though they had been prepared by his publicity team.

He liked the electric-blue walls: blue always represented the colour of the future. And while he felt free from the dangers of re-earthing, he none the less found himself increasingly concerned with reconstituting the life he had known in the past. Memory associations were beginning to form a coherent pattern, as though dormant brain cells were being revitalized to provide the necessary information. His life as an android had led to the deoxygenation of areas of his brain vital to temporal functioning. Being here was a process of continuous retrieval.

There was a persistent blip on his interplanetary Walkman. The headphones were clear sound all the way to Diamond Nebula, the rhythmic patterns transparent in their audial frequency. The machine offered both visual and coaxial digital inputs. The tiny screen relayed the caller. The ovoid face was cushioned by earpads. Protective glasses sat on feature-less contours. An android bug jumped clean out of a Miró painting, the transmission was direct.

'You are rehabilitating. The location we have chosen for you is not accidental. You lived here in retreat in 1977. Reacquaint yourself with everything before returning. There are supercomputers capable of a trillion operations per second, embodying a parallel architecture. We expect the same of the new species. We are looking for galactic informa-tion highways. You are one in a million.'

The transmission went dead. The photonic network con-tained within his nervous system allowed him global com-munication without the constraints of physical wiring. Like the autonomy of his music, he could be anywhere and everywhere.

Part of him was fascinated by the prospect of rehearing his music. He purposely delayed re-entry to that audio-visual universe, the one in which he had excelled as an alien. Despite his flirtation with the other arts, his regularly announced defections to acting and painting, he had remained a singular innovator within the field of rock. There wasn't anyone else who had enjoyed his persistent success as an assimilator of contemporary modes. His amalgamative talents had allowed him to anticipate and outstrip fashion. He had cultivated a mystique that had separated him from his rivals. He had become an astral traveller, someone who had still to create an interplanetary music, one which combined cybernetics with a Martian language. The David Bowie continuity was not earthed, its future influence extended to the stars.

He thumbed through the miscellany of press cuttings. In all of them he recognized himself. Someone called David Robert Jones had been superseded by a genetically transformed David Bowie, to be replaced in turn by a biomorphically recon-structed alien. He looked at photographs of himself with a comparative reluctance to let them go. Parts of his mind con-tinued to celebrate the fêted superstar, endlessly planning global tours, facially reconstructing himself for the image that accom-panied the project. He was mauve-haired, red-haired, blond, peroxide yellow. Transvestite, emaciated, militant, inhuman, but always the face that suggested a way forward.

It was weird to be here without the accompanying adulation, the incessant buzz of telephones, photographic appointments to be kept, reporters to be circumvented, material to be discussed and rehearsed, his mind endlessly alert to the intake of new musical concepts. He had been used to raiding and assimilating the avant-garde, and then reprocessing the formula with a risk that the originators would never have dared. What he had learnt now was so far in advance of his contemporaries, if they were still alive, that he almost feared its unlimited potential.

He thought of his one-time fascination with Hitler's bunker, and how this nuclear dug-out was his own temporary base. There was a minifreezer stocked with bottles of champagne. There was a medicine unit containing lotions, skin creams, tranquillizers sealed into sachets, disposable hypodermics. Someone had stocked a cabinet with canned and powdered foods. What was here, represented the short-term rations for a people who would never come out alive.

He felt in his pocket for his thought processor, a compact system that allowed him electromagnetically to transfer thought directly on to a screen without the intermediary process of a keyboard. It would make the inspirational process of writing song lyrics something autonomously controlled rather than linguistically contrived. More direct than Breton's experimentation with automatic writing, revisions would respond to thought independent of language.

He watched the white lines waver across a blue screen.

> Tomorrow's twenty million stars away
> the mutants live on Diamond Nebula
> I left my wardrobe in a Zurich house
> I need it now before I get away.

He saved the four lines and reviewed them prior to continuing. He had always dreamt of never growing old, of achieving a youthful permanence that would transcend death. And now that state had been implanted in him; he was programmed as an extraterrestrial who would also continue to visit earth for as long as there was a recognizable planet. He was a visitor to a recognizably devastated enclave, a coastal area where the survivors had gone underground or else lived as the embodiment of their psychoses.

He blanked his mind out and meditated on a single diamond point of light. The miniature planet showed up in his head, its blue facets mirroring a cool mineral scintillation positioned in the galaxies. It was the internalized punctum that centred him in inner space.

He got back to the idea of the song.

> I'm wired to live on TV everywhere
> so many stations strung out across space
> transmission goes direct to astral nerves
> it regenerates Andy Warhol's face.

And having stored the lyrics, his idea was to record them and send the tapes back on the next planetary shuttle. His mix of earth and android influences would create a controversial intergalactic music. He would be the first of his kind to relay a computer-based lyric music to the unnamed, the invisible planets, the binary stars in which a white dwarf drew its luminosity from an attached red companion.

When he had lived here in the mid-seventies, he had been too dissociated to notice the constrictions. He must have painted the walls cerulean to coincide with the writing of 'Sound and Vision'. His depression had been terrible in those months, he had avoided everything, people and things. Only Coco and Iggy and Brian Eno had remained constant in a world of manic variables.

He found himself picking up infrasound and recognized the degree of his solitude. It was the image of Xenia occupied his mind. He needed to locate her to discover if she too had undergone the migration to aliens. The vision of his people in coveralls, the emblem of a winged serpent visible as a logo on the left arm, invaded his mind. Crafts operated by reverse electromagnetism, the occupants shooting greenish gas from ray-guns, was just one level on which the extraterrestrials functioned. His was a superior role, for he served as an intermediary between earth and Diamond Nebula. He was needed by both, and his potential as a musician was still unrealized. Tin Machine had been a partial experiment after his years as a chameleonic solo artist. The name was another hint towards saucers, metallic discs, the future of rock as he conceived it in terms of galactic relay.

He lit his first cigarette, one of the preserved Gitanes, and savoured the acrid aroma of cooked tobacco. It was a symbolic re-earthing, a savouring of a former addiction and acknowledgement that the kick could still get him high. He relaxed, his silver boots resting on the table. A cassette of 'Low' had been put on board the Pioneer spacecraft in its journey out of the solar system, together with directions from earth to various pulsars – along with codes for their frequencies. The information aimed at giving alien astronomers the date and place of origin of the spacecraft, would also provide the recipients with evidence of the music on which he had collaborated with Eno. A sci-fi mix of lyric montage and synthesizer.

There wasn't any Coco to call and enlist personal support. She might be anywhere, occupying an office floor in a block recently split off the coast of California by a seismic upheaval. He pictured her waking to find herself miles out at sea, a turbulent surf breaking on the narrow white beach adjacent to her window. Or could she also be out there in the maze of film props that constituted Arc's psychotic vision of the future? The space-age architecture might have been devised as a model for a series of biospheres on Mars.

He was waiting for other walk-ins like himself. It would be a gradual but meticulously planned take-over. Alien intelligence would infiltrate across the continents. Someone would open their silver eyes in a museum in Moscow, at a summit meeting in the White House, on a spiral arm of the Milky Way, in a street market in Marrakesh. The moon-eyed people discovered by the Cherokees in the Tennessee hills, and who were unable to see by daylight, would reappear as a cult who adopted black shades, occupied strategic positions of global power, and who would pull the switch on governments.

He was conscious of this period of adjustment, of the need to earth himself by concentrating on density, rather than periodically dematerializing, existing as though he were back on Diamond Nebula. The biogenetic engineering responsible for creating humanoids had also provided for his partial conversion to the physical state in which he had lived as David Bowie. He thought of how he could put a new music through the twenty million frequency channels flashing through digital processors computing the cosmos. The chemical high he was getting from his first cigarette was confirmation that he would record on earth again. He uncorked a magnum of champagne, intended in the surroundings as a source of pre-euthanasia euphoria, and experienced the reassuring lift in his head. He was coming alive after the second, the third glass, his thoughts going off at a dipped tangent, travelling back to places he had known, a street market in Kyoto, a private visit to Moscow in 1977 with Iggy Pop, a crowded night in New York's Ocean Club, his anonymous globe-trotting, discovering the world after overcoming his aerophobia, disappearing to remote corners of Australia, Africa, South America, always conscious that money could solve all unnerving predicaments. He realized that the brain recorded everything on mental film and that, selectively or autonomously, the past that he had experienced was on visual recall. It was like continuous cinema. Only he had to learn how to systematize projection, relay things chronologically, editing out the unconfrontable, the trivia that obscured the vital realizations. Once he had mastered the technique, he would have selective control over memory. Things could be cancelled in the way that words are revised and reordered on a screen. He could use his thought processor to help construct a selective model of experience.

He was beginning to feel the absence of live performance. So often in the past he had declared his intention never to tour again, only to be attracted back to the circuit by huge financial gain. And there was the stimulus of lighting up on-stage, being sick afterwards, keeping to the baroque interior of a hotel room, jet-lagged, nervously exhausted, but addicted to moving on. In the almost amnesiac unreality of touring, he had come to believe that there were parallel worlds, continents across which he had never played, airline flights unknown to his promoters and record company, and the undiscovered islands out there in the blue, invisible land masses that pilots flew over before disappearing into the Bermuda Triangle. His was the music they were anticipating, the sound that would instil in them the recollection of their alien heritage.

The more he learnt to filter thought impressions, the more he became aware of his past contact with UFOs. He remembered how out of the car window in LA he had observed, articulately, precisely, the shapes of two saucers seeming to stay level with the car. They were distinct by way of red lights illuminating the circular discs, and what looked like fins protruded as stabilizers as the saucers accelerated away at great speed over the coast. And at the time he was convinced that he had seen someone crouched at one of the cabin windows, a uniformed snoutish face appearing by way of a sign. He had put the happening down to the side-effects of cocaine, but had awoken later in the night to find the figure in his room, stepped direct out of his dream into reality. The man also had vertical slits for eye pupils, the one distinguishing mark of the alien that still persisted in his present features.

There had been so many persistent recurrences. Multiple green lights sighted outside his aircraft window *en route* to Melbourne, ovals that appeared to be tailing the 747, jumping in and out of his visual field while the aircraft inexplicably lost height, the pilot remaining silent about this demonstrative extraterrestrial probe. And once a car that had appeared out of nowhere on a deserted highway, the road running like an ironed black snake towards the next town, a silver car had effortlessly achieved a parallel position, stayed there, only its dark-green windows were opaque, and instead of hopping into a forward position, it had taken off vertically, climbed on a rapid ascending trajectory and hurried away as a speck into a sculptural oblong of white cumulus. The driver might have been J.G. Ballard experimenting with the first UFO-Cadillac, but more probably he attributed it to links with Cape Kennedy, a deranged trainee astronaut lifting off in a car for Jupiter.

The space in his head was doing weird things with the effects of the champagne. He discovered his old file marked DARYL – Data Analyzing Robot Youth Lifeform. In it he reclaimed his notes about cybernetics and cyborgs, his comments on linear perspective vision, and how we have become astronauts inhabiting technological space, creatures distanced from both the world and our bodies. He had seen himself as a potential leader of Robot Youth. Not only would his musicians be automatons, but he would instruct his audience to recognize their superiority. And they would liquidate dissenters. He had introduced mutants into his stage act, but the audience hadn't seen them. They had assumed that his imbalance was taking over, the knowledge of his brother's madness, his own drug-stretched androgyny, there had been speculation. People had avoided confronting the issue, and he had modified the truth about his real identity in order to retain his commercial popularity.

His old files were full of pictures of saucer sightings, copies of the confiscated photographs taken at Maspalomas in the Canary Islands, in which a spiralling, rocket-shaped object had exploded into an orange asteroid and remained visible above the sea for over an hour. The government had suppressed all findings after an official report had ruled out the possibilities of a local electromagnetic field or atmospheric disturbance as having contributed to the phenomenon. He had guarded his private copies, stored them amongst the mass of evidence that helped confirm a belief in his people.

He riffled through newspaper clippings, articles photocopied from sci-fi journals, pictures of himself dressed in red zoot suits, costumes he had adopted as part of his visual image aimed at impregnating humans with the idea of alien intelligence. What had been seen as an act was a reality. And if at one time he had feared madness, had conceived of himself as the single occupant of an interstellar message, then later on he had come to confide a peripheral area of his fears to a Zurich analyst.

He could still see the room, the pale-green walls imparting an air of serenity, the analyst dressed like an accountant in a dark pinstripe suit, only he was tieless, his white button-down collar shirt open at the neck. Blue light had planed in from the lake outside. The analyst's imperturbability had shocked him. The man showed no element of surprise at his confessions, he had spoken of the necessity for psychological polytheism, the admission into the psyche of fictional visitants. And of the need to converse with mythic creatures, accept the plurality of the subjective cosmos, and to bring him notes of his dialogues with mutants, his dreams of being instated as a leader on Diamond Nebula. Jung had called the psyche a structure of multiple scintillae, something which in his, Bowie's case, clearly involved contact with other centres. There were constellations in his psychic structure which, clearly, he had to explore.

He had spoken of the constructive state implied by disintegration, and how madness as a pejorative term was the creation of secular psychiatry. And that archetypal psychology as it had been re-envisioned by James Hillman was an adjunct to creativity.

He could see himself sitting there, listening, self-conscious of his silence and the need to punctuate it with words. He had talked about the occurrence at Cape Kennedy that had instigated the whole thing, and how the person of Major Tom had come to possess him on-stage, then to become a double, someone putting words and ideas in his head, and in time attracting aliens to the binary star they shared in Bowie's mind.

All his old notes were in a file marked *Major Tom: Analysis*. He had taken to typing up his dreams preparatory to consultation. He had even attempted working his dialogues with Major Tom into a proposed film script, something altogether more authentically bizarre than Roeg's creation *The Man Who Fell to Earth*.

He stopped reading. In the sessions with his analyst he had been encouraged to introduce Major Tom into the room. They had both addressed the latter as a third party, a presence with a justifiable contribution to make to their discourse. Each time he flew back to Berlin he felt certain that the aircraft would be hijacked by aliens. He had nervously scanned the aircraft window for signs that he was being followed. He had gripped the supports of his seat with sweating hands. And each time they had landed he had entertained the fantasy that he would be detained, stripped by security, and denounced as an alien.

He had tripped through airports, a white-faced somnambulist going somewhere that the others weren't, back to this hermetically sealed dug-out, his meditation space in which he wrote up his dual life, devised the music on which he had collaborated with Brian Eno, drank, called up his closest friends, and remained disconnected from the commercial aspects of the record industry. 'Fuck their formulae for programmed hits'; he had made himself very clear at the risk of losing his label. And they in turn had tolerated his cryptic phase, believing that it was a temporary aberration, and that with declining finances the artist would see sense again.

At the time he had relished both the perversity of his reclusion in terms of loss of record sales, and the fascination when it wasn't too obsessively disquieting of his evolution to a sci-fi mutant. The analyst had helped him accept the realization that he was on a metamorphic dimension, that he was involved in body consciousness, a somatized awareness of his migration to another species.

He had sat here so often, one foot on the chair, his head resting on his hands. He had dressed up in military uniforms, Yves St Laurent dresses, catsuits. Other days he had gone over to the apartment he rented and spent the afternoons painting. Addressing the canvas with his anger, he had projected a sort of post-expressionist portraiture as representative of his frustration. Colour was his primary interest, heightening tones, exploring configurative planes, attempting to find a way of speeding a Rothko to a series of kinetic images. The paintings were always taken back to Zurich and stored in his archives. It was as though they were executed by someone else, perhaps the figure of David Robert Jones whom he had locked away in his psyche, dismissed as someone dead in the interests of his career and the multiple personae who inhabited David Bowie. And there were imaginary portraits, the luminous oval and rectangular faces of aliens who came into contact with his mind.

113

And where was Zurich now? He couldn't be sure how long he had been away. It was rather like waking. There's no difference between five minutes and ten hours, the shut-down of consciousness eliminates all awareness of time. And on Pluto a year could conjecturally be the equivalent of two hundred on earth, and on another planet, according to its composition, a year might equal twenty-eight of our months. He had painted a generation of Hollywood stars resurrecting themselves from cryonic burial. Blanked into ice storage, their imperishable bodies confronted a world in ruins. Massive earthquakes had fissured the whole Californian coast. Upended architecture had landslided into ravines. These celebrities, shovelled like fish from their deep-freeze vaults, stared inanely at a holocaustal horizon, vaguely looking for their limousines, the security guards whom they expected at any moment would come running to their assistance. What he had tried to convey was their absence of any sense of time. They might have been coming round after a drink-induced siesta, only they held serrated fragments of ice in their hands. Glacial splinters and shards lay at their feet as though they had walked clean through a window.

All of his contempt and loathing for Hollywood had been channelled into these paintings. Liz Taylor was seen running naked across a rubbled villa site. Joan Collins and Frank Sinatra stood shielding their eyes, looking up at great dust-whorls suddenly obscure the sun, rust and burnt sienna coloured drifts that seemed to originate from some planetary eruption. All of them were in the process of realizing that there was nowhere to go. They might have been trying to clear a space inside a dream, wondering how it was they had woken up within a prolonged state of unreality.

He had worked on these canvases for long stretches, sometimes exhausting himself so totally that the need for the drug disappeared, and when he emerged from the bunker it was dark outside, the city's lights showing in the sky. The Wall had been there then, that grey, divisive imposition that he had got into his song 'Heroes'. The atmosphere had been charged with political tension. He realized now how big a part fear had played in his emotional vocabulary. Fear of becoming a declared monocrat, of goose-stepping down the street proclaiming his intentions in a glossolalia of invented German.

He realized too why Zap's paintings had so fascinated him, and why he remembered most representations of art with an almost immediate recall. He had thought at one time of abandoning everything and just painting. He could lose himself in that medium, go on exploring his interiority until the transition took place. Like someone waiting for death, he was anxious to be absorbed to a point whereby he wouldn't know the change had taken place.

On other days he had drunk himself ill. On-stage for most of his 1976 tour, he had been out of it, too intoxicated to check his incoherent asides between songs. In this dug-out he had drunk as though it was his last and only support. He would uncap a bottle of bourbon and realize three hours later that he was attempting to pour a half tumbler from an empty bottle. And it seemed a trick, as though the liquid purposely wouldn't flow, or would return to the bottle if he looked away. He camped for days by a hazel-coloured whisky lake that seemed to have swamped his mind. There wasn't anyone who could join him there. That far out and one is reborn. Another life connects with total dissociation. The chimeras, hallucinated faces on the other side of drink had fascinated him. He had actively set out like Rimbaud to attract derangement, systematically to disorganize his senses. His notebooks and paintings reflected a concern with self-destruction, a defiant courting of the abyss. He had written free association prose poetry, stringing together images in a cut-up style, using concepts as a kind of automatic montage. He looked at the coloured inks he had used, felt-tip flourishes scrambled loopingly, geometrically across the page:

Stardust in a sachet . . . America encountered at the speed of light . . . 297,600 kilometres per second and I'm still balancing a microphone . . . A saurian stands on the roof-top . . . Betty sings the blues through a psychotronic transmitter-translator . . . Another diamond glacier outside the Hilton . . . Hitler is in a

115

mad ward in Rio . . . Psychotic visions of his armies
masturbating . . . ejaculating the white crosses that fill
cemeteries . . . Electric blue skies arching above
cerulean swimming-pools . . . A man with one centred
conical breast suns by the pool under a violet sun . . .
A gravitational well inside my mind . . . Bill Burroughs
floats up out of that black hole . . . The proclaimed
leader of the Milky Way shows up on a computer
screen . . . Berlin outside, so grey, so grey. . . .

He had planned a novel called *Sound and Vision*, and his
exercise books were full of notes, phrases for the latter. He
had been up all night sometimes, crystallizing the blaze of
imagery that had burnt his mind. It was a way of directing the
out-of-control nerve impulses on to the page, a translation of
ideas that came in a visual rush. The music would follow
later. He had intended to create a rock opera out of his
fiction. The book and the video would be marketed in one
package, a synthesis of new-age versatility. He had held to his
literacy in the face of rock music devolving into cliché, lyrics
that stated the obvious with an insulting banality. Punk had
launched its anti-élitist, anarchic front at the time of his mental
crisis. He had listened to tapes of Patti Smith, the Sex Pistols, the
Clash, and picked up on their deliberate immediacy, their
speed-freak monotonal delivery, their gutter fascism, their subversive credo to incite social revolution and a plethora of body
bags. His method of circumventing that untutored adrenalin
rush was to withdraw into the minimally oblique, the avant-
garde music he had created in Berlin. He had insulated himself,
the world of art affording a protective igloo.
    In those years he was humanly suicidal and psychically opti-
mistic. Music, *per se*, had failed to interest him. His collabora-
tions with Eno, most of which had remained unreleased, were a
sort of robotic means of keeping in touch with the careerist in
his ego. He couldn't eliminate the latter entirely, try as he did. A
survivor waved from the bottom of the glass, a diminutive,
Chaplinesque figure with a cane and hat. This persona was
dwarfed but invincible. One day he would return to life size

again, rake the angle of his hat and resume his role on-stage.

What was so odd was the way the landscape had changed. He wondered how a segment from his past, this old Berlin retreat, had ended up in a hallucinated resort controlled by a mad director's mind. Moving about these streets, parting the luxurious fauna that grew side by side with sci-fi constructs which would have pleased the most fanatical xenologist, was rather like having Max Ernst screens incorporated into one of his archival Diamond Dogs stage-sets. This was presumably another transition period, while he awaited news either of eventual recall to Diamond Nebula, or instructions as to how to proceed on earth.

He lit another cigarette and settled into reflection. As a member of DARYL and SETI, he had been conscious of speaking of realities which to the others were half-truths, germinative mythologems, astrophysical data cushioned by unprovable speculation. Their suppositional bases for the existence of life on other planets – the presence of sugars, amino acids, nucleotides, or climates at liquid nitrogen temperatures in which by human reactions it would take hours to inhale and exhale a single breath, weeks to digest a plate of pasta – remained theories. Without enzymes, the human would live in a state of metabolic refrigeration.

He had attended meetings, listened to those who had argued in favour of external phenomena, and those who had supported the claim that mutants were present on earth, and that they represented alien intelligence housed within the human. And he had used his wealth to buy confidential documents out of the Pentagon, to amass the folders of photographs that were stacked on the tables here as though it was still *circa* 1977. His dialogues with Major Tom had continued. They were conversations with an elected instructor. Teachings, preparatory guidance, information from a star-guru. Major Tom was there to help him complete a successful mutation. 'You are the chosen one' had reverberated in his head.

And the documents. One purported that the real Marilyn Monroe's ashes had been taken to the moon and buried there. In that way there never could be a final autopsy.

Interdimensional travellers had surrounded a crash-landed Boeing in the Arizona Desert. A speed-up recall dart fired into the pilot had him divulge everything he knew of avian development. It was an experience equivalent to hearing his mind played like a tape at the wrong speed. Everything he had thought forgotten about his life was instantly related. Working late at night in the White House, the President had looked up to apprehend a walk-in. Too terrified to buzz for security, he had later committed to a confidential report that the intruder had alternated in colour from blue to red, had opened cabinets containing secret reports by directing a light beam that broke the lock, had transcribed the entire contents on an instant codifier machine, and faded in the way a television goes blank when the power's disconnected. The President had been found off-beam, in a state of temporary aphasia. The incident had been buried as part of the continuous myth of disinformation. A double on autocue had stood in for him on next day's important address to the nation. A hair-stylist had spent most of the night matching the number of grey hairs in the President's black shock with the silver-dye tints necessary for his simulacrum. No one would ever know.

His information was universal; Martians, Venusians, Jupiterians, extracts from the authentic reports made by Armstrong and his crew on the return of their Apollo mission from the moon. What they had really seen was censored, but excerpts existed on audio cassette. To have allowed a leak might have resulted in global chaos. In his state of mind the extracts had been unhinging. What had been cut from the edited film was the discovery that others had been there first. As with the gold plaque in the Pioneer, depicting a human, so another civilization had left its insignia behind. They had discovered it inside an eroded capsule deposited in a canyon, a medallion featuring what was taken to be an interplanetary traveller. The body was diminutive, compact, oval. There were no facial characteristics, the eye stalks appeared to be set in the top of the head and to extend into antennae. The name of their star was given as Diamond Nebula, but its exact sector on the galactic disk was not recorded. Frequencies of surrounding pulsars were coded. The script was otherwise indecipherable. It appeared to relate to the wavelength of visual sensors.

His stimulus for contact had been alerted. They were really out there, mostly wide of the electromagnetic spectrum, the attuned ones, those who had set up a signal pattern in his brain rhythm. In the recording studios he had felt energized by the need to register an extra impulse, to motivate a music that would defy his critics. Odd, bizarre, he had channelled his creativity into something that had been construed as Dada minimalism. What he had attempted to communicate with was his idea of an extraterrestrial audience. Humans were marginal, predictably limited in their expectations of a hit formula. You brought in the hook to support a suggested narrative, repeated a guitar riff, and the song was swallowed as pop. He had smashed that concept. Pieces like 'Warszawa', 'Art Decade', 'Weeping Wall' and 'Subterraneans' had been aimed for those living on the fringes of a black hole.

Something of his old impatience to anticipate change was returning. He missed the impulsive channelling of his energies into creativity. There was a music to be had from the silence of this fractal landscape. It was moving in on him as an aura, an atmosphere, in the way that dense sound had descended on him in Berlin. His surroundings had always been trans-lated into a musical texture conveying mood and local en-vironment. This time his sensibility was in perfect accordance with the surreal fragments of a beach resort, the truncated segments of a town through which the psychotic floated in search of an exit from themselves.

His equipment fitted compactly into his silver leather top. He checked his hair, his face, before going out, dusted his eyelids cobalt from an old Charles of the Ritz container, and surfaced from the dug-out.

Reverberation from guitar feedback hung on the air like the rumour of storm. He found himself spontaneously looking up, scanning the mauve planes of sky for signs of his people. Migrationary sophonts were all the time working along the clusters of the Milky Way. There was no reason why they should break their interstellar silence. It was his adopted race on

Diamond Nebula who had sent walk-ins to monitor progress on biotechnological innovations. Their primary concern was that of developments in artificial intelligence. They were looking for robots, and instead had discovered humans.

He immediately encountered evidence of Arc's obsessions. A five times life-size publicity shot of Ballard had been placed on a filling station roof. A shot of Warhol sitting with his hand over Parker Tyler's cock had been positioned on a billboard. And a photograph of himself backstage *circa* 1976, brushing his hair flat to his skull, was elevated to a position of prominence outside a cinema. *Showing tonight: David Bowie and the Extraterrestrials.*

He moved on, realizing that the caption was right. His future musicians would be aliens. His imaginary ethos had grown into a reality. The street was littered with cans, hypodermics, advertising flyers. A mannequin had been placed in an alley, legs wide open, a toy rat positioned in the divide. The entrance to a street market, its stalls heaped with leather and suede jackets, hats, jewellery, pointed another way into a prismatic maze. An enlarged photograph of John F. Kennedy collapsed from the assassin's bullet and falling into Mick Jagger's arms had been mounted as a celluloid montage. Jagger's shock-haired performance gestures were disconnected from the President's head-slanted collapse.

He was pulled up by the sound of voices. He heard them before he saw the group sitting cross-legged around a radio as though it was a fire. There were four of them. He thought they must be his own people, but he couldn't be sure. Dressed in blue metallic helmets with holes for eyes, they had clothes clearly picked out of shop stores. Two of them wore black glitter leggings, the others jeans and boots, all of them had chosen leather flying jackets. He imagined them adopting these clothes in order to infiltrate. Or were they the cast of Arc's disbanded film project? Actors who had migrated towards mutant identities? They sat equally spaced around what he saw to be a transmitter alive with leakage signals. They were picking up on frequencies that had travelled from a galactic station.

He stood screened by a car, ready to dematerialize if they

should spot him. He couldn't make out the language in which they were communicating, and they spoke indirectly, without individual focus, as if each were interpreting the microwave frequency according to his own referential range of knowledge. There was a feeling of non-sharing, an exclusivity that suggested a solitary, self-contained black box of genetic experience, parthenogenesis rather than birth by a parent, non-affiliation rather than monogamous or heterogeneous relationships. These beings were frozen into themselves. Even if they kept together, he realized it was for purposes of travel and reconnaissance. They were clearly without emotional ties.

He sensed a fear of these people. Whatever the transitional stage of his being, he was still strongly attached to earth associations. At one time he might have invoked these aliens as a video clip to a live performance, contextualized them as an adjunct to his act. But now they were realities, creatures down here to participate in the change. He watched their self-orientated responses to the transmissions. They were reflectively animated. But none of their moods corresponded or synchronized. They might have been looking at the earth through infra-red and ultraviolet filters, scanning it for the endless possibilities buried in the substrata – fossil rivers, monoliths deposited beneath the Sahara by interstellar voyagers.

He found himself retracing his steps back through the alley. Having encountered one group of migrants, he expected others. Johnny's guitar was still screaming intermittently from some deserted concrete shell on the high-rise skyline. It sounded like a sonic wound, a post-Hendrix assassination of a three-chord distorted fuzzbox. When he made his way through what had been an urban shopping complex, he found himself abruptly on an airstrip. The reinforced surface had been broken up by the underpinning of roots, the proliferation of totemic cacti. Tyre ruts were written across the concrete like forgotten avian graffiti. He thought of engine nacelles, the sonic roar at lift-off, an experience that had never ceased to create a pit in his stomach. Even in the deserted, assassinated landscape of what had been an airport with its surrounding perimeter roads, he felt an apprehension, a sense of hidden danger. He kept waiting for the silence to be broken by the whine of a taxiing Boeing.

He knew he should tune in to his interplanetary Walkman, but he resisted the impulse. He was on the look-out for survivors, planetary migrants, the enigma who was Xenia.

He turned his back on the distant complex of terminals and went in search of the town centre. On the way he passed by Cindy and Zap, who appeared to be moon-walking. They had linked arms and were walking dead centre down the road. Each looked so irretrievably shocked they could have been the two survivors of an air crash, walking away any-where, nowhere, aimed for a time-trap.

They must have been looking for the road that led to the beach, the Grand Hotel standing out like a miniature world headquarters. They were too frozen into their own vision to see him. The reality of their situation had begun to leak through, the awareness of what had happened and their mutual interdependence had them appear like children shocked to find on pushing open the garden door that a world in ruins lay on the other side.

It was the chopped, sawing guitar noises that attracted him, dissonance as he hadn't heard it since the time of his recording 'Scary Monsters and Super Creeps'. The human part of him was already getting high on the stimulus. He had known from the beginning of his music career that certain sounds were the atonal eloquence expressive of the end of a civilization. The guitar and the synthesizer interpreted disintegration; they courted the death of harmonic structure, the introduction of a fragmented universe. He felt assured of his intuition. Johnny was celebrating the temporal ruins that formed a bridge into space.

He wasn't hallucinating. Over and over again he heard the riffs to 'Up the Hill Backwards' shriek through the dead air. Johnny was spooking him into announcing himself. He felt as he had done so often in life, that he was an actor on a film-set. He had the sensation that he was being watched from roof-tops. Ahead of him he could see the four figures who had sat around the transmitter, checking both sides of the street in a reconnaissance patrol. They were stopping at store-fronts, scrutinizing the interiors of cars. Their manner was brutally objective, empty of all emotional filter. He watched them disappear into an arcade, headed for a software megastore.

He clipped on his headphones and listened to the transmission. 'You are invisible to aliens. Their biological optimum is a transitional one. Their saucer is waiting on the beach. You have encountered Jupiterians before. We are considering your return as optional. All future recordings are to go to Diamond Nebula. You are the chosen one. You can revert or evolve.'

The contact went dead, the great interstellar spaces pushing their silence into his head. He was aware for the first time of a volitional freedom, the choice given to him to remain or go. His feet instinctively toed the earth, kicking up a dust-cloud from the parched earth ripped across by fissuring roots. He knew there would be others, extraterrestrial refugees, faces escaped from television screens, actors touched by Arc's monomaniacal dimension. The realization of his own 'Cracked Actor' song, inspired by his first visit to America. His prophetic vision of reality had occurred in his transitional state between human and android.

He stood dead still in the street as part of his earthing. His mind was running with images, it was like a speeded-up film-reel. His chance had come to make the songs that would alter music finally. He felt in his pocket for his thought processor, switched on control and let the autonomous ideas flood the miniature screen. Then he moved over and sat on the bonnet of a blue and chrome Cadillac. He looked up as though from a trance and saw the four aliens hurrying in the direction of Johnny's guitar noise. They too were searching for the electronic core to this town. He heard their footsteps echo through an alley, and then the crackle of flame they left in their wake, cars incinerating, melting to a buckled sculpture on a warped chassis. He needed to get out of the precinct, but resisted dematerializing. The impulse to stay was strong. He relocated to a looted record store and sat down behind one of the cash check-out points. He had all the time he needed in which to create. The fires were still blasting off in the centre of town.

123

Chapter 9

Johnny slammed the microphone in its hold in order to hear the loaded voltage reverberate. He got down on his knees and crawled across the stage, an insane cross between Iggy Pop and Charles Manson, he imagined himself burying the entire colony together with Marilyn out in the stone forest. It would be the culminating ritual to the suite of songs he was recording.

He had progressively recruited more mannequin extras into the audience. Taking one of the more ostentatious of the abandoned cars into the still accessible areas of the town, he had salvaged male and female models from display units and the store-rooms of large departmental stores. With his power to extract thought, he would be able to implant it into his still-life audience. The impregnation of the cybernetic by the human, thereby speeding up the creation of a transhuman species.

Johnny's manic raids on shops like Sadie's Basement, Lowlife, and the jewellers Star Gazers had been undertaken with one of his wrecked Fender Strat guitars. He had stood back elated from window-fronts as a central star fragmented itself into sparkling geometric planes. And there was the stimulus that he might have been watched. At times he felt that a detachable eye rested on his shoulder. There were so many posters connected with Bowie, Ballard and Warhol about the place, a plethora of eyes watching him from wall angles, street corners, the bottom of emptied swimming-pools, table-tops hidden amongst rioting sunflowers.

Arc had disseminated his obsessions everywhere. The three faces were beginning to infiltrate into Johnny's moods. They were complicitous, accusatory, indifferent, condescending, impassioned according to how he read their features. And they were omniscient. Arc had established them as the new gods – a triumvirate representing the future.

Johnny picked up his Martin M38 acoustic. He took the low E string off and tuned to G, D, G, B, D – the old Keith Richards formula made popular by Southern blues men. His five-string G tuning allowed for the use of minors. He wanted to lay down a melody for the lyric White Beaches, an old studio demo from the short-lived interstellar Polaroid, which he had around since the band broke up. He saw the song as superior to its acoustic prototype – Lou Reed's 'Pale Blue Eyes' with its blend of street lyricism and Warholian pop. He scanned through the loose but orderly quatrains, the sheet trembling in his uncertain hand. He began to try some of the lyrics without accompaniment:

> The sand is bleached blond
> as we reach for the stars
> I can see through the blizzard
> white tigers sitting on cars.

Johnny had really seen them; white tigers with blue eyes sitting on a line of parked cars that had escaped being buried under debris. They were there on one of his downtown raids, unmoving as statues, caught in a split-second still between imagination and reality.

And the Euro-beach was the old resort he had known. Blonde Swedish and Danish girls had sunned there in thongs, while red and white striped beach umbrellas had shaded tables on the sand. He remembered tall glasses, the green of mint julep, the ruby of sarsaparilla. But mostly his song looked for misconnections, nerve-ends that buzzed.

Johnny fumbled his words. His vision of himself as the ultimate rock genius outstripping the death-motivated Jim Morrison was beginning to collapse under his disordered nerves. His thin torso showed a diagrammatic skeleton beneath his open leather jacket. He tilted the bottle of Jack Daniels to his lips and blinked himself into a state closer to temporary nirvana. The stage was littered with dead bottles, a surf of cassette shells marked with his own haphazard chronology of recordings. In his mind he saw someone cataloguing these demos; they would become as valuable as the posthumously released Jimi Hendrix tapes.

Johnny put the second string up a semitone and tuned to the root and fifth intervals which fitted D, A, D, G, A, D. By working with alternate tuning he could rely on the unpredictable and avoid playing repeated patterns. He wanted to use the bottom E as the drone and create the effect that Pete Townshend does on 'I Can See for Miles'. Old songs rerouted themselves in his head. 'Eight Miles High' by the Byrds, the secular vamp of Marc Bolan's 'Give Me Love', the spookiness of 'Wheels on Fire' by Siouxsie and the Banshees. He wanted a song that opened up inner space, one whose edge lay open to an indefinite future.

Johnny went out to the packed mannequin audience, his guitar in one hand, and chose a blonde-haired, leather miniskirted girl from the front row. He scooped her up and carried her to the stage. With a red spotlight trained on him he fitted her legs over his shoulders. They rested there in sheer black stockings, the scarlet toe-nails showing through. She was Scarlet, the girl who had tracked him through thirty cities, to end up in the Peppermint Suite as one of the select audience given access to his recording studios. She would listen enthralled to his live versions of the Doors' 'People Are Strange' and the Velvet Underground's 'Sister Ray'. He needed to concentrate, to modulate the drug so that it afforded him a creative energy rush. In the lucid intervals his guitar would feed the void. He would bring the android to his studios, and then enter the race for transbiological superiority.

Johnny withdrew from Scarlet. The faces stared back at him from the audience. He knew them all – Ciona, Debbie, Lucinda, Jade, Ultraviolet, Candy, Flip-over Cindy and Long-legged Mandy.

He smashed into an amplifier, swinging back on his arc to come face up with the microphone again. He split his lip on the metal and blood zigzagged across his chin. He hunched into his leather jacket, pushing the collar up into his black, spiky hair. He knew that Bowie would be listening to him. And the dead would be waiting for him. Rock music as an apocalyptic manifestation of absolutes. The sky would open to reveal a gallery of stars. Jimi Hendrix parachuting out of a purple cloud to electrify a desert amphitheatre; John Lennon sitting at a piano in the middle of nowhere; Elvis Presley performing the automatic gesture of flicking his hair back; Billie Holiday still lurching towards an intangible handhold.

Johnny kept changing his guitar, discarding a Martin acoustic twelve-string for a Les Paul Junior – a cutaway sunburst with another humbucker added in the neck position. He wanted to startle himself alive. He was the man in black tuning to devastate the audience. What if Bowie were concealed amongst the mannequins? Johnny knew that his virtuoso primitivism, his crazed guitar power was more exciting than computer music. He would bring the survivors here and extract their thought processes.

Johnny lurched offstage in order to heighten the anticipation of his return. There would be the frantic buzz set up in the audience concerning the possibilities of his overdosing. Johnny backstage applying gel to his blue-black hair, oscillating for lack of a centre pivot, his mind full of the silver mutants waiting for him on the edge of the desert.

He cleared his way through the girl mannequins sitting legs arched, toes resting on the sill of his make-up unit. He faced himself in the multiplying mirrors – moving from panel to panel, surprised by the person who stared back at him, his black pencilled eyelids, the white foundation he had sponged on his face to accentuate its lean angularity. He had dressed the girls in back-combed orange and pink and blue wigs, leather and plastic microskirts. They were his passive, suppliant partners. Their sexual geometry could alter according to his fetish. Some of the models had detachable arms and legs, and for special pleasure he used one of the inflatable latex dolls he had selected from a sex store. Lolita with the bright-red lips and china-blue eyes waited for him in a room upstairs. Once or twice, while performing Iggy Pop's 'Some Weird Sin', he had brought her on-stage in a copulatory ritual, but mostly he reserved her for psychological comfort. She was a focus for his often wounded emotions, a silent minder when his habit grew dangerous.

Johnny wanted to bring Bowie and the survivors in various parts of the town out of hiding with the aural distillation of his electronic rage. His blitzkrieg tonal indulgence was meant to outstrip Lou Reed's Methedrine orchestration on 'Metal Machine Music'. The latter experiment, which had almost cost Reed his commercial credibility, was a direction that Johnny saw as necessary towards total artistic alienation. His work would comprise an electric signal to alien frequencies, a blip transmissible through deep-space networks. Once he got beyond cosmic radio noise and the microwave window, he could establish interstellar communications. Rock music would take the place of SETI, his polarization proving exact in contradistinction to the random search in the cosmic haystack.

He stripped off his leather jacket in preparation for going on in a black T-shirt and open-fingered, elbow-length gloves. His mind was in attunement to dissonance, the cool white vibrations that came after taking crack. The world was congealing around his warmth and then thawing around his cold. He might have been anywhere, but he had to come out and play. And nothing had changed; the catatonic faces continued to stare. They were waiting for the unexpected. Johnny could hear the music building inside him; but he still couldn't connect. He searched for the bullwhip he had placed on a side-chair and unleashed savage cuts at the microphone.

The whistling lash of each successive swish appeased his nerves. It was a powerful offensive, one that he followed by unabbreviated noise, a sonic guitar drone with exaggerated feedback.

He was searching for the dissociated lyrics to his song 'Ecuador', an oblique cut-up piece he had dedicated to Henri Michaux. It was the song he'd written sitting in a fuelless Citroën parked between gapped house walls and a spreading forest of sunflowers. At the time of composing it he had felt as though he could sit on his nerve-ends, balanced there like a spider's web in the grass. He scrambled the words, feeling the possible gaps in his articulacy as two of the stanzas arrived.

He could visualize the landscape as he performed. A giant iguana was crouched on a rock shelf. A naked woman shivered in a state of levity. When the iguana breathed, it blew out the sun. His guitar gestured towards apocalypse. The manic shriek of something building irrepressibly. His pulse was overspeeding, growing dangerously irregular. It felt like somebody tripping down a flight of stairs, regaining his balance only to lose it again. Johnny felt like someone coming at himself from either side without a centre. There was so much drift that he was without arms or legs. The latitude to left and right was the opening of the two deserts. And in the middle he had the sensation of a vertiginous hole, a telescope stood vertical and took him to a reverse perspective of space, a sky as deep as it was correspondingly high.

His tunnel vision was beginning to narrow in on the dead. It wasn't only Marilyn, her frozen body stylized like a hooker in a car seat, but faces from the old world that he knew he would have to bury out in the stone desert. They were calling him. He was the one who could cross dimensions, while Arc remained immobilized as the president of a cine-state. He would take the dead to their resting-places under a mauve sky. The valuable ones would be restimulated, wired to brain-support machines and shipped out on the shuttle service.

Johnny realized he had become the legend of his own invention, the man shooting up to edit out the lucid intervals in which he might have created. His boundaries were growing transparent, and while silence has no opposite in noise, so he found himself the prototype of a species answered only by the blank vacuum of space.

He was too preoccupied to know that two of the aliens had entered the building. The transhuman reconnaissance group were right there, each listening in to a personal transmitter. They were round the back in the manager's office, helmeted, leather carapaced, and rifled through drawers with the exacting scrutiny of minds programmed to discard all trivia. Old posters, accounts, duplicate copies of contracts, photographs, these were peeled off as debris. The wall safe housed the cashier's takings from the last week of concerts played in the Peppermint Lounge. There was an automatic in the right-hand drawer of the desk. Various articles of signed memorabilia. The two aliens were searching for something else. One of them thumbed through a line of books on a shelf, paperback biographies of the musical glitterati. With a kinetic incisiveness, he extracted the book that would impart the required information. He held the wedged book in a metallic-blue, gloved hand. He flipped from the dust-jacket image to the corresponding photographs on the back. The green-eyed face with arched sensuous lips positioned beneath THE DAVID BOWIE STORY STARDUST was an illustrator's impression of the man depicted in triplicate on the reverse of the jacket. There he was photographed on-stage in a kimono, face reddened by blusher, his hair the inimitable red of his Ziggy period. The same face ten years on, planes highlighted around high cheekbones, was seen with short, peroxided hair, a stylish boater offsetting the memorably alien features. Two stage shots, which contrasted with a natural photograph, no make-up, taken when Bowie must have been in his mid-thirties.

The figure had found what it wanted. It rapidly flipped through the pages scanning the chronological diversity of images that the photographs displayed. The other one was busy picking up on a transmission, listening intently, automatically, a robotic receptivity allowing for no questions, not the least vacillation over the instructions supplied. Neither conferred with the other. The second one showed curiosity over a missile-shaped desk ornament. An aluminium spacecraft

130

modelled on the lunar Apollo model, it was handled with interest before being pocketed with an unemotive gesture.

Absolutely focused, they turned the room over with the rapidity of two fish darting in opposite directions across a tank, their fluency coming to an abrupt halt as they recognized each other. There were two and not one. Two cobalt helmets, bruised leather flying jackets, black glitter leggings.

There was no contact. One of them opened the zipper on his jacket to reveal two square nipples, a blue rectangle and a red. The blue one came on alert, lit up, pulsing as a sexual receptacle. The other figure moved in, adjusted its helmet and directed a ray at the nipple. The act was performed with the motions of impersonal sex. Something of the genetic earth instinct had been converted into a transbiological process. An electromagnetic wave frictionalized with another to induce a nipple orgasm. A light bleeped and went dead.

The two figures resumed their search as though the incident was supererogatory. They moved out of the manager's office and into the cloakrooms. One of them systematically opened the three black-painted door cubicles. A red heart had been placed above the central mirror. Someone had written up in candy-pink lipstick, the scrawled message WENDY LOVES JILL FOR EVER.

They itemized the contents of the room with objective scrutiny, an immediacy that assimilated without questioning. Fast, immediate, they picked up on nothing that suggested the least interest to them. They were out and gone into the corridor, hearing Johnny's guitar chop with its delayed fuzzy wowwow before entering a room that contained the mixing-desk unit for recording live concerts. The technology was too simplistic to be of interest to them. Master tapes had been neatly shelved, but the alphabetical wedge yielded no return. The small club artists who had played here were scanned as expendable names.

What did occupy the attention of one of them was a small, grey, tank-shaped CD player with the lettering PROCEED PCD2 marked on its plastic casing. With its analogue and digital electronics on separate boards, and its input circuit maximized to reduce radio frequency interference, the design seemed to arouse the curiosity of the alien. Deletable in time, the product none the less merited disinterested inspection. Synthesized knowledge told the alien that the designers had chosen to use eight-times oversampling digital filtering on this machine. The framework was also noted for its protective casing. The construction had incorporated some of the principles architects use to protect buildings from earthquakes. It would be worth taking back on the saucer. A memento of terrestrial hi-fi.

The alien marked it for collection, while the other stared at a poster of Madonna in tiny gold metallic panties. Her mouth was shaped as though it were in the act of giving passionate head. It was the metallic sheen of her underwear that attracted the alien's attention. The poster was selected as a salvageable curiosity.

They cleared out of the room and headed towards the swing doors marked *Exit* which gave admission to the club basement. Through two glass horizontal panels inserted into the black-painted wood, they could see Johnny on-stage under a wash of red, blue and white spotlights. The frequencies he was using charged the compressed space with sonic disturbance. His overloaded reverb set up an electric dissonance. The aliens watched intently. His sound was too disorganized to warrant analysis through a frequency modulator. It was his movements that attracted their joint attention. Johnny was crouched bow-legged into his playing as though the noise screamed from his solar plexus. It sounded like he had wired his nerves to amplifiers, and that when the circuit burnt out he would drop dead on-stage and incinerate there in a charred frazzle of autocombustion.

They scrutinized Johnny's fumbled retuning before hearing him scratch another distorted riff, his chording stacking a feedback apocalypse, his skeletal callisthenics having him appear more like an animated aura than a body. They could see clean through him to the impulsive autonomy of his nerves. His aura was haloed around him, a black ring graduating to minimal blue and purple.

They could see the mannequins grouped around the stage. Some of their bodies had been truncated or smashed to fragments. Johnny was automated with tension. In his own mind he was playing to an auditorium of the select dead. Locomoted in spasms, he was moving from left to right of the stage as though the point to be reached was the visible end of the world. It was a somnambulist's achievement, a man arriving with his guitar to a continent in need of aural conversion.

The two aliens kept immobile. For decades pop station wavebands had been picked up by extraterrestrials as unwanted interference, signals that specified an urgency about this particular planet that was not evident to reconnaissance missions. Radar images had suggested that earth was not in a state of terminal chaos. It was simply a biosphere progressively drained of its natural resources, a dust-bowl with rootless forests, war scars written across its continents, concrete blocks converging to form a universal suburb. Their interest was in certain individuals who could be relocated. Bowie was an obvious choice, and there were others like the futuristic writer J.G. Ballard who they knew would adapt to a creative life on extrasolar planets. They were partial infiltrators, men who brought to the earth a realization of alien culture. They were the adjustable ones, the neurobiological mutants. Their lives were extensible because they acknowledged deathlessness.

Johnny's chemistry lacked advancement. They could perceive the drug screen that filmed his nerves. His mind was like a deoxygenating fish in a chemical tank. But they could also perceive the electromagnetic power within him, his faculty to mindbend, direct someone's impulses into his own brainstorage system. They could read the spiral arm of the galaxy in his brain cells, and how chemicals had shaded areas like computer artefacts. Johnny was like a supernova remnant, a mass cooling to a red dwarf star.

They continued to watch as he loaded the air with a surcharge of decibels. His introspective histrionics worked in his favour. The potential for his mutation was questionable. Drugs should have killed him a long time ago, and by surviving a toxic surfeit he had acquired extrasensory faculties. The two of them had stood in on Madonna's 'Blonde Ambition' tour. Impressed by her dance troupe, futuristic costumes, the erotic calligraphy of her body gestures, they had observed it as no more than an act, right down to the posturing on a red velvet bed which was lifted hydraulically from the stage. They had omitted her from any conception of interplanetary transpeciation.

But Johnny fascinated. He was not as intellectually advanced as another of their migrational conscripts, William S. Burroughs, but he possessed something of the latter's ability to monitor the implosive dialogue established by narcotics. A voluntary experimentation had made him hypersensitive to inner change, to the hallucinated images that free floated across his consciousness. Whatever his original intentions, he had become preoccupied with the kaleidoscopic visions that punctuated rational thought, and finally preoccupied by inducing them, relying on artificiality to generate reality.

They decided to review the situation later. There was still the possibility that Johnny might OD on-stage. He flickered between motory arrest and hyperactive stimulus. And even dead, his extrasensory facilities could be transplanted into a robot and computer analysed.

They moved round to the other side of the building and flipped upstairs. They entered a room in which a mattress had been placed on the floor. Cassette shells littered the wooden boards, together with bottles and empty food cans. The wrinkled snake slough of several pairs of leather trousers were lying as stiff exhibits in a corner. Old copies of the sci-fi journal *Interzone* had been stacked on a chair. There was a pharmacopoeia, a slew of disposable syringes, the contents of narcotic plunder spread around this improvised bedroom. As if from an old habit, Johnny had hung a black drape over the window. Even in a world without police, he intended to screen his privacy with a junkie's mania for secrecy. The place had the compressed aura of a person who sealed himself into a tin can. The whole mechanism went inside, compacted, taut, and then reappeared, slicing a circular groove for release.

A pyramidal dune of cigarette-butts had formed as the overspill of a metallic ashtray. No possessions, as Johnny existed by regular looting. They knew he could have lived anywhere along the coast, but he had chosen to retreat into the constrictions of a single room, to spiral upstairs after playing and make the long dark drop into unconsciousness as exhaustion took over.

It was like disturbing a pharaonic burial chamber. They had been everywhere in their reconnaissance of the fragmented universe, excavated the past, taken radar images of geophysical strata, monuments, and they had shown an immediate dismissal of everything that could not be converted to future use. But what was here in this makeshift room was compelling in the way that Johnny's chemistry was wired to an electronic apocalypse. Aspects of him were sufficiently weird to be convertible.

They left Johnny communicating from his amplified umbilical and got back to the street. Transmission told them that the other two of their party were searching the tenements for Bowie. Something about him didn't connect with their frequencies; rather, he deflected their signals and existed within his own set of communications.

They decided to head for the coast. Arc's film archives were important for clues as to Bowie's mutations. And there was the artist and the girl, the two of them wandering through hallucinated dimensions in their search for a way back to time. They had seen them mentally travelling on zebras through a landscape of truncated statuary. In their shared vision they were making for a lost city. They had only to blow on the dust covering the buried site and the architecture would resurrect itself. They would travel for ever, passing out beyond the Grand Hotel and walking in search of the inaccessible horizon. They wouldn't see the saucer, their minds were too fixated by the metamorphic visuals of their psychosis.

The two of them moved with automatic rapidity through the multi-set streets. The town was the shape of a twenty-third-century Gaudí construction, a space-age baroque that exteriorized the contents of Arc's mind. There was a design behind this that had occurred with the same sort of accidental providence that had allowed Warhol to find an art expression in a Coca-Cola bottle. Their interest lay in this area of Arc's mind, the intuitive function that triggered off an expansive sequence of visuals. A world transferable to software images, a microstructure they could analyse back home on their planet. An exhibition model of psychosis. They had already discovered how synthesizer sound was similar to the background noise of the cosmos. Madness might also represent a sound classification of one or more stars in the Milky Way.

The way to the beach was like a Hollywood constructed from fragments of Dali paintings. They inspected only what provided intimate clues to Arc's hallucinated fetishism. The long black shop wig placed over a steering-wheel, the looping curlicues of graffiti, the constant allusions to J.G. Ballard, the proclamations of Bowie as a new world avatar, of Warhol as having survived his death.

They got to the beach and stood looking out at the hotel. A shift of terrain had placed it signally offshore, distinct from the holiday villas that were set into shallow dunes along the coast. The place stood out imposingly as a headquarters. There was music issuing from it. It was the message of a cyclic obsession, the signal of a man walled in by his mania.

There was a bronze convertible parked outside a side-entrance. It looked like an object of the space junk they frequently encountered on interplanetary travel. There was no sign of anyone, just the eerie transmission of music placing a protective envelope around the building. They could see from an isolated plume of smoke that the other two from their reconnaissance saucer were off somewhere, gutting an apartment block. They knew Arc was watching them through closed-circuit television, a source they could instantly de-magnetize, leaving him facing a rectangular black-out.

There was no hesitation. Arc's circuit was defused by the emission of wave frequencies from a transmitter gun. They knew he would be staring into the black hole he so dreaded.

Their singular objective was to check out the Bowie ar-chives. They crossed the beach as they had the dust surfaces of so many planets, always inquisitive, mechanistically selec-tive. They had encountered the absence of beaches on Mars, despite water flowing in intermittent epochs. The oxidized red soils rich with maghematite deposits were something they had rediscovered on earth. But here they faced sand, quartz granules refined by aeons of oceanic pressure, a mauve poly-gonal sky. None of them had been willing to test the atmos-phere without a life-support system.

They entered the hotel, switched off transmission and waited. There was a hum in the air. The music appeared non-localized, as though it were part of the micro-environ-ment rather than the issue of a sound system. Arc's metro-polis started here, the videoscape emporium over which he presided. Wall photographs were neatly captioned, print from newspapers forming a subtext in the montage. They took in the faces on a video camera the size of an automatic. Bowie formed the dominant image. His body had been positioned in the galactic centre of Grote Reber's contour map of celestial radio noise. In that way the singer stood at a microphone in the middle of the Milky Way, a spiral of cigarette-smoke diffused above one eye, his extended arm signifying the dramatic gesture accompanying a phrase. Orbiting radio telescopes were like a constellation of saucers around his body.

They went up a floor. Logograms were on every wall. The place was being converted into an imagined biosphere by its occupant. A metalanguage was becoming Arc's means of codifying his manic fluctuations of mood.

With customary methodology the two entered an unlocked suite. The room had already been overhauled. Dresses and high-heel shoes were rucked in a disorderly mound on the bed. The wardrobe was open, to reveal what looked like an altar. The numerals 666 had been transcribed in silver over a globe devised to incorporate areas of the moon into the earth's continents. Beneath it Arc had copied out a text that they committed to film, interested in converting its archaic symbols into the equivalents of neuroscience.

The replicable dialectic of Arc's mind advised them against close scrutiny of individual rooms. They knew that Johnny's victims would be packed into the hotel's freezer, or buried in the metallic shells of cars that littered the immediate sand. They flashed up two floors to the fourth. They could blow Arc's whole system, but they chose to wait, select their data on Bowie and record Arc's brain rhythms to analyse their correspondence to the electromagnetic spectrum.

They could hear him working in a room facing the hotel's sea view. He would be adjusting potentiometers on a console, frantic to have the video circuit come alive, a coastal villa step into his visual field to the exclusion of all other concepts.

Bowie's 'Ashes to Ashes' had been programmed to repeat. It would go on playing for as long as Arc remained in that obsessive groove of consciousness. The cut-up components of the narrative were recycled into audially fixating atmospherics. To Arc it was the only sound in the universe.

The two of them got into the room he had established as a film archive. Audio and video cassettes formed a random spoor across boards that had been painted silver and blue. Drag shots of Bowie looked down from the ceiling. There were files everywhere, exfoliations from books, press cuttings, photographs. Sophisticated lightweight camcorders were scrutinized for their serials: Mitsubishi MSCXI, Sony TR-105. Palmcorders equipped with six shutter speeds, hi-fi stereo sound, date/time recording, the compact electronics associated with a certain point in technological advance. Equipment they got on to film as curiosities, things deleted by their own culture, but of interest as artefacts, correlatives to man's creative interiority.

They scanned video processor units, systems that incorporated channels for creative editing, detail enhancement, colour control. The studio was lined wall to wall with television screens.

Their search was here in Arc's ritualistic inner sanctum, the boundaries of his psyche translated into video footage. The sound off, they watched as forty different images of Bowie jumped into view, each phase of his singing career represented in all its diverse and conflicting modes of expression. Bowie was seen sitting at press interviews, making up backstage, being driven across America, an emaciated mutant slumped in the rear of a limousine.

One of the two selected a video tape marked *Cape Kennedy Rehearsals October 1973*. There was a second tape balanced beneath the first: *Cape Kennedy Concert, Transbiological Mutation*. The tapes had been copied, triplicated. A blue glove placed one of each in a spacious, light-sealed backpack. They

selected a variety of related items, footage from private sana-
torium films showing the singer in the company of his personal assistant, a casually dressed, dark-jacketed, blue-jeaned
psychotherapist sitting in a rocking-chair, his dark glasses
lifted into racemed curls, his hand holding a cigarette with
the extended gesture of a conductor. They snatched the brief
impression of a clip, then flicked through copious files
marked either *Bowie, Ballard* or *Warhol*. Arc had amassed a
disorganized slew of papers, his own red felt-tip notes conflicting with a mass of reportage, a system they would have
committed to microfiche.

Ballard concerned them in a way not dissimilar to Bowie.
Research had shown them he had adjusted the easier of the
two. His anticipation of deathlessness, interplanetary life,
was an involuntary acceptance of the mind's continuity.
Bowie's rebirth had been more difficult, lacking the cellular
substrata that Ballard had come to incorporate into his chemistry from the time of writing his first novels. His transition
would be effortless. His central nervous system was already
attuned to deep-space frequencies, his imaginative current
answered by pulsars. Warhol had been designated his planet.

One of the two aliens operated a mini colour screen. The red and
pink surface of Jupiter was suddenly there like a magnified eyeball.
Turbulent storms were moving across it, a dust-cone was hanging
above a bright central belt. The red eye was cannibalizing smaller
spots. The wrong atmospherics for transmission. He blanked the
picture out and returned to investigating Arc's chaotic archives.

They left the paperwork, selecting only audio and visual
items. They could hear Arc absorbed in his own schizoid
videoscape. 'Ashes to Ashes' was still repeating.

For a long time the individuals in this resort had been viewing
nature from a point in the universe outside the earth. Their
bodies had begun the migration towards the transhuman.

Johnny's victims were in the hotel's kitchens. They had
abandoned their bodies long before he had driven them here,
unloading them from open convertibles in the way that stores
had once been delivered to the side of the hotel. It was time to
catch up with the other two, get back to the saucer.

Chapter 10

Arc heard the sonic roar of a car out on the coast. A crazy, stunt-car driver's zigzag negotiation of surfaces. The noise crashed through the silent zone he had come to accept as a permanence broken only by the music that fed his nerves. His interpretation of Bowie's sound as a musical annotation of the future, an invocation to the new species, was being realized through his construction of a video city.

Arc was busy revising blueprints for architectural innovations. He wanted a city that would represent the salient features of a Ballard novel. When he welcomed Ballard through a door in the purple skyline, he wanted to introduce him to an environment that would be inseparable from his fiction. He had already begun to devise elaborate fictions into his set, imaginary cities incorporated into the videoscape.

His three icons were to be the legislators of an interplanetary metropolis. Arc would make films of their various creative contributions. Tapes of these would be placed on board space shuttles aimed for the near planets. There had to be cars for Ballard, airports, launching pads, film studios modelled on those at Shepperton, high-rise car-parks, submerged forests. And for the resuscitated Warhol there had to be back issues of *Interview*, sites for prospective Factories, a reconstructed Bloomingdale's, an endless supply of candy. And for Bowie, make-up artists, recording studios at the Grand Hotel, videographers, a studio in which to paint.

Arc was attentive to every need, every idiosyncratic fetish of his triumvirate. The map of his head was to be the design of the future. He no longer knew who was alive out there; his reclusion didn't allow for others. He, too, would leave the earth for the near planets.

His work was to construct a videoscape that would harmonize with their creative sensibilities. Arc's paramount need was to detain them long enough for the shooting of the film he had in mind. He wanted to be isolated with the three so that together they could exhaust the possibilities of film before enlisting the permutations made available by the resources of Mars, Jupiter, Neptune.

Johnny's intrusion impressed on Arc the need to hurry. The singer's drug-fuelled psychosis was channelled towards a Manson-type autocracy. Arc expected all the time to hear the car detonate in the gullies, an impacted velocity of metal sheeting into flame. And if Johnny survived one crash, he would come back with another car, line it up on the shore and use it as expendable weaponry in an impulsive gravitation towards a maniacal point in inner space.

Arc busied himself in touching up a series of Warhol portraits. It was the fixed mortuary quality of the shots that fascinated him, as though the subject portrayed had never really lived. The porcelain skin, the platinum hair, the refusal to concede to overt emotion, the realization that all nepotistic *ingénues* are as fraudulent as the illusion they satellite, had somehow made him a caricature of his own entropy. Andy was there and he wasn't. Whether caught in a photograph by Anton Perich at Studio 54, or snapped by Christine Sorley, Gerard Malanga or Victor Bockris, Arc came back to the notion that Warhol would make a perfect candidate for the new species. Warhol had only pretended to be alive; his real existence would happen within the context of Arc's meticulously constructed universe. He imagined Warhol shooting film after film of the new city.

And Ballard. He was already a contemporary myth, someone operating on so individual a plane of consciousness that he was without contemporaries. In his books the imagination was inseparable from reality – the parallel universes he had established were quantifiably identifiable in an unlimited dream future. In Arc's mind, Ballard would lead the sea in from its ultimate point of recession. The whole pantheon of the novelist's protagonists would materialize and cross the barrier between inner and outer space. They would walk in across the beach, disorientated like astronauts emerging from their capsule after splash-down. Arc imagined their saying, 'Hi, we were always there, only you couldn't read us into the same space as you occupied. Now we're here. We've been waiting a long time for this.'

And Bowie? Arc was fixated by his chameleonic mutations, the physiological changes within him which seemed always to anticipate possible states of deathlessness. He knew he was out there in the ruins, a transhuman caught between worlds, inhabiting his past and future with equal facility. And in time he hoped to create autonomous Bowie clones, computerized images that would acquire independent lives. Arc would process them so that the stages of Bowie's earth life could be projected into a continuous cycle of return.

He trained the circuit viewfinder to its maximum reach, but couldn't pick up on any change within the radius of the beach. The same ruins half buried in sand presented their uninhabitable but geometrically arranged façades to the unrelieved silence that flooded the screen. He half expected to see Johnny, abandoning a Buick or Porche, his leather figure hunting the foreshore for a way out of the drug-trap imposed by his mind. Or the silver-jacketed figure of Bowie appearing momentarily on the sands, music announcing his presence, the air buzzing with extraterrestrial frequencies. He was picking up unconsciously on some intrusion into the vibrational

142

envelope that sealed his headquarters. Foreign impulses had flickered through his private space. Neurons, electrons, photons pulsated like amplified explosions in his oversensitized sensory field.

When he stepped out to the beach, it was like moonwalking, a remove to another planet. Arc wasn't sure how long it had taken him to get from the fourth floor to the ground. He might have set out yesterday, or it might have been years ago that he began the journey to the planet he had created. The bronze Jaguar had been side-tilted, and Marilyn's body was missing. He stood there, immersing his feet in the drift, watching the fine dazzle sift whitely over his boots. In earlier times he and Marilyn had sat outside the hotel at a circular table, high on each other's physical anomalies, watching the waiters come and go with drinks trays.

Arc kicked his leopard-skin toes in the sand. They had travelled so far since that summer in which they had decided to edit and augment Buñuel's Cape Kennedy film of Bowie. They had seen a world altered beyond recognition. And where was Marilyn now? Arc was struck by the unreality of death. One moment you were breathing and the next you were somewhere else. There weren't any logical connections between the two states. His toe turned up a rusted Coke can. It lay there as a memento of the old world; something vestigial of beach holidays, advertising, Andy Warhol. Or rather the dead Warhol. This time round Arc imagined the pop artist painting astronaut food-drips, sunflower heads poking through smashed glass, extraterrestrial sightings above the Empire State Building.

Arc scuffed his way back to the terrace door. He was a transvestite god awaiting the arrival of a new race. Everything visible to the eye was his own ingenious fabrication. When the time was right, he would divide his power with the three progenitors of his mutant race.

He went back inside. It was like reclaiming a planet after an intergalactic mission. The hotel's imperturbable silence swallowed him into its depths. His vanishing-point existed outside linear, single-plane reality, that old cultural habit of the mind. Instead his window on reality had become the dream, that admission to the interior where he would reclaim Marilyn.

He knew he would have to work furiously to rearrange the desert landscape so that Johnny would get lost in the maze of labyrinthine reefs. Arc wanted Johnny to die out there; he was the last of his temporal embarrassments. Johnny's retroactive mania stood as a barrier between Arc's conception of the new and the old. The archetypal rock-and-roll figure, trafficking between overreach and suicide, would be chromosomally phased out by musicians receptive to biological mutations. For Arc, only Bowie possessed the innovative chemistry that would correspond to mutants living with a more advanced technology.

Arc's mind was speeded up to live in a subliminal future. In the way that Warhol's portraits seemed to circumvent the present and situate his subjects as icons awaiting a future, so Arc was already living in an unconscious world that had still to materialize. He negotiated the corridor in the direction of the lift. Already he was losing gravity, space telescoped into the six billion light years encompassed by a telescope – he was heading towards the idea of a planet in his mind. His studio was a radial punctum existing outside the universe. He had so far to travel to get there. He was conscious somewhere along the way of the dead. There was a body laid out on the kitchen floor. Was it Marilyn's? There wasn't time to stop. He had to keep on journeying if he were to reach his destination while still alive. There must have been innumerable bodies back there in the untraceable dark. Did he search the freezers? He couldn't be sure, only that he was drifting towards the impression he retained of himself as someone identifiable, tangible, situated at the Grand Hotel.

At some stage he found himself back in his hotel suite. His Warhol videos were neatly shelved – *Blow Job*, *Screen Test I* and *2*, *Horse*, *Vinyl*, *Hedy*, *The Chelsea Girls*, *Trash*, *Lonesome Cowboys*, and so forth, and the films that he and Marilyn had made on a corresponding 16 mm were attached to the Warhol cassettes as variations on the singular and

144

obsessive. Arc had plagiarized Warhol's method of snapping three-quarter profile shots with a Polaroid for future portraits. He had also devised a method of shooting photographs from photographs of his three heroes for a series he called *Visitors from Imaginary Space*. Arc's method of physiognomical distortion lay in first making an exposure of the negative with the right half of the printing paper covered, and then changing the image over, reversing the negative in the enlarger and exposing the other half before developing the print in the normal manner. A dissociated Bowie or Ballard could be recognized only by drawing an imaginary line down the centre of their bodies and covering the right-hand side. In the new world anything was possible. Bowie trekking in a silver space-suit through the communications centre to pick up an intravenous macrobiotic from the drugstore.

Arc needed to re-edit and revise the landscape. He had returned obsessively to the big change; the opera-house roof, the filming of an environment that had been so radically altered as almost to disappear. The audio mixer had captured the roar of the big wind coming out of the back of space. Marilyn's laughter slashed across the pauses. She was hysterical. He had forgotten that. Together they had acted out the role of spectators to a millennial apocalypse.

Arc backtracked through unedited tape. He had repeatedly zoomed in on Marilyn's face, almost as a perverse fetish, exposing the stubble beneath the matt foundation, the sweat runnels leaking into her carefully graduated make-up. It was a subversion of the accumulated aeons of macho-autocracy to have a transvestite and a transsexual preside over the end of the old scheme of things.

Arc bit his tongue at the citric thrill of it. His old films of Hitler, Stalin, Ceauşescu and Margaret Thatcher, the principal tyrants of the twentieth century, together with media monomaniacs, industrial barons, publishing magnates, were eclipsed by this statement that contravened nature. Arc recalled all the humiliations that he and Marilyn had suffered at the hands of the collective. Deprecation at parties, street insult, the outraged PR man who had urinated into Marilyn's wineglass at a roof-garden party, coercion by their professional colleagues to get straight.

Arc worked at the processor with its selection of hard cuts, soft fade-overs and special effects. He wanted to enhance the edited image, and by alternating between the master machine and the slave video his intention was to achieve the refinement of two independent shoots. He would superimpose his own takes on Buñuel's master of Bowie's transformation into Major Tom.

The idea of Johnny continued to disturb him. By the use of a montage projection Arc conceived of devising environmental traps. He could float a new architectonics on the old, have the gutted cottages, huts and cabins appear to have become a beach colony's props floating on the tide. In Arc's mind Johnny would be lost underwater, the car headlights still shining in a channel between reefs, two yellow moons attracting inquisitive fish.

Arc needed time in which to perfect his film. Staging a millennial end, a last terminal to the stars in which he lived as the invincible technician of a resort created out of visuals, demanded above all his own indestructibility. Buñuel's film, repeatedly studied, would offer him the clues to undergoing the mutation that Bowie had successfully survived. He was already aware of his own displacement outside time. He could do with his body volume and energy what photographs from Hiroshima had made all too clear, that matter at some distance from the ground becomes a shadow. His inner momentum would establish the trajectory by which he would overtake and transcend himself.

Arc suspended the image of anticipation in Bowie's eyes, as the latter launched into the Cape Kennedy live version of 1984. Aluminium and paper skyscrapers were the backdrop to a show that was to initiate Bowie into a new dimension, the ballistics of inner space rather than that of the outer preoccupations of the astrophysicists.

Phallic antennae, model missiles were on-stage. Buñuel had succeeded in freeze-framing rehearsed emotions, then allowing the spontaneously acted to be injected into the footage at a modulated higher speed. A quirkiness that transposed the viewer from slow-motion mime to accelerated callisthenics.

Arc watched Bowie go through the motions of 'John I'm Only Dancing', the ambivalent lyrics pronouncing the singer's androgyny. Bowie's face was washed by a silver spotlight. The involuntary change-over was already being activated by his chemistry. Something within his psyche had been anticipating the change, had lived with it as a potential reality, an inner state, long before the thing had occurred. What looked like drug strain, fatigue, emaciation, was the back-brain alert to a subliminal signal.

Mick Ronson's thin, angular face, fringed by platinum hair, jumped into view as the guitarist doubled with Bowie on the vocals to 'Jean Genie'. Arc had forgotten the back-up group in what was a film singularly devoted to Bowie's face and body expression. All extraneous admissions read like an intrusion on a focal centre.

Bowie's brief disappearance was for a costume change. When he returned, he was wearing nothing but a silver thong, fishnet tights and thigh-high red boots. An hysterical assault on 'Panic in Detroit' followed, before the band moved into an equally manic 'Cracked Actor'. Buñuel had made it seem as though the lens were directing the change. The director was discarnate, an enigma who happened to be a spectator to the events occurring on-stage.

Arc was also conscious of how little attention the old film-maker devoted to the theatrical stage-set that Bowie had brought with him, insisting in pre-concert interviews that the props had become incorporated into his psychology. Their elaborate construct was an internalized artefact, a miniature future that Bowie purported to inhabit.

Buñuel's declared impatience with prefabricated cinematographic beauty was apparent in his turning the camera round to focus continually on isolated characteristics of the singer's face, turning an eye into a magnified planet, having the sound appear as though it issued from this one point, the mouth still having to be anatomically invented. Or he went in under a depilated armpit, exploring a forest reduced to pointillist bristles.

Arc was reminded of some of the shooting in *L'âge d'or*

and *Un chien andalou* in which Buñuel's sense of subversive outrage had found full expression. The eye razored open in order to admit the new vision, the world stood upside-down, the right way up, the imaginative undermining of all conventional orders. It was little wonder that Buñuel had recognized in Bowie's image and music the continuity of a revolution that was now directed towards questions of gender. The ageing director had lost none of his insurrectionary qualities. He had constructed a film out of Bowie's body. The genitalia were a suggestive volcano, a protruberance so tightly housed on-stage that the camera had transformed the bulge into an ovoid, a silver reptile contracted into an erogenous radius. Nothing was missed, the pitted craters of skin that showed through white foundation had been made to resemble something as pronounced as a snake's markings, so too had the hands, the angles of the knees been transformed into an erotic science fictional geometry of a body no longer bound by time, but dispersing itself through the cosmos.

Arc viewed the film with critical detachment, searching for technical blemishes, material to be dubbed, images to be edited. Bunuel had only half completed the film he had made from the live recording, superimposing on Bowie's dynamism his own visual genius.

Arc switched over to the interviews and rehearsals, and an equally made-up Bowie confronted the camera, sitting knees up in a bucket chair, defending his beliefs about the inner planets with an oblique eloquence. His red hair was shocking against the white face, and the lack of focal synchronicity in his eyes added to the impression that the man was an alien. One who chain-smoked and spoke with a Cockney accent, but whose central nervous system blueprinted alien intelligence.

Arc watched backstage shots of Bowie making up, trying out various facial images, using his face the way an artist textures his brushstrokes. He was clearly searching for someone, attempting to make visible his sense of extraterrestrial identity. And again, there was the sense of unconscious awareness that something was about to happen. His eyes were searching for something in the way that a reader attempts to anticipate the development of narrative. He was trying to read into his life the possibilities of existence outside it.

Arc wondered if it were Bowie who had returned here and examined the contents of his studio. There were no signs of anything gone missing, other than a number of video triplicates. For some time now the red-haired android hadn't showed on the beach, his enigmatic materializations leaving Arc strained towards the vision. At such times he knew his studio was a universal headquarters, a locus for the change-over of the species to mutants.

Arc felt his pulse accelerate. He knew Johnny was out there, closing in, despite the silence, the absence of a motor gunning for a gap in the convoluted landscape. He was being spooked. He had seen Zap and Cindy walk off towards the horizon, eyes fixed on an invisible point. He knew they had gone for ever, that they would join the other nomadic packs of psychotics who would die before they reached the end of the visible world.

He was too distracted to continue editing. He felt like he was speeding full tilt at a giant lens. If he kept on travelling, he would reach the sun.

His adrenalin was burning too fast to have him stay. His lipstick was smudged like a crushed raspberry. Not since his early raids to loot all the available film in town, and to requisition new camera equipment, had he left the Grand Hotel.

He ran outside to the bronze Jaguar convertible and checked the fuel-gauge. The tank was almost full, suggesting that Johnny had topped it up on that day he had driven out to the beach, a week, a year, a century ago. The ignition key had been thrown on to the red leather passenger's seat. Arc worked the clutch and heard the engine falter before firing to an upbeat tone. His mind was jumpy with flashbacks – Marilyn's lips as they closed over his cock, her slow, drinking-straw manner of giving head, their globe-hopping trips together on film excursions, her dead body arranged in a position of sexual abandon in this car, and then her disappearance. Suddenly the sky was alive with nuclear warheads – he could hear the jets crash over low, as though they had punched holes in the mauve sky. He knew he was audio-hallucinating, but it threw him. He got the car on to the flat and nursed the accelerator. This time he knew his trajectory would take him right to the edge of universal power. In the course of eliminating Johnny he would realize the expression of his supraconsciousness.

Arc could feel a centre return to his mind. The automatic shifted to third as he spun the car out of a sand-drift and on to the flat. The sand blew to an overhang, a dust-cloud that trailed his acceleration towards a divide between two reefs. It felt like he was driving through Johnny, or that by some freak connection he had become him. Arc was driving into the alienation of the world he had constructed. He felt confused by distances, unsure if the horizon was no further away than the glass wall of an aquarium to a fish, or whether it was as far out as the moon. He stalled the car repeatedly as though expecting an imminent crash. Several times he threw his arms up to protect his face, expecting the windshield to shatter with the impacted dazzle of a breaking wave.

And now that he was exposed, he missed Marilyn. She seemed to come at him in so many ways, erotic, consoling, conciliatory after his temper exploded over a film hitch, outrageous after they had attended a drag ball, fagging back in the early hours and making love on the back seat on the top of a high-rise car-park as the sun lifted red above the sleeping city. They had shared their perversity.

Arc's mind oscillated between past and present. He was still working out the connection between inner and outer in film, thinking how someone could be cock-sucking while watching a lunar landing, and later on the sequence might find a fictional coherence, so that in the inner takes it was the couple who were moon-walking, and the astronauts who were engaged in sex at the bottom of the alley stairs.

Arc equivocated. Part of him wanted to go back and reclaim his rights. He imagined his archives being looted, his work in progress being irreparably slashed by a knifeman, the hotel catching fire in a furnace roar of sheeting flame.

He swung the car round in the direction of the hotel,

150

describing a whip-coil of sand, a viper-tailed flicker of dust that hung in the air. His heartbeat was fast, a persistent bass chord that seemed to rise from the depths of the earth. He floored the accelerator and burnt a trail back towards his headquarters. He couldn't be sure how near or far away he was, or if he had entered a parallel dimension, the centre stretching away like a black hole, and time becoming elongated as he tried to align his vision. The idea that he might have been travelling backwards through a distorted duplication of the world he took on trust, flashed across his mind as a speeding blip.

He pulled up in front of a reef. There was a figure waving from the hotel balcony. He could see distinctly it was Johnny in his cracked leather suit, his affected posture angled for an invisible audience. Johnny's indifference allowed him an off-centre, lethally accurate focus.

Arc got free and chased off in an erratic, impromptu burst of speed. He could hear music issuing from the stone forest. And this time it wasn't Bowie's voice but Johnny's ragged guitar shriek. Arc could hear the chords of Hendrix's 'Purple Haze' being picked out and relayed through a fuzzbox. The guitarist was jamming. He switched through a number of tunes, deliberately phasing one into the other.

Arc cut the ignition and sat with his headlights full on. He needed to recruit his heroes and quickly. He didn't know why he'd switched the lights on, it was an old reflex habit of blazing a way into the future. He found himself listening for the imminent descent of a helicopter that would touch down on the beach, its whirring props blasting Bowie's red hair to a contrary swathe as he exited through a side-door. Ballard's resigned sense of elation in response to a proven landscape, and Warhol's modestly snapping the other two in their immediate surroundings, was a scene that Arc had referred to again and again.

It was the silence that amplified Johnny's chords. There wasn't any other noise in the universe to contradict his virtuoso pieces. The music had established a solitary discourse with space. It was spiralling skywards as a form of electric kundalini.

Arc conceived of the idea of running at Johnny with a

camera and filming his own death as the guitarist fed bullets through his diaphragm. Instead he sat in the car and waited. He trained his camera on the continuation of the causeway between reefs. The stillness, when the guitar cut out, the unrelieved mauve of the sky, the coast with its villas cowering into dunes, its mirror cities, labyrinthine constructs; he and Marilyn had presided over this in a state of drugged indifference. They had created a new architecture: blocks built in the shape of cameras, moon-shaped film and recording studios, a world in which inner space was an inhabitable reality.

The vicious guitar wail started up again. Johnny was playing against himself, sawing on the strings, twisting the chords to strangulation.

Arc rolled the car forward on the down gradient, the headlights focused like those on a lunar landing-craft negotiating an uncertain surface. And the landscape could have been the moon. He braked the Jaguar and abandoned it. The Grand Hotel looked like a doll's house built on the edge of space. For a moment he imagined he was too tall to enter it again; his proportions had grown while its dimensions had shrunk. His foot might fill the baroque entrance hall, the balcony rooms form ridges against his legs.

He found himself returning to the car for reassurance, touching it and flipping off again. It was his one point of surety. The convertible had become an extension of consciousness, an artefact balanced on a thought-ray.

Arc moved forward to a vantage-point from which he could see Johnny through his lens. The wire-thin, drug-smashed guitarist was stripped of his leather jacket. Green and blue snake tattoos flickered across his torso. Arc was filming the bizarre rites, homing in on Johnny as he abandoned his guitar and stepped out to the cobalt Mercedes he had parked up against the hotel. After so much editing and cutting, Arc was shooting direct again, and the experience thrilled him.

With the cool indifference of a spectator he watched Johnny lift Marilyn out of the boot of his car. Arc followed the posture of her dead body with his camera. He was so stimulated by the act of shooting new film that the subject-matter was irrelevant. Had he once made love to this artificial woman? He couldn't remember anything about their past intimacies. She might have been Bardot or an anonymous Pigalle transsexual.

He watched Johnny return to the car and offload three other bodies. His lens found Cindy and Zap interlocked as though engaged in an obscene death-rite. Arc isolated each of the group individually. He didn't want to know them other than as a series of angles, planes, weirdly fabricated sexual geometries. He had picked up from Ballard the art of dehumanization, of freeze-framing his subject into a study of poetic robotics.

Arc moved in fractionally closer. Johnny was looking back over his shoulder, staring away towards the horizon as though he were searching for something, someone, the mutant figure of Bowie to appear as a kinetic image on the sands. Johnny was using a shovel to scoop a shallow crater in the sand. But his work was misaligned, his weight leaning back when it should have been forward, forward when it should have been back. He was persistent, a man prospecting above the abyss. The cutting edge would ricochet from its groove and run up his spine as a series of shocks. Arc kept connecting with the idea that the last man on earth would have to eat and bury his contemporaries. The dawn of the mutant age would arrive, the old species represent an obsolescence. Arc realized that it must have been like this at other periods of the earth's evolution, in the split-second transition between the extinction of one species and the arrival of another. Only this time it was the earth that was suspect. The future lay in space, the colonization of the stars, the inhabitation of the asteroid belt.

Johnny went back to the Mercedes at intervals to rest or snatch at another beer, drunk straight from the bottle. Arc imagined the label blown up to an apocalyptic logogram in the studio. Another terrestrial curio that might prove of interest to his three interplanetary visitors. They would all have to undergo cryonic repair to survive the ravages of subsequent millennia. He could imagine Bowie selecting stage costumes for his opening night on Phobos, the red moon that orbited Mars. Replicated earth-props would enthral the

Phobos mutants crouched to their life-size video screens.

Arc watched Johnny attempt to deepen the burial trench he had dug for Marilyn. Cindy and Zap were still interlocked in their inseparably weird embrace. It was as though they had died making love. The fourth figure remained resiliently acrobatic, inert but suppliant to however Johnny manoeuvred her anatomy. Arc realized that Johnny's partner was a doll. He straddled this fetish without penetrating her. He must have been saving the consummation for the last perverse rites.

Johnny threw down the shovel as though compelled to return to his guitar. His chords ascended a scale from gut-wrenched blues to melodic notes that might have been picked from a sitar. He appeared to be elegizing his drug-ruined body and the dead bodies he had accumulated around him.

Arc was getting it all on film. The camera gave him the power of pointing a gun. He was shooting history, micro-second by microsecond. He needed only Bowie to appear as a silver-jacketed mutant and the sequence could be worked into the Cape Kennedy films. Arc narrowed in on the increasingly bizarre ritual. Johnny was unpeeling his tight leather jeans and playing his cock like a light-fingered jazz pianist, the finger-points hitting the sensitized nerves. He was on his knees now, hunted by his own death. His nerves were beginning to slacken, something irreversible was closing in on him, the shutting down of his system from a misregulated overdose.

Arc remained silently filming, executing his documentary art with Warholian hauteur. He was detached; the lens was his unflinching eye on anything and everything that entered the camera's radius. Arc realized that Johnny must have been digging his own grave. He was within touching distance, lying down flat to freeze the dying man's collapse into himself.

Arc lifted Marilyn into the back of the wing-battered Mercedes and filmed the car from all angles. He would keep it as an exhibit, a symbol of Johnny's pathological obsessions. He needed to get back to his studio and work on constructs for his imaginary city.

Chapter 11

Her name was Xenia. He had found her, but at first she wouldn't stay, drifting in and out of his dimension, a visual illusion, a screen image such as he might have used in an early promotional video. Her black hair appeared to be blown away, even in the absolute calm. Her curves were moulded by an emerald-sequinned dress, a second skin that fitted each contour. She was silent, a transitional person like himself, someone who had stayed on in the ruins, attached to the place by memory associations, not yet willing to go. They were at the same state of transhuman mutation. They could take it a dimension further, adopt an android identity, the step forward that would relinquish earth ties, allow them to migrate to Diamond Nebula.

For a moment he found himself about to rehearse his old stage lines from the seventies. 'This song is called "Changes", and my name is David Bowie. Good evening.' It had become a presentation format in 1976, a means of stressing his own chameleonic identity.

Like him, Xenia had undergone the change by unconscious presentiments during the time she was living with Zap. At first she had hardly noticed the increased light that had resulted in intense migraines, back-brain zigzags which had her go off moody, uncommunicative, walking the beach for hours. She had feared schizophrenia, interpreting the intrusion of voices as a pathological symptom, an interference that messed with her clarity of thought, her fluency of expression. But the directness, the incisive relay to which she was subjected, assured her of its objectivity. There was nothing confused, contradictory or irrational about the messages. They were precise, formulative, exact in their information.

He sat looking at her across what had once been the television room in which she and Zap had watched videos, or stared at the panicked blue screen on which a late-night film had devolved into inevitable violence. He had come back to this house, knowing it was the place to which she would in time return. Her vibrations were here, the nerve-impulses that had dictated her human life, so too the tangible map of objects, clothes, personal items that had furnished that life.

They were near and far from each other, cut off from direct contact like two people attempting to emerge from shock, the earthquake scars visible around their feet. They were comfortably uncommunicative, cushioned by their isolation, each approaching the other with unhurried caution.

He kept on thinking about transitional states, and how people spent their lives fearing death, not realizing that the change-over had probably occurred unconsciously, years ago, so that they had already died but forgotten it in a black-out, dream, a momentary shift of consciousness.

He knew he should have tuned in to his interplanetary Walkman, days, hours ago. He was negotiating danger by severing communications. He was risking an intermediary state of psychosis, a world in which he belonged neither to the android nor human species. And in Xenia he saw the same non-polarized magnetic field, the drift of someone still undecided about whether to stay or go.

And they shared a metalanguage, speech and the commitment of images to thought processors. In that way they really could visualize the inside of each other's heads, translating thought into automatic concepts when language appeared to have exhausted its potential.

Xenia's change had led to her progressive alienation from Zap. Something within her demanded remove, dissociation, a period of intense solitude, heightened by sexual excesses, and for the latter she had picked out strangers, casual pick-ups in bars around the coast. She had been used on beaches, in alleys, the back-seats of cars, had simultaneously front and back by two men. It was a period of self-debasement, a valediction to the world of the senses. She had walked into a modelling interview by cracking open the zip on her tight skirt, arching her legs on the desk and letting the scene take over. Zap was the first tie she had to sever. The communications had helped her with this, they had placed her elsewhere, speaking right at her interior, signalling a response to the inner fictions she had left unrealized.

She told him of her first meeting with the aliens on the beach. They had instructed her to visit a deserted part of the coast. She had driven there in a white Lamborghini, time seeming to reverse into slipstream, the future opening out as uninhabited space, a telescopic dimension awaiting her on white sands. She had got there, her car radio no longer transmitting current pop, but the articulation of a voice filtered through pulsar frequencies. The voice had instructed her that her code name was PSR 1257 + 12, that Diamond Nebula was situated within the constellation of Virgo, fifteen hundred light-years away, one of three planets orbiting a fast-spinning neutron star.

She had walked out on to the beach and waited. She could hear radio emissions in the blue air. They demanded her attention against a backdrop of measured waves, surf pushing lazily across a flat gradient. From where she was she could make out the façade of the Grand Hotel further round the coast. A white, imposing landmark, a place she knew from fashion shoots, her body stepping out on to a balcony in a pink-sequinned bikini. She had done a session for *Vogue* there with Helmut Newton, another for *Harpers*, and one for *Playboy*.

157

Her instructor had materialized more as a voice than a personified presence. She had caught sight of two androids flitting in and out of vision; dressed in metallic blue and silver, they had only a millisecond permanence before intermittent fade-out.

She could feel the deacceleration of her pulse. Body-time as it was measured by heartbeats was altered out of recognition. The alternation of systole diastole was spaced over a long interval, one bass note resonating slowly through the body, to be succeeded much later by a rhythmic counterpart. And correspondingly her senses were changed, she could hear cosmic frequencies, a whole range of radio emissions transmitted by pulsars. And there was one in particular that connected with her audial field. It was the sound of what she had come to know as the planet Diamond Nebula. All random electron motions were edited out to permit a centralized incoming data. Interstellar transmission had found a direct lead to consciousness. Received signal strength grew to a constant pulsation, an indicator that the code had found a corresponding cell cluster in her brain.

And at the same time her body lost the restrictive parameters that she had conceived as its limitations. She had visualized an arm, a foot, her head, her quantifiable mass, and now these boundaries were meaningless, she was an extensible part of the galaxy, a directed energy flow in touch with a pulsar. Each conceptualized visual image stayed suspended, so that she could view a thought as though freezing it indefinitely on a screen. And whatever instruction was given her, was translated into a fractal image. The whole planet came close up, a violet, blue and green spheroid on which she could make out the populated areas, a detailed topography of the geometric blip constellated in her mind.

She didn't know how long she had stayed there on the sands. There was no conception of time. She had stepped into a parallel universe. A quantum jump had contacted the gravitational distortion that allowed her to live in space-time. It was like a tape winding backwards and forwards at the same millisecond, the audio-visuals neither regressing nor travelling into a recognizable future.

What Xenia couldn't find speech for, she committed to her thought processor. In that way he could read the complex structure of things that eluded language. Their communication was of the advanced nature he had conceived in his earth life. Drugs had given him a peculiar insight into other people's heads – a sense that there were no longer barriers, and that while someone was speaking to him he was really inside that language, behind it, proving the lie. There was no paranoia in his relations with Xenia, all sense of contrived or deceptive mind games had disappeared.

He was still occupied with rethinking his past. How and why events had happened. Was the android gene inherited, or was it an anomaly not dependent on implant but a tangential existence evolving from life-style, awareness, gender orientation, an expansion of consciousness into the extraterrestrial dimension? How uncertainly he'd begun as David Robert Jones, only he'd always been aware of an inner conviction, a purpose that had separated him from others. Only he didn't know what it was, this keeping himself apart, waiting for the unspecified change to happen. It was a microdot he couldn't locate in his brain cells. He had unconsciously prepared himself for the role he was to live out, even at school. His first incursions into music, his concerts at the Marquee and the Beckenham Arts Lab were the beginnings of a realization that was to gain in momentum until he had achieved his ultimate catharsis – the projection of the Ziggy Stardust persona.

Xenia was all that occupied his consciousness at present. She stood between him and the emptiness of space. She was only a stopping-off point, a terminal on his journey, but he had to pass through her in order to progress. They would meet again on Diamond Nebula, he was sure of that. The present was also an engagement with the past. He could sense in Xenia as in himself a gravitation to stay. He recollected the song 'Stay' he had written in the mid-period of his career. The lyrics, which had appeared ostensibly directed at an oblique love affair, had also served as a reminder to himself to live, distance his mind from excesses which threatened him with psychophysical dissolution. That concept had taken on a meaning he couldn't have anticipated. The choice of leaving one planet for another had never presented itself as a feasible option.

Xenia was re-earthing in her old surroundings. He could watch the associations flicker and connect, not so much curiosity as an awakening to facets of the past. It wasn't that she was trying to retrieve things she had forgotten, it was more that she was fascinated with how the new related to the old in terms of experience. She was looking to assess the power of combinations, one over the other. Engaged in a form of metalogic, her mind sighted details before sensory curiosity demanded validation by touch. It was enough to perceive the infrastructure of things, to formulate the image independent of the object observed. Ever since the voices had arrived in her head, she had understood the disparity between personal and collective vision, and how the informed arrived at the cosmic window with a self-created realization of externals, while the majority decided things in advance of their appearance according to a preconceived order of experience. Life on Diamond Nebula would be too immediate for earth consciousness. Johnny, Marilyn, Zap, Cindy had died in the intermediate state. Their body mechanisms hadn't adjusted to the change-over. Johnny's greed to siphon off intelligence had pathologized his mind. His killings were in part the result of a gene overdose. She remembered watching him in his room, her body invisible to his manic perception, his voice intoning a mantra to power, to deathlessness. She had seen his ego as a square, windowless black room. Each time he attempted to rush the walls, his body grew to the exact proportions of his confinement. Rage, ejaculation, altered chemical states, nothing could take him through and beyond.

Xenia watched Bowie reclining in a bucket chair. She felt the slow electroneural transmission pulse resonate through her nerves. Zap's death created no anxiety in her. She wondered if his neurology would be remastered on another planet, and if the stored sense impressions that had allowed him to create would live again as electric impulses charging a body. She played ideas into her thought processor. Zap,

160

automated without a biochemistry, threw up a white, tingling image on the screen. A shape, but compact, differentiated from space by reason of its being bounded, quantifiable. The image blanked out and was succeeded by a blue eye, as though that was all she would have remain of him, just a single reference point as a reminder before she began the journey away from a metabolized body. Initiation into the secret of death, as it was individualized according to the evolutionary progress of a habitable planet, would come later.

Xenia adjusted the control panel on her processor to rest cycle, and avoided further confrontation with death as the notion of image. She could see Bowie dragging on a cigarette, acquainting himself with the half-life of the experience, the inhalation no longer feeding the nerves. He had poured himself a tumbler of bourbon, his old habits persisting as shadow acts, theatricals to appease a subdued earth consciousness. She could sense his dormant eroticism finding central authority on a psychic plane. The curve of her bottom moulded to green sequins was one remove from physical contact. Subject to earth patterns, they would have already been intermeshed on the bed, her body undulating in a belly-dancer's rhythmic circles as she stretched towards orgasm. But a new order was instating itself by way of attraction, she could feel the rush of pheromones to her brain, the impression that he had stepped into her head, and was perfectly accommodated to that space in the way that her body would have fitted itself to his penis. On a cube-shaped screen in her head, she watched his hands release the zip along her spine, the motion pursuing all the way down across her bottom, so that she stepped out of the dress by standing still. He released the hook-and-eye fastenings on her bra, and she watched as the left hand slipped into the back of her black panties, and the right into the front. He sat down on a chair, lifted her by her bottom, and splayed her legs to either side of him. The rhythm was slow but exquisitely deep. She was lifted higher and higher with each demanding thrust. Each propulsion took her nearer to the unrestrained shriek which she knew was building inside her. And when the spasm came, it repeated itself, flooded her endlessly, left her head hanging over his shoulder like a wounded bird. And then the screen cut out, their miniature bodies were extinguished as visual images, her hands searched the abrading sequins sitting on her skin to assure herself it hadn't occurred physically.

She was still standing wide of him, disinterestedly staring out of the window, but a complicitous friction of shared energies vibrated from both their bodies. Her eyes encountered objects she had once thought indispensable to her existence – the stopped clock, the appointment book, the burgundy-coloured leather wallet in which she kept her credit cards. Everything had the air of historic deletion, a postmillennial amnesia had settled on the town. The open suitcase she had ransacked for immediate costume change, weeks, months, years ago, now seemed an improbable receptacle for travel. Bruised, bulky, an old Swiss Air label visible on the near side, the thing was consigned to the gradual dissolution of objects.

Bowie was absorbed in picking up signals on his interplanetary Walkman. At first she hadn't understood his curiosity to receive ETI transmissions from near the hydrogen line frequency. He was looking to establish contact with the sunlike stars – Epsilon Eridani and Tau Ceti. He used the spiral arm of the Milky Way as a keyboard, experimenting for accidental contact as though he were still in the studio, looking for the spontaneous dissonance of chords that made up his musical texture.

When Xenia looked round, he had left the room. She could hear him upstairs in the studio, his silver boots resounding on the wooden floor. She feared his withdrawal to a microcontinent situated in his mind. He had told her of schizoid informers in the galaxies, voices that leaked the news of cosmic imbalance, the approach of a catastrophic end to the earth. A rise in temperature causing galaxies and stars to dissolve into nuclei and radiation, and then to protons and neutrons, and finally to interacting quarks and leptons. He claimed that the idea of mental illness in aliens had been suppressed as part of disinformation. She imagined a scream issuing through her set, ululating dementia travelled all the way from Jupiter.

Her easy drift of thoughts was broken by an abrupt crackle of flame. An office block on the near horizon had jumped feet first into fire. Xenia could see an upward-growing creeper of flame lick from the inside to the outside of the first four floors, the smoke dragging, lifting to a black jet trail.

The raids were occurring with greater frequency. Xenia wondered if Arc were assassinating his own film-set, or if the terrorist hits were being conducted by the reconnaissance party from Jupiter. They would be systematically eliminating sectors of the town in the hope of forcing Bowie out into the open. The central fire was spreading to a supermarket adjacent to the high-rise. Flames were peeling the roof back, running like tigers across the flat surface. There must have been fires lit all the way round the coast.

Xenia could feel an increased frequency in the pulse directed to her from Diamond Nebula. It had doubled, trebled, was observable in the way palpitations would have been. It demanded her attention. She turned round from the window, hands instinctively supporting her head, and felt the transmission buzz alive. Something had gone very wrong. There was interference, as though a wrong connection had crossed with the frequency fed her by her planetary custodians. Her mind snowed silver with static. Billions of mathematical computations were happening each second within her receiving system. She wanted to be sick, but her body mechanism had dispensed with the discharge of poisons. Her panic accelerated; electricity was buzzing through her nerves. When the blizzarding static slowed, a head stepped out of it, a luminous ovoid, featureless until the blue membrane slit open to reveal eyes and a mouth. Xenia realized how these had been protected from the intense frequency shocks. There was no visible mouth, and no turning away from something addressing her from the inside.

She waited for contact, shocked that someone from so different a cultural frame should be constellated in her mind. And for a moment she was reconstructing fragments of her past, watching her earth body race across the beach, seeing her father's interrogative eyes scan her figure, doing in his mind what his instincts forbade him, and shocked, when on meeting Zap out shopping, he appeared to her as a stranger, as though marital ties existed only in the familiarity of their home. Out-takes from her life flashed in and out of consciousness.

Then the mouth came clear, was unzipped along four lines to form a rectangle. Her eyes were directed to this focal point. She had the feeling she was staring into an aperture that opened out to space. It was black inside, and constellations swarmed in the interior. The red one must have been Mars, a chip on a microscreen. She was still looking direct at the interior when the scream began. It started as a low-pitched, almost inaudible whine, increased to a shrillness that was uncomfortable but not intolerable, then grew in intensity until Xenia felt herself feet lifted, blown back across the room as though she had strayed on the airstrip at a point just behind a jet's open throttle ascent. She was stood outside the opposite window, static above the vertical drop, and by an inverse frequency of sound brought back into the room and deposited on the floor. The frequency could do with her what it wished. And as suddenly, it went dead. The face was out of her head; her body shook from the confrontation with this infiltrator.

Xenia wanted to go up to the studio and tell him of galactic psychos, weirdos who messed up frequencies, but she delayed, oscillating between two- and three-dimensional vision. She was paranoid that Bowie might have been instrumental to the experience she had undergone. What if he were an informer, an android whose concern it was to instigate mind games, planetary warfare conducted by sound frequencies, nerve viruses? She kept on wondering why he hadn't picked up on her crisis, his interplanetary Walkman should have informed him of her danger.

There wasn't any sound coming from the studio. The isolation was sealing her in, as though her existence were contracting to a self-contained biosphere. Xenia kept flipping in and out of old and new patterns. Part of her wanted to revert, to live again the sensually hedonistic life she had followed as a model, pouting for the photographer, strutting the catwalks in transparent tops, while the other part longed to rush out into the streets, join the party of looting aliens and adopt their identity.

She kept on being drawn back to the window that gave access to the street. There was someone out there, a figure in a blue helmet and a scuffed flying jacket was kneeling down staring into the wing mirror of a black Mercedes. The figure was fixated by the presented image. It had placed a compact transmitter by its side, and was curious to the exclusion of all other signals. Xenia could see a light pulsing in the miniature video screen, but the figure ignored it and continued to stare at its reflection.

Some sort of ritual was taking place. Xenia watched as two gloved hands removed the helmet, lifting it tentatively, revealing the facial ovoid she had confronted inside her head, the same undelineated consistency of blue membrane, only there was some sort of lesion at the back, as though the face was incomplete in its transhuman metamorphosis and still carried a symbolic blood wound. It was this that the alien brought up close to the mirror. A diagonal discolouration extended from the top of the head to a point above what would have been the left ear, only the latter was replaced by a retracted aperture. There was a sense of urgent fascination about the inquiry, and a secrecy attached to it, indicating that the alien had detached itself from the reconnaissance party in order to be alone. All incoming signals were being ignored in this act of intense scrutiny. The alien was recognizing an earlier existence, scar tissue that remained from brain surgery, or a wound acquired in the process of transpeciation. It was a prolonged moment of recognition, the head tilted forward as though remembering, the gesture one of concentrated recall. Then the helmet was placed back over the featureless membrane, the zipper checked on the flying jacket, the transmitter retrieved and consulted. The alien remained crouched down, one denimed knee raised, the other supporting the body. There were clearly no emergencies, for Xenia watched the figure orientate and disappear into the opposite house.

She felt unnerved, the area was being methodically searched, and she half expected to see the other three aliens arrive as back-up. She caught sight of the alien dispassionately scanning the contents of a second-floor conversion. Telephone, television, sound system, none of the technological innovations applied to each seemed of any significance to this polarized intelligence. She caught visual cut-ups of the search, the figure was looking for something independent of gadgetry, it was pursuing a tangent that suggested flashbacks to the human, a sensory field activated by association with blood. From Xenia's vantage-point the alien looked like a hydrocephalic insect blown up to human size and feeling its way towards some tiny association with memory. Several times it froze, cut a movement dead and appeared to be assimilating energy traces. All the more obvious reference points were avoided. Domestic objects went unitemized; the alien was cued to the invisible.

Xenia anticipated their arrival before they materialized. She could see the other three members of the group appear on foot, cautious, exploratory, working with the imprint of the territory. They had lost interest in cars and seemed dissociated from their surroundings. The three entered the building with militant authority. Xenia watched the party, detached, but unified by a stellar impulse, disappear into the house. She could see the android on the second floor panic, kill the idea of escape, and back off into the window end of the room. There was no attempt to avoid the confrontation. Xenia realized she was a voyeuristic party to a Jupiterian death hunt. It was like watching a sci-fi film, the events unfolding as visual dialogue. She watched the three form a triangle in the room, their spacing one of exact symmetry. The interrogated figure was being ordered to remove its helmet, the hands going up in slow motion, the surrender final, incriminating, the wound an instant exposed, and the liquidation immediate.

The three came back to the street. Xenia saw them look directly at the floor below her, marking the place as though they knew he was there, and that the time wasn't right to move in. She was aware they had been found out, and that

166

the party would return again after consultation with base.

She recalled Bowie speaking of video disks placed on board spacecraft launched towards Jupiter and Saturn on trajectories that would eventually shoot them out of the solar system. The sophisticated message would travel on through the galaxies until it was apprehended by extraterrestrials. Something of that sense of itinerant isolation had entered into Xenia. Bowie remained her only contact in a landscape ravaged by fire, policed by aliens dressed as street-wise vandals. She thought of Arc's neo-Dadaist mania, his obsession with Ballard's fiction, the pathological hubris that had him manipulate reality into a giant film-set.

The slow bass note of her received pulse from Diamond Nebula had her restabilize. The transmission was stimulating the production of endorphins in her chemistry. She was still confused by the notion of disembodied orgasm, thought processor relayed images, the transitional state in which she found herself. Something kept holding her back from rushing up to the studio and demanding Bowie's response to what she had seen. There were big jumping lights fizzing in from the skyline. Xenia was moving amongst reflected flame, her body chasing across cold shadows. In a human state, this would be madness, she told herself, but she was removed from emotional involvement by the gradual switch-over in her thought processes. In her mind she could see Zap wandering off into the desert, looking back at his butchered body, unsure of his direction, only that he was someone or something else now, an energy without the constraints of a physical body.

Xenia worked her way up the spiral stairs to the studio. She remembered how she and Zap had made love up there, her body arched on all fours on a wooden table while he entered her from behind. No matter how intensely he was involved in the interiority of a painting, he would leave off instantly as she entered the room wearing nothing but black suspenders and silk stockings, and the two beauty spots she had pencilled on her bottom.

She felt an opposing force testing her momentum. It was the same resistance she had known when swimming, the water imposing a density that was combative but fluent under physical pressure. She was going forward because that motion was marginally stronger than the backward tilt into a head-over-heels plummet down the stairs.

When she reached the door, her transmitter was flashing red, the emissions from her nerve impulses connecting all the way to a planet scintillating in Virgo. He was inside and had his back to her, he was crouched over the dead body of an alien, tracing a finger along the detailed map printed on a foreshortened back, the vertebrae pushed up high to accommodate the predominantly hunched posture of an interplanetary voyager.

Xenia realized instantly that there must be others. The reconnaissance party was either out to eliminate defectors, or it was one isolated unit from a series of landings along the coast.

Bowie didn't look up, he was too preoccupied by his search of the walk-in's body. The skin envelope was blue, and Xenia could see the outline of a microwave map shaped like a green heart drawn up in intricate detail on the alien's back. She wondered if the red spot at the left was Jupiter. Cosmic dimensions had been reduced to a compact heart in a circle.

He went on ignoring her presence, as though her vibrations were closed to the sealed rite in which he appeared to be conducting a ceremony with the dead alien. He had let go his thought processor, and Xenia watched images colour and disperse on the screen. He was lyricizing, animating the human and part-silicone intelligence that allowed him to exist between planets.

Xenia started to back off, the cerebral fractals transmitted by Bowie's mind were being sustained in image duration. They were mostly coloured red, the superimposed details standing out in blue and white, as though he were able voluntarily to isolate components of an image map. It was like cosmogony through impulses. He was transmitting back to source a visual relay of how thought is conceived. The informational singularities were being processed on Diamond Nebula, she assumed, a sequential library of four-dimensional thought replacing the randomized data generated by the multiverse.

Xenia was using her own thought processor to read his images. Death for him signified a black oval, the unrelieved pulsation deepening rather than expanding into fragmented split-offs. She interpreted these ten to twenty pulse meditations as unconceptualized reflections on death. And music wasn't entirely forgotten. Several times she encountered manic snatches of melody linked to thought associations that were too rapid in their transition to follow. Then he would return to the black void, stay there in the expectation that he could translate death into an intelligible vocabulary, before taking up with other, more immediate stimuli.

Xenia could hear him intoning. He was working himself into a trance state, officiating over this body with its failed life-support system, its metabolic regulations formulated in a code she imagined he would crack.

He had spoken to her in the past, when her own knowledge of mutant existence was only first realized, of life-forming compounds, the complex chains of molecules necessary to the human organism, the hydrogen-bonders nitrogen and oxygen, and of the possible chemical combinations needed to sustain beings on planets distinct as Diamond Nebula and Jupiter. He had spoken of low temperature liquid nitrogen oceans, and of life speeds altered by the absence of enzymes. He had told her that it would take Jupiterians weeks to digest the hamburger that humans metabolized within hours. He was constantly searching to resolve questions relating to interplanetary contact. She was frightened of his overreach, the manic voracity for knowledge that she hadn't yet acquired.

The body he stooped over was small, light, and probably concealed within a protective blue envelope. She didn't want to be there when he stripped it of the insulating membrane, the portable body-bag in which it was dressed. She feared alternatives to the human, the anatomical adjustments that she too would undergo in the journey away from this coastal town.

She watched Bowie conducting death rituals which were relayed to Diamond Nebula. His role appeared to be that of an informer, someone giving away secrets as to the qualitative

infrastructure of thought, the continuous blips that punctuated consciousness. Freeze-framing ideas had eluded science,
and Xenia was reminded of Dali's intention to invent a
thought camera, a mechanism that would isolate the autonomous image.

The atmosphere was too pressurized. Xenia took off her
shoes and ran back downstairs, collected a number of items
for her bag and hurried out to the street. Conspicuous in her
emerald sequins, she looked around for signs of the maraud-
ing aliens and hurried into a side-street. She could smell the
smoke hanging along the coast, a lazy black mushroom
roofing the white buildings.

Something had snapped within her. The code-name she had
been given, PSR 1257 + 12, seemed inoperative. There was more
of the human Xenia than the figure who had lived in a
state of disembodied transition before finding herself back in
the house she had shared with Zap. For the first time for as
long as she could remember, she was experiencing sweat
again, in runnels under her arms, chasers across her bottom.
It was as if she were running back into orientated consciousness, aware again of the earth biting her feet, of the solidity of
empty buildings surrounding her. And correspondingly she
was re-experiencing fear, submitting to a suggestive paranoia. She kept thinking they were behind her, or that one of
the three would be waiting at the end of an alley for her,
materializing slowly from a warehouse, the mask focused
directly on her eyes.

There was nowhere to run to, and she toyed with the idea
of taking a car and heading out to the coast. She was caught
between Bowie, Arc and the unknown. She didn't know how
long it was since she had last eaten. Her basic survival instincts had been attenuated by the frequencies fed into her
mind. She was afraid the face would return again and liquidate
her by the volume of its scream. Part of her wanted to revert to
human, the other was still excited by the prospect of bending
intelligence to a trajectory that linked with the stars.

She jumped back from a parked car, thinking an alien was
sitting there, watching her from the passenger seat. But it was

only a dark coat someone had left draped over the head support. Xenia couldn't rid herself of the obsession that she was being watched. And what if Bowie came after her, immobilizing her through his knowledge of transmitted frequencies? She anticipated autocombusting, the voltage burning her to a black, gristly core.

Xenia was beginning to feel a systolic beat assert itself in her diaphragm. The electric impulses feeding her heart were intermittently refunctioning, independent of the bass note reaching her from source. She could see a tassel of ignition keys left behind in the dashboard of a silver Montego. She marked the car for future reference, reassuring herself that mobility was at hand. Anxious to be free of her constricting dress, she entered a clothes shop opposite and wriggled into black leggings and a green cotton top.

When she got outside she heard something drop from a roof, a dead, untranslated echo that forced her into a doorway. She expected to see someone appear on a flat roof-top, a figure challenging her by its cold, automated response. She waited, and there was no uptake of the sound, there were no itemized footsteps moving in on her with a calculated, authoritarian suspense. She pushed out of the doorway, surprised by the intimation of music in the air, a recognizable snatch of Bowie's voice which she assumed was being relayed from the coast. It might have been the thunder of Arc's speakers, she told herself, his windows at the Grand Hotel open on an uninterrupted white beach. But it was nearer than that, the sound moved in and backed off, wanted to make itself known to her, adopted the insistence of a bird beating around her head, its point of attack never made clear.

Xenia picked her way along shop-fronts, using the line of parked cars to conceal her from the other side of the street. What she discovered dropped conspicuously on the pavement was a jewel-studded bird. The size of a town pigeon, its blue feathers were studded with minerals. The thing was still warm, as though it had just spiralled out of the sky, its life silenced on contact with the concrete. Xenia weighed the bird in her hands, holding it in the early stages of its death. And as she did so, she had visions of flying, she was streamlined, an avian dipping in and out of open windows, pursuing a trajectory above the beach, joined by a storm of birds similar to the one that was turning cold in her fingers.

She held on to the bird and continued to map out the precinct. It was a talisman reminding her of life, the pulse spots that throbbed beneath skin, blood in its coursing of veins. She would carry the bird with her towards the realization of a new future.

And as she continued down the street, she had the growing conviction that she was narrowing in on a personal apocalypse. She told herself that this time it would really happen, her mind would turn white with vision – she would step out of herself and the sea would rush back to her feet. Anything and everything was contained in her brain cells.

Once or twice her eye was drawn by an article of clothing in a shop window, but she hurried on in a state of animated trance. The urban and the immanent were fused in the weird chemistry of revelation. Nothing could stop her now. She knew that she was expected on the beach, the same abandoned cars still parked by the wrecked beach-huts, the Grand Hotel standing off as a possible headquarters to galactic control. She imagined she was the catalyst to change. On her arrival, Arc would throw his final self-annihilative switch, the beach would fulminate in white light, and out of the fragmented film-set a stranger called Ballard would come to meet her, followed by a new species.

She didn't know who had implanted this conception in her, only that she had to realize it. She was telescoping direct into the vision as she hurried forward. In her mind, she could hear the scream of the birds as they built to a dense, undulating cloud above the bay. Dramatically apocalyptic, they flew in and out of the Grand Hotel windows, long streamers of film attached to their beaks. They were dismantling Arc's projects, going off in a whip-curled parabola to a location further down the coast.

Xenia could see it happening. Orange fires stood like a mountain range in place of the town. The sky ceiling was cracking, and big blue spaces rushed in, clouds pushing over in leisurely convoys, the wind returning as an abstract force, lifting her hair, rushing the sand grains into ticking grit. She was living through her own reading of events, as though the dead bird had precipitated the autonomous stream of imagery colliding in her head. She wasn't afraid any longer. The idea of being apprehended by an alien psycho was no longer a threat. She knew her vision would carry her through, right to the end.

She moved quickly down a side-street, picked her way round chairs left outside a café, and joined the coast road. The houses were fewer there, the vegetation raffish, cars were spaced out like abandoned exhibits from a dead century. In another time, she would have picked up the iodine scent of the sea, the juniperish tang carried by a warm wind. But she was getting there, dodging impositions from her past, and replacing them by an imagined future. She was travelling into light, its abundance burnt inside her head. She imagined thousands of deck-chairs floating over in the sky, their old-world inhabitants dead, and then mountains, forests crashing through the clouds in their exit out of time.

Xenia broke into a run. The old blue and white boarded beach café seemed in its isolation to be a monitor station on Jupiter. She had the impression she had been here before, the information stored as a film-frame in her mind had recycled itself, and deposited her back in the past. If she stood still for long enough, everything she had ever known might come through, a continuous stream of consciousness flicking to an end before she blacked out.

She sat at one of the café's wooden tables and placed the jewelled bird beside her. An empty, lipstick-smudged glass was positioned next to a Heineken bottle. Whoever had sat here had been reading a summer 1990 edition of Paris *Vogue*. The cover model looked as if blueberries had been crushed into her lips as pigment to her bee-stung pout. Xenia was sitting amongst the remnants of a summer she must have lived through as someone else. Topless, sitting on the beach smoking a black Sobranie, men had circled her, sat off at a distance, searched for the eye contact she had never given them.

Lighters, cigarette packets, sun-glasses, the clutter of human ephemera was all that remained of that time. Xenia searched the mauve sky for birds. From her chair she could see the outline of the Grand Hotel in the distance. She half expected to see it lift off into the sky, a white cube moving effortlessly towards the horizon. But it stayed, a bizarre, surrealistically juxtaposed slab of stucco, something escaped from a Magritte painting to isolate itself on the sands.

Xenia rested. The excitement in her was burning up adrenalin. She would have to continue down a road flooded with vision. The world was re-creating itself in her head, formulating a new filmic vocabulary, a visual eschatology she would follow in its trail towards dead planets.

She got up and continued. Somewhere behind her she could hear a car negotiating a way through the alleys. It stopped and started like a wasp browsing over a bruised fruit. The driver was living off ricochets, bouncing the bodywork off parked cars, obstacles littering the street. She could hear the reckless, dull impacts stall the car temporarily, before the wheels shrieked on the uptake.

The panic in Xenia's head told her that she must get to the beach. Only there, revelation would occur. She would run out of a film-set into the new reality. She held the bird and got off the road, pressing herself back against the wooden boards of a bungalow.

She could hear the car getting nearer, a bug zipping from alley to alley, a tormented crescendo of dead metal tuned direct to her wavelength. It was like the thing had found her and was hunting her into the back of her head. And beyond her was the potential future, a curve leading away to the hundred billion stars on the galactic spiral.

Xenia sighted the dust-cloud. The car was enveloped by an energy field of sand glitter. Her vision shot towards it, as though mentally she was racing to throw herself under it, collide head on with its trajectory. She couldn't see the driver, the interior was screened by smoked glass. The thought flashed through her mind that the car was programmed to find her, automated to liquidate obstacles in its search to destroy.

174

Headlights on, a blue, bullet-nosed convertible negotiated a car slewed across the road, climbed into the air in avoiding a tip which had been dragged into a traffic obstructive position, shifted to a diagonal tangent, and screamed towards her, the streamlined bulk lifting to take in the pavement, the slight gradient to the garden, while Xenia hologrammed her energies into light, flew wide of the impacted metal tearing into a dry wood partition.

In her mind she was travelling faster than the speed of thought, she was overtaking her life and connecting with a future incarnation. When she came to rest, chin down on the hard dirt, the bird was still beside her. The car had come to a smoking halt, its savage assault having twisted it inside the living-room. Xenia expected to hear the roar of spontaneous combustion, but there was only the delayed breakage of objects dislodged by serial vibration.

She sat up in the aftermath to the crash, silence returning as though it had never been away. It was so quiet she could hear herself breathe. Hesitantly, expecting at any moment to encounter a whiplash blaze of lit fuel, she searched around for her transmitter, retrieved the incidentals scattered, and made her way towards the wrecked car. Her earth memory had her anticipate blood, multiple cranial lesions, the driver projected through the windscreen.

The room was littered with glass, upended furniture. A glass cabinet had fallen across the bonnet as the car made impact with the opposite wall. Chairs, tables were trashed, a black spill of oil was seeping into the wooden floor. Xenia was looking for the driver, knowing all the time that there wasn't one, and that the car's programmed death-run had been devised by Arc's computerized intelligence.

There was no one. A body's ejected flight path would have been obstructed by the facing wall. Xenia felt herself to be the targeted victim of a psychopathic mind. What if she were tracked by cars right across the open sands? She imagined a converging circle of self-automated cars closing in on her. The red one would take her from behind, the black one pick her off the front. They would play with her, lift her on to the bonnet and drop her again. She would begin running, only to be repursued, and they would force her into a complex geometry of moves as she struggled to reach the Grand Hotel. And when she dropped, it would be under the wheels, the car raking her across the sand, her bones cracked by each driverless vehicle in succession.

She dream-walked her way back to the road, listening out for a second car zigzagging through the town's outskirts before it homed in on her circuit. The atmosphere was charged with her waiting. Anything could happen. The sky could blow apart and drop on the town in heavy mauve fragments. She was free to meet the random chances that contrived the future, the possibility that thirty thousand parked cars might come in pursuit of her.

Xenia drifted towards the beach, a mutant decided on neither race, her transformative properties demanding completion. He didn't see her, although he was travelling on a parallel dimension. She could see him, although the divide was uncrossable. It was the same Bowie, his red hair pushed back in contradictory strands, his silver flying jacket open at the waist, his interplanetary communications system wired lightly to his body. She could have touched his hand, but it would have taken light years to do so. She supposed he had come out here to view the wrecked car and was now travelling on towards the Grand Hotel. He would use it as a headquarters for his race. There was no reaching him ever, but she felt assured now that the cars wouldn't launch an automated offensive. They were in parallel worlds, headed for the same destination.

Xenia could hear her heart beating in a normal rhythm again. The endlessly sustained pauses punctuated by a single bass note had disappeared. A new sense of vivifying euphoria was asserting itself in place of her uniform mood of alienation. She was headed for the new world. There was a big screen in the centre of the sky. She could see the dead on television. Arc was interviewing Warhol. When the picture phased out, she understood what it meant to die.

Chapter 12

Arc brought the window-smashed, crippled Mercedes to a halt in the hotel car-park. He had loaded the car boot with film and videotape; the back seat was glutted with cases of spirits and canned foods scooped from a supermarket. A humming-bird flickered across his vision, brushed on his consciousness like an eyelash.

Arc pushed his way through the giant hemlock, umbels big as radar dishes, which had formed a miniature forest at the back of the hotel. His mind kept on switching dimensions, jumping from time to space and back again. Who was that man at the top of the fire-escape looking down at him? It must be Ballard. An early arrival, checking out the possibilities of the cine-landscape, and how the desert could be better improved by the introduction of Brancusi sculptures. And that man down on one knee, the camera aimed at Arc's crotch; it had to be Warhol or a trick of the light. And was he hallucinating the figure descending out of the sky with flaming red hair?

He got inside and loaded his boxes by the elevator door. Arc was high on the realization that his life no longer intersected with anyone. He had dispensed with the idea of shooting films for the earth; it was with the galaxy that their future lay. His chosen subjects had all transcended the temporal and established a trajectory that aimed for the stars.

Arc pushed the lift button for his studio floor and shifted the film cartons into his room. When the door snapped shut behind him, it was like a signal to enter a trance state. Now that Marilyn was dead, he wanted to experience what it was like to be her. He put on one of her long blonde wigs, and free associated, imagining the electric tips of her fingers mapping out the nerve-points in his cock. He knew that even dead, she would still satisfy his extreme fetishes. Arc would keep on opening up the dimension of sexual transference between incongruous psychic planes. In the same way as he had created his own landscape, so he intended to make inroads into disembodied sex.

He could sense a friction coming alive in his stomach, energy lines were jabbing his penile nerves awake. For a moment he could feel Marilyn's lips begin to ingest him, then he was suffocating, resisting being dragged into a vortex. There was too much interference on the communication channels. Arc realized that he couldn't function psychologically without a camera. Unless he was creating the world he saw, he was being seen. He felt overexposed. What he couldn't manipulate visually, threatened. Marilyn might have too unlimited an access to him. Arc needed to quiet himself and begin filming again before he could go out to meet his arrivals. His mind buzzed with the conceptual architectonics of his future city.

Arc was beginning to notice a variation in the light. It was no longer so intensely violet. Leakage from the atmosphere was starting to find a way through. He thought he could hear an aircraft go over within hearing range, its flight course marginally up above the mauve ceiling. If there was still a world out there, he was alarmed by the possibility of its familiarity. The plane was receding, following a route along the coast, the passengers looking out, unaware of Arc's private videoscape, the animated zone he had established for extraterrestrial visitors.

Arc's camera was growing to be a gun. He needed to keep on shooting film in order to convince himself that he was alive. In time, he would remove Johnny's victims from the hotel freezer and have them buried in ice, before facilitating post-cryonic repair.

He had already photographed Marilyn dead. He had taken close-ups of her nasal bridge and red-glossed lips. Every detail of her physiognomical irregularities continued to fascinate him. He told himself that Warhol would find in her the perfect subject for perverse still-life portraiture. Andy would photograph the inside of her nostrils, the cavernous roof of her mouth, the dark forest leading to her anus. Transsexual necrophilia would appeal to Ballard's constant breaking down of sexual barriers. Arc considered the body to be obsolete. The humans included in his iconic pantheon would all have to undergo a biological mutation to aliens. Transcription factors produced by the cells would learn to recognize new DNA sequences, advanced genetic permutations leading to deathlessness.

Arc sensed the premonition of impending confrontation. He checked out the rooms on his studio floor. They were still the same ransacked rooms, only they appeared to admit too much light. He ran up the blinds on each, checked the adjoining bathrooms and locked each door with meticulous care. He took the elevator down a floor, and couldn't remember when he had last visited this wing of the hotel. And were there others unknown to him? What if the building had altered its dimensions to claim extra territory? He might discover extensions that led into space, a corridor that would take him direct to the heliport where arrivals would gather.

He was searching his mind to find out if he had constructed the hotel, and why the vinyl sacks in the corridors had been left standing there. He realized that he must have abandoned this floor a long time ago. The sacks contained disposable rubbish for burning on the beach. Or were they body-bags, prophylactics for Johnny's victims?

Arc shifted down to the second floor. The whirr of the descending elevator sounded a brief note of activation in a time-warp. The residents along this coast were either dead or waiting for the world to start up again. People might come pouring out of the desert, bits and pieces missing, with bloody bandages, imploring that they are not forgotten. They would see Arc as their healer, the one who could provide them with the model anatomy they were missing.

Blown-up publicity shots of Ballard, taken for his late seventies' books, stared back at him from the walls. Arc remembered printing the image light and dark, and the familiar black and white features of his understated cultural icon looked out of an isolated moment in 1977.

Arc felt safer here. He broke the seal on Room 89 and reacquainted himself with the evidence of Marilyn's reckless pilferings. Suitcases had been emptied and the contents spilled over a bed. Prosthetic devices had been prominently displayed on the bedside table; a black mamba, an equally conical vibrator. The contents of the room looked like *disjecta membra* blown out of a crashed aircraft.

Arc snapped random images, his mind incessantly plotting animation, his eye searching to register a continuous history of concept. What he recorded would become a documentation to the near planets. And someone journeying to this earth, thousands of years from now, would discover his photographs sealed in metal containers and begin all over again speculating on the last days of a species who had lived on this coast.

Arc entered a room further down the corridor and checked himself in the mirror. It was nearing the time when he would have to relinquish his solitude and initiate a working relationship with his mutant team. The black cashmere suit he was wearing, slashed by a silver belt, and his leopard-spotted boots accorded perfectly with his transitional role as a film director awaiting humanoids. His eyelids were dusted silver. In his symbolism it represented the colour of the future. Ballard would drive a silver car to the interior and return with news of a chromosomal formula for deathlessness, mutants waiting in the desert to exchange intravenously injected helium for cocaine.

The glare outside was beginning to seep into the hotel. Confronting it, Arc was reminded of emerging from the tail of an aircraft to meet brilliant white sunlight. He checked the monitor screen he had established in each corridor. The rectangle showed the same blank uniformity of sand, black rocks protuberantly poking through like sculpted fins. He found himself facing his own preconceived image, as though it were an X-ray of a thought. He nursed the vision of a future launching site, an interzone between his city and the galaxy. He had outgrown possibilities of human sensation. No amount of sex, drugs, filmic experimentation could appease his nerves in their quest for ultimate power. He would have to go beyond himself, be integrated by another species; he had exhausted his sensory repertoire.

Arc noticed the fissures zigzagging along ceiling and wall. The hotel was beginning to crack, as though the foundations had walked under an earth tremor. A crevice was written into the floor, a spine had furrowed the red carpet. Arc discovered footprints in the finely granulated plaster dust. They might have belonged to the last man to leave the hotel in a hurry. Outside, he would have dematerialized in the wind.

Arc stood and faced a landscape of his own creation. He stared out of the window at a beach receding to marine desert. And suddenly there were birds, a whip-coiled parabola translating itself into individuals, as wedges scattered across the sand, birds braking short on touch down, settling to agitated spurts, finally coming to rest and policing the area adjacent to the hotel. He could see the sparkles in their blue plumage, the mirror flashes shaken out of a lifted wing. Things were happening outside his control, a world of involuntary events was infiltrating his fixed system. Arc returned to the screen. He was convinced that in the desert he would discover Ballard's solitary heroes. Like him they would be searching for their author. And who was the Ballard who would arrive at the Grand Hotel to take part in the ultimate fiction, a reality constructed from his novels? His world of deranged film directors, brain-damaged astronauts, solitary protagonists exploring the frontiers of inner space would have become translated into a textural quality of life.

Arc found himself requisitioning memories. Buñuel's lost film had served as the initiating factor to extraterrestrial contact. He could see himself again editing and doctoring the incomplete document, finding somewhere a serial that suggested humanoids lived on the flip side of consciousness. They were walk-ins to the receptive. Marilyn hadn't been able to go far enough, she had reversed her progress, run back on herself. He could see her again sassing down the corridors, terrified of what they had invoked, but odd enough to go on with it, welcoming any species other than conformist humans. And Johnny, burning out with his ingrained narco-mania, sensing change, but retreating into a world in which the guitar was an extension of his pathological need to kill. Arc viewed their faces as if on a contact sheet. Zap, unable to adjust to the environmental changes, attempting to reorder a landscape that had vanished, internalizing his old habits, strung out as an intermediary between two uninhabitable planes of consciousness. And Cindy, moon-walking her way across the beach, transposing the contents of her mind to dramatic treatments, her short skirts no wider than belts as she went in search of her own imaginative reality. Arc wanted to live with the idea of their respective deaths, assimilate the possibilities before he let them go and affected his own change-over to deathlessness. He would have Marilyn conserved in ice, subjected to cryonic suspension before she was resurrected. He would perform the rites over her resuscitated body. A transsexual rebirth. Wherever her consciousness was now, it survived independent of his control. He imagined her in a dream state, unaware that her body was dead, the sequence of oneiric events running like continuous film. She was swimming underwater, discovering a statue between weed-forested reefs, picking the coral encrustations from its body, the eyes coming alive, starting to blink, showing green lights round their black pupils. She knew she was on a journey of discovery, only there seemed no stopping-point, no reference back to her sleep quota. She was encountering a lost city, inquiring of a race that materialized from the deep. Somnambulists came to her across the sea-bed, she opened their eyes by removing shells from the closed lids. She wasn't afraid, but her unconscious informed her of the lightness with which she travelled, as though she were out on a long lead of precisionally unravelled thought. There was no opposition, no weight of a body to retrieve her fluency.

Arc brought himself back from drift. He was feeling increasingly unnerved by the lateness of his arrivals. All the signs were there, but the beach was deserted. He wanted to people the screen with the advent of his new race. He was wired to start filming. His old headquarters was beginning to crack. He feared the building's dissolution would spread through his organism, and that he'd wake to discover an accelerated process of ageing had worked itself across his skin. He was paranoid about the possibilities of immediate age, seeing his skin collapse, shrivel, decompose in a matter of seconds. They would find him on the bathroom floor, a compact wrapper of skin that could be picked up and carried in the hands.

Arc's solitude was beginning to track him with malevolence. The pressure of it had built to the idea of a disembodied double. He could hear the other fixing a drink, taking a bath, riffling through papers at night. He was being pursued by someone who in time might subvert his power, demand his body, take over his identity. The parasitism on his energies was beginning to exhaust him. His double escaped the lens, eluded the complex system of running cameras he had set up in the hotel corridors. Once, he had apprehended a flash of blue light, an instant dematerialization as he had turned a corner on the fourth floor. It was like a brain conception – a psychic transference that tailed him with the cold detachment of an assassin. And if the process was reversed, Arc feared he would be his impostor's shadow. He would watch him sitting in a chair, snorting cocaine, debating on the risks to be taken in shooting a film about arrivals. And the exchange might go on indefinitely, one becoming the other, and in that way avoiding the issue of death, two halves dependent on paraphysical energies.

Arc vacillated between going out to the beach and maintaining his control at the studio. He had brought his microcontinent to the edge of the future. In his mind, the hotel was already transposed to another planet, it was a biosphere situated on Mars. He had still to visit the red canyons, the slopes of the massive volcano, Hecates Tholus, the three-dimensional acrologies built in place of two-dimensional conurbations, the pyramids approached by undulating foothills. Mesas, mortuary chambers, high-rise buildings free of blast shadow, Arc had the main city areas mapped out in his head. Biological constraints were no longer operative, the inhabitants were informed by indestructible genes. Arc would have Marilyn taken out to the hills, and there venerated as a transpeciated humanoid. And in aeons, reports would filter across the galaxy of earth escapees, those who had come to make their lives on other planets. Data in their sperm banks would be analysed for structural items, intraspecies selection, origins that suggested a planet away from earth and in orbit about the sun.

Arc was engaged in a ceremonial valediction to his colony. His mental window looked out on a new landscape. No longer inhibited by the perspective of linear, single-plane reality, he had entered a dimension in which imagination presided over the surreal. He was the heir to a building designed by Ernst, a baroque ruin honeycombed with mirrors, stashed with the works of Chirico, Dali, Tanguy, Picabia. Arc's studio was the archive for the lost novels of Poe, Lautréamont, Rimbaud. A discarnate hand that had continued with automatic writing since 1916, tracked endlessly across an unfailing ream of paper, caught up in the transcription of an inexhaustible poem. The bathrooms had windows by Chagall. Roses scrambled over the furniture, big cats lay on guard in the hall. In his bedroom he lay on a pink cloud for a cushion, one which changed colour from white to grey to red according to the dictates of light up above the mauve sky ceiling. He fed rats to the python he kept in Marilyn's old bedroom. He expected stones to flower and forests to walk out of the sea. Eagles would cluster round his camera; the wind would return in the form of an orphaned child, squeezing a rusty harmonica.

The light was reaching him with disquieting consistency. Again, he interpreted the flight path of a low-flying aircraft. He listened for the drop in its engines, the standing still before swinging into an arc, which would be the signs of a reconnaissance plane. But the vibration was travelling, making distance between him and it, buzzing inland, headed for one of the bigger towns at the interior.

Arc returned to image manipulation. The suprareality environment he had established would open up the channel to have him leave earth ties. He'd loaded film and his favourite 35 mm camera into a leather satchel. He was prepared to pull the plug on the system if communications broke down. He saw himself defending a last outpost, in the way Hitler had been driven into an underground bunker. His was the autocratic command that would either instate a new consciousness or burn out the first positive, interplanetary relations. Arc had attained cosmic intelligence, his discourse through image had superseded silicon devices. His power was in a circuit he could cut.

He was waiting. A self-created humanoid, he had outdistanced his own race. Reprisals were too negative. Once he got clear of his colony, received instructions, he would never come back to this planet. He would hear news of its death in a thousand years. An ash cone, revolving under an ultraviolet stratosphere, the last survivors dead in the high altitude zones, he would remember briefly his time there, as the information was received across the galaxy. He would recall intense, isolated moments, snatches of music, bedroom scenes with Marilyn, the conspiratorial atmosphere of darkrooms in which he had printed up still-life negatives, car rides along the coast, fellatio on the hotel diving-board, storms banging around the coast; and then the associations would be gone for ever. Already he was disconnecting himself from ties, programming his emotions to a set of dispassionate responses. He had survived the upheaval which had left the others as bodies stashed by a butcher in the deep freeze. He had arrived at a particular mental state that yogis backed out of, psychiatrists left uncharted, and the insane feared, for without his rational manipulation of the tuning, he would have joined the suicidal mad, the psychotic staring at a lion shaving a bone inside his head.

And suddenly the screen was coming alive. Two figures, side by side but apart, had entered direct into his visual field. They were still the length of the beach away, despite their walking between his eyes and into the room. He recognized the one on his left as Bowie, red hair and silver boots, while the other was an unidentifiable woman, black hair, proportionately curvaceous figure, hands clasping what looked to be a bird, its crumpled plumage lit by jewels. Arc was looking beyond them for Ballard and Warhol, expecting at any moment to register their arrival, followed in turn by those who had crossed the divide. It must be like that, he thought, when you're awaiting rescue. The idea of a face grows to be a reality, the imagined person steps out of the snow and seems to have been born for nothing else but to be present at that moment in time.

There was no communication between the advancing figures. They might have belonged to separate worlds, and Arc was quick to make the leap to the possibility of parallel dimensions. If this were the case, neither would know of the other's existence until each acclimatized to the possibilities presented by the Grand Hotel. It might take years for the two to join hands, get a tactile sense of each other's body, grow aware that they shared a language, a proximity, a skin surface that could be explored, brought alive by fingertips.

Arc waited on the curve of his own evolutive future, the angle of ascent increasing imperceptibly, the dazzle surrounding his private mythology standing round him as an aura. He could sense the firing of neurons in his double, the circular impulses emerging from the nervous system into the muscles, and back to the nerves via the sense organs. It was like the triggering of an assassin's gun.

He feared that if he left the hotel, his double would shoot

him dead on the sands. He'd walk out to welcome the infiltrators and crumple at a bullet fired with the silencer on, the lack of report making the event spookier. They'd find him leaking blood through an immaculate suit. Preserved in ice, he would be taken to Jupiter and resuscitated. But there would be brain-fade, impairment of memory, a dissociation from the events leading up to his death. Arc had accepted this as a possible concomitant of cryonics. Deoxygenation might cause partial amnesia; he had to keep living in order to make the transition to deathlessness.

The silence was building, packing him in like snow. The two advancing figures appeared to hang immobile in the backdrop. Arc was searching for others; he expected the screen to blacken with arrivals. Once the radio signal was out that walk-ins could get through, his colony would be invaded. They would come from all over the galaxy. He was feeding his tired nerves amphetamine, loading his circuit so as to keep alert to the possibilities of danger. None of the universal threats to the planet, like deforestation, desertification, water pollution, ozone depletion, Aids, had touched Arc's consciousness. He had disinherited carbon man for his conception of androids. No longer earth-bound as he was in his manner of thinking, his nervous system had adopted the interplanetary rootlessness of silicone devices, things whose natural habitat is space. Free of the constraints of gravity, Arc would discover areas of his mind that were sealed off from pre-death experience. He would walk direct into his dream. Giant fern and ginko trees forming a three-dimensional forest would serve as the initiatory threshold to a secret base. The lake surrounding the building was so concentratedly hallucinogenic that one millimetre of the solution represented a million times its equivalent in peyote. The miraculous swimmers lived in it, engaged in unending vision, swallowing the liquid, diving to meet cities exploding in orgasmic supernovas. Myths and cosmogonies occurred in that lake, civilizations erupted and simultaneously died. Arc imagined himself being rowed out in a glass-bottomed boat and pressing his face flat to the partition dividing him from unlimited creative turbulence.

On the screen now there were four distinct figures. Arc could make out Ballard, soberly dressed, the antithesis of Warhol, whose familiar platinum hair, jeans and tailored jacket remained with him as a post-death walk-in. The two seemed not to have noticed each other. Like Bowie and the woman observing a parallel dimension, neither showed signs of departing from a singular objective – the distance across the beach to the Grand Hotel. Arc, too, realized that he was living out of time with his arrivals. They appeared to be indefinitely suspended, as if their own progress wasn't relative to his conception of linear advance. Arc could feel his nerves shifting to overdrive, panic was setting off weird messages in his nervous system. He imagined running out to the beach and proving invisible to the four arriving here from different points in space. He would never reach them. He would light fires on the sands, which would go unobserved. He would watch them in motion day after day, year after year, travelling without pause, four figures who would never coincide with his own life. Hallucinated entities, they would grow to keep on walking inside his head. He feared never being able to erase the image of the fixed, peopled screen from his mind. His consciousness might come to adopt precisely those proportions. This was his idea of madness. A vision he would have to take with him to the stars.

Ballard was walking diagonally across Bowie's path, going off at an unpredictable tangent, as if distracted by a subjective event. Warhol was sitting on an oblong-shaped stone, loading his camera. He was taking in particulars of litter visible in the sand, candy wrappers, Coke and beer cans, flotsam jettisoned by the last sun-worshippers on this coast. Andy was sifting through ephemera, as though reacquainting himself with a forgotten past. He was examining objects with the naïve immediacy of a child. He was retrieving items for his satchel. A rhinestone brooch sparkled on his black lapel. His hair was the same unnatural white. No one ever got that platinum except in a dream. Arc watched his film mentor affect the same casualness he had adopted as the monosyllabic spokesman for the Factory generation. Death hadn't altered his external characteristics or outwardly modified his obsessions. Introspectively shy, he was none the less resolute about that in which he believed. Arc could see that sense of surety written in his features. He might have been away on vacation, taking a long spell of Indian summer in a villa on the coast, and was now back, still not anxious to summon his entourage, taking time out to explore the boundaries of his art. He was appraising the deconstruction of a civilization, a trashed culture by which he had grown fabulously rich. Now he would have to begin all over again, not as a designer of shoes and fashion accessories but as an emissary between planets, someone sorting through meteor dust, dead cities, looking for substance through which to define an extant or recolonized race. Arc watched Warhol's inquisitiveness, his constant rooting for clues to a new expression. There was so much to reclaim, re-evaluate. And Ballard had begun to do the same, only less obsessively. He seemed already to have adjusted to suprareality. Ballard's immediate acclimatization to a fictional landscape was confirmation to Arc that the imaginatively creative would experience little trouble in conditioning themselves to the change-over. They would cross from one extended state of reality to another.

Ballard too had paused and was taking in his surroundings. Arc had constructed a maze of elaborate arches, relying on *trompe-l'oeil* artifice, to serve as a screen between the beach and the town. Ballard stared at a jewelled column that appeared to lead to an autoscape of scrapped cars. A debris of twisted metal had been sculpted into a pyramidal monument to the machine age. Bits of Cadillacs, Chevrolets, Volvos, Buicks, Porsches, Citroëns were recognizable in the junk. A solitary figure, which might have been Vaughan, as the embodiment of psychopathic obsession in his novel *Crash*, had been crucified on top of the pile. A jagged, viciously serrated cross telescoped from the roof of an autopsied Bentley. The body was upside-down, thousands of car rivets peppering the abraded skin. The carcass was an open sore, the man's long hair twisted into a plait of caked blood.

Ballard stood there, unshocked by his discovery. The

entrance to another arch, which appeared to recede into a diminishing perspective, showed a series of Hollywood models grouped round a black-tiled swimming-pool. Dressed in sequinned thongs, the girls were collectively drawn to a single red leather leg swimming across the surface of the water. No other part of a body was visible, just a detached leg propelling itself from one length of the pool to the other. Ballard stood there, looking on, noting the action as though he were editing information for a novel, his mind compelled to return to a singularly fascinating image.

Arc picked up on Bowie's movements. Making no headway in his journey across the sands, the singer was sitting, hands locked together, eyes directed towards that interlocking cat's-cradle of fingers, at the entrance to a strategic arch. A leopard slept by one of the columns, and by the other a black mamba the size of a pine tree was penetrating the image of an oriental girl's bottom. When Bowie got up and investigated the view inside the arch he was confronted by the façade of a building covered by reflective glass. The mirror surface showed fractal images, cloudscapes shaped like ribbed canyons, a black ovoid planet standing off in space, a vulva open to reveal an eye, in the foreground. A depersonalized dimension, the futuristic intimations suggested by the imagery had Bowie take up a position at a central viewing-point. The leopard continued to sleep. Time stood still as it does in the silence of a painting. He knew he would never reach the building, that it existed as an idea that would forever elude him. He retreated back to the remains of a sand-castle, fluffed out of glitter, its turrets partially collapsed, matchsticks forming flagpoles on the battlements. It represented a symbol of the naïve past. He had travelled a long way and was waiting to return to his people. His interplanetary Walkman would instruct him how to proceed.

Arc watched Bowie contemplate the immediate within whatever time-zone he was experiencing. What Arc detected wasn't so much resignation as disinterest in his surroundings. Bowie was consulting compact gadgetry he kept in his stars-and-stripes jacket. He seemed to have abandoned his march on the hotel, and the unidentified woman had stopped short too, her hands thrown up at the entrance to an arch in which two headless figures were shaking hands on the steps to a square, windowless building. She stood frozen in the moment of apprehension, shocked into immobility.

Arc monitored the console. The four figures were all temporarily suspended in their progress. Quadruple universes that could be extended to billions of individual awarenesses. He was obsessed with the notion that no two individuals had ever shared an experience in common. The isolation implied by human consciousness found a corresponding degree of separation in death.

Arc wanted to question Warhol about death and to learn from Bowie the secret of deathlessness. He himself was one of the immutable race. When his heart slowed down to ten beats a minute, and his respiration acquired the slow rhythm of hibernatory mammals, then he knew the transition would come. Cellular decay, organic dissolution, would be corrected. He would adopt the time-scale of indigenous Martian evolution. He would explore impact craters on the red plains, disappear through one planetary skylight into another. He saw death as the psychological product of humans, a preconception transferred from one generation to another, thereby instating an artificial time-clock in the genes. Free of earth, Arc knew that his consciousness would expand to accommodate life across the galaxy.

Arc kept his focus directed on Ballard. The novelist was writing the landscape into his head. But the process was different from temporal writing, for the quantum leap into imaginary space was met direct by his surroundings. He was adjusting to this. Instead of having to create externals, he was reversing the order, assimilating the dream contents Arc had established as a videoscape, and editing factors out in order to impose a sense of his own inner space. Arc watched the transformation taking place. Ballard was learning a sense of mental balance. Warhol was still inquisitive, but the changeover from death demanded a more complex approach, an earthing experience that suprareality did little to provide. Andy was still living on the surface of things. His hands had become reflecting mirrors for every small thing that invited his obsessive curiosity. A child had abandoned a rubber duck, close to a red and white striped towel, and Andy was entering into a conspiratorial dialogue with the toy, personalizing it as though he were reliving a tiny fragment of his childhood. He went from thing to thing, rather than assimilate the landscape in entirety. Once he had exhausted the associations, so he moved on. His path across the beach was erratic and dilatory. He paid attention to nothing but immediate apprehension. His findings were inexhaustible – a can, a shoe, a tube of Ambre Solaire, paperback books, Walkmans, handbags, hold-alls, magazines, cigarette-stubs, newspapers. Each contained the individual narrative in which he could read the expression of his former life. He was connecting again in the manner of someone restringing a necklace. He needed the sparkles to shine like a piece acquired from one of his long ago shopping expeditions to Bloomingdale's.

Arc refocused on Bowie's movements. The latter was consulting a pocket gadget and appeared to be processing direct thought. His preoccupation with this excluded further discovery. He must have been checking his inner and outer orientation. Most landscapes must have appeared possible to him after the change-over to being an android. He got up and headed for another arch: the way through presented an industrial forest, a metal labyrinth in which iron stacks escalated above equally metallic buildings. In a near quadrangle two cars were mounted on a plinth, as though joined in a weird coitus, the bonnet of one raised to the rear of the other. The whole place was sealed by an air of impenetrability. Its steel interfaces presided over absolute silence. Even the water in the municipal fountain basin had solidified to metal. He stood there contemplating the dull glare of the metallic streets, and backed away, unwilling to lose himself in a town in which metal birds sat on the roof-tops. He appeared not lost but searching for the way forward to Arc's base, that white hotel which had suddenly become obscured by a maze of possible entries. The hotel had come to represent in his mind the same sort of temporary refuge he had found in an apartment in Berlin in 1977.

Arc watched Bowie equivocate. Perhaps he was picking up on the presence of others, for the screen was suddenly snowing with birds. They wheeled over in a jewelled, clustering wedge. Arc saw Xenia launch the dead bird from her arms, throw it into the air, the feathers catching, the upward spiral immediate. It flew away quickly to join the blackening mob.

And now others were coming. Arc watched two Range Rovers arrive on the beach, high suspension bouncing the wheels over loose pebbles. Aliens, dressed to resemble the paramilitary, jumped out of the two vehicles. Arc counted ten of them. They assembled in a loose circle, faces concealed, except for eye-slits, their manner diffident, impersonal, their information fed to them by radio bands. Their gestures were automatic. They appeared to be receiving collective instructions, squatting down, extensions of the one source, primed for action.

Arc was facing the materialization of his inner world. There was plenty of time to remove the bodies from the freezer, to photograph the maniacal lesions administered to the skin, as a form of post-death body art. Memory blocks had him forget so much. Was it he or Johnny who had performed weird rites on these butchered victims? Arc couldn't account for so many days spent exploring the hotel's expansive labyrinth. What he had done had escaped being stored in his memory cells. There were events belonging to no one, an automaton might have bloodied his hands in the hotel kitchen, and gone on distracted, walking out across the sands in a time-warp, to return much later, oblivious of anything but his own obsessive need to be the progenitor of a new race. It would take Arc millennia to decode his brain cells, to scrutinize hypnotherapeutic discoveries, the linked associations allowing him to relive the past and, by his distance from it, deepen his sense of accelerating through the future.

Arc left the screen and took the elevator up to his studio. Since the first raid by alien infiltrators, and the pilfering of the Bowie video *Transbiological Mutations*, Arc had taken to devising methods of disinformation. He had stored visuals within counter-visuals, protecting the image by a superimposing fractal. He loaded his research discs into an aluminium attaché case, checked the contents of his medical case, and looked over the chests he had prepared for shipment: his cameras, film archives, the stash of valuables that he and Marilyn had taken from the hotel safe, the journals he had kept as a record of his life in the suprareal videoscape.

Again he found himself unconsciously looking up, as though he could see the aircraft mentally through the studio ceiling. This time it appeared lower, the engines modulated, so that the sound droned, hung off and reverberated, took up a circular course, the flight path aimed above the hotel, and was now returning to make a closer inspection. He could feel the vibrations come alive in the stucco walls. Objects were jumping on the near table; a minor earthquake temporarily threatened the roof. This time Arc sensed the flaw that had opened up in his biosphere. They were closing in. Someone had cracked the videoscape, and the pilot must have been looking down at the coast, the yellow shock of sunflowers, the giant thistles and ferns telescoping up towards the sky. The pilot would have seen the labyrinthine maze Arc had constructed, the imaginary cities leading to no conclusive interior. He would have mistaken the Grand Hotel for still another illusion in the complex, metamorphic kinetics of a coastal landscape. Arc imagined the pilot freaking out at sight of the interminable desert, the masses dead in their search for refuge, meteorites spotting the surface, no one around, but the pressurized atmosphere building above the sands.

They would never find him. He assured himself of his invulnerability. Even if they sent in a landing party, they would come up against the same obstacle of incongruous time-zones as his alien arrivals. His accessibility was no more apparent than the dead. They could shoot him from point-blank range and it would be a simulacrum which dropped. The autopsy would show a body without organs, someone composed of anti-matter. Arc was high on his own sense of deathlessness. He would go out to the beach and locate Ballard, and having once enlisted the novelist in his supreme design, together they would attract Bowie, and lastly Warhol, whose subtle interrelationship between planes had to be treated with psychic deference. The girl would be the last to occupy his immediate concerns. They would elude the alien reconnaissance party. Where they were travelling was outside the latter's scope of location.

Arc felt the anticipation build within him. He had been waiting for this for centuries. In his mind he had lived for ever, he had burnt out reincarnation after reincarnation, left them littered as shells on the floor, as he quickly assumed a new body, another identity. He was part of the deathless ones, like asteroids generating new stars in the spiral galaxy. He hunted around for last-minute collectables, objects that might serve to remind him in the distant future of his life at the Grand Hotel. He selected a pair of Marilyn's red stilettos; she would look for them after she had undergone cryonic resuscitation. He heaped an assortment of her jeans and sequinned skirts into a suitcase and placed it beside his archival repositories. Marilyn's sense of *outré* panache would remain as a predominant characteristic on whatever planet she lived in the near future. His mind kept returning to the paramilitary who had arrived in Range Rovers. He was sure they couldn't crack the seal to reach him. They would hurry across the beach and enter into one of the illusory time-zones established by his videoscape. Their progress towards his headquarters would be on an infinite curve, with no reverse contraction of the spiral returning them to their starting-point. They would hang suspended like flies in his web. They would see him as a cat does a fish in a bowl, as motion from which they were divided and could never apprehend. He would personally guide his select arrivals through the optical labyrinth.

Arc heard the glass explode before he was conscious of the simultaneous gun-shot. A star-shaped fissure stood out in the studio window. His dementia told him it was nothing. If the patrol was closing in on him, he would dematerialize. They would end up shooting at nothing. He could be on the other side, watching their pointless attempts to assassinate nobody. He picked up a splintered shard of glass and turned it over in his hand. He didn't bleed on contact with the serrated edges.

He had gone beyond that. His transphysical body was impervious to cuts. Part of him wanted to go out on to the balcony and offer himself as a target to the infiltrators. He would dress for it, put on one of Marilyn's clinging, sequinned skirts, and flaunt his indestructibility. He would walk out through the planetary invaders and secure Ballard's attention. In the course of that hour he would retrieve Bowie and Warhol. He would go back for the girl, an expedition that would be repeated whenever a walk-in showed on the screen. At a given moment, he would liquidate his enemies, but not until he had sufficiently demonstrated the facility of parallel worlds. He needed to be seen but never touched.

Arc moved around the studio with rapid gestures. His database of expert systems had been established with technical mastery. He wanted to ship his findings, no matter the technological advances he might discover on the inhabited planets. There was an attachment to his surroundings he hadn't anticipated, a sense of abandonment that stuck despite his exhilaration at the prospect of breakthrough.

He went back to the screen. They were really there. He saw Bowie flick his hair back, his gesture stylized, conscious, as though he knew he was under camera scrutiny. And Warhol was walking with a surer direction towards the hotel, his initial fascination with ephemera gone, his eye picking up on the skyline. Arc reassured himself that Ballard was still within view. The novelist was snapping a lighter to an angled cigarette: his mind was recording incidentals of the dream landscape. Arc conceived of the action as magnetized tape, a little coil transmitting messages to the memory cells. He wished he could relay the accumulated contents of Ballard's mind in a speeded-up series of visuals – a lifetime's imagery exploding across the screen as billions of implosive supernovas. Arc wanted personally to experience this. It would be the equivalent of a sustained and accelerated acid trip, every crystallized image stored by the novelist, encountered as replay. The novel would be replaced by a laser disc recording the intrinsic excitement of creativity. Videos of the process would come to exist as an interplanetary language. Arc could see himself editing the contents of Bowie's mind, Warhol's, the experimentalists on Mars, Pluto, Jupiter. It would be his ongoing project in the spiral journey through the galaxy.

The sound was returning again, the irascible drone of engines, coming closer this time, so that he assessed the flight path was at roof-top level. The engines appeared to be fanning the building, thugging the glass in the frames, a wall of sound moving inwards inside his head. Arc knew he was untouchably located in a parallel universe coexisting with the pilot's own, but accessible only through tangential points. He would go outside and crack the entry codes to admit his heroes. He imagined himself disappearing from base in a craft operated by reverse electromagnetism, the speed of getaway allowing no chance to the inert helicopters bugging the sky above the beach. One after the other they would crumple in flames, their metallic debris detonated across the inshore reefs and sands. Arc was laughing maniacally. He startled himself into silence and the belief that the mania was generated by his double. The other one was pursuing him with increasing vigilance. His body was heavier for the double's taking refuge in him, his thoughts were beginning to split along a line, a dual sequence that created a double concept of vision. He had received audial instructions about future catastrophes on earth. He had been told that the land masses comprising Canada, the Great Lakes and the Mississippi to the Gulf of Mexico into Central America would be changed. The tilting of land to the east would throw up mountains along the central states. The Aegean Sea would recede in the manner of the sea in Arc's videoscape, revealing subaqueous pyramids, landmarks to a future species who would claim the earth. Only the inhabitants of parallel universes would survive. He imagined the Hollywood megastars attempting to colonize the suprareal – Michael Jackson, Madonna, Elizabeth Taylor, a convoy of chauffeured limousines heading into the mountains towards a given location. They would migrate on a bronzed afternoon, a mist coming in from the Pacific, their cars loaded with jewels, costumes, memorabilia, a cortège driven towards a state of perpetual unreality, Michael Jackson lifting a gold-braided sleeve to salute the death of stardom in the old world, the advent of fame in the new one.

And all over the world, the message would reach the select ones. Colonization of parallel worlds would begin, isolated pockets would establish themselves in the busiest quarters of cities, and in the wilderness of the American deserts, the rain forests. Arc would return to visit them. They too would find the inner trajectory to the stars. Remote mineral constellations, previously only inexpertly glimpsed in the night sky, would take up clear residence in the brain cells, become identifiable future homes to suprareal devotees.

Arc was nearing that breakthrough. The demonstrability of it was a private, internalized thing. Going beyond humans entailed the sort of loneliness that few ever experienced, it involved an implicit trust in his alien guides. He left the studio and stood in the baroque bathroom attached to his suite. The gold taps were in the form of dolphins. He stood there facing his mutant body, burying the human reflection, watching his skin radiate silver. He splashed himself in Oscar de la Renta, lifting on the pungent woodiness, feeling his nerves respond to the cooling stimulus. He had stood here so often, ritualized the process of identity by staring his image into distortion. Now he let the transformation work itself out in full. He watched his facial planes adopt a perfect androgynous symmetry. The lines under his eyes, and those mapped idiosyncratically across areas of his face as an expression of ageing, were erased for contourless skin. The lips were sensuously reshaped to resemble a triangle of dark cherries. Immediate telemedical repair was happening to his entire body. He was acquiring the curves that no cosmetic surgery could provide, waist, hips, legs, his flat chest emphasizing the exactness of his proportions. He continued to watch his metamorphosis. The transbiological mutation was removing him from all contact with the earth. If the patrol got into the hotel, they wouldn't find him. Instead, they would be confronted by a humanoid who would pass invulnerably through them and begin his journey across the beach to retrieve his chosen arrivals.

Arc stepped back, complete. His green eyes were like a cat's staring out of aluminized features. He could have been making up for a cyborg shoot; eight robots positioned round a table, the central exhibit, a computer showing astronomical formula. He had lived through a long period of preparation to arrive at this state of transformation. All the old UFO findings that had gone into *Project Blue Book*, all the information about sightings assembled under high security in the Blue Room were intimations of the world he had discovered.

In the bathroom, he was insulated from helicopter reverberations. This room was the last of his inner sanctums, he told himself. From it he would emerge as the undisputed leader of suprareality. And in time he would return to the earth and visit the colonies established by others who had anticipated a future of transbiological mutation. And one by one they would evolve sufficiently to make the journey across the galaxy in pursuit of new and higher life forms. He would narrate to Michael Jackson his excavations of the pyramid cities on Mars, his observations of the Cydonia Complex, the subtleties of telepathic sex in which he would engage with Marilyn in transport stations across the red planet. Arc's mind buzzed with anticipation, he was anxious to have outdistanced a future he had still to experience. Parallel processing had allowed him to connect with the android dream, a neural circuitry that had demanded a new body to further its advance.

He stayed a long time, measuring his transformation to alien life. The helicopter – or were there several? – had gone off on a slow reconnaissance movement. He knew it would return, the pilot opening throttle, a trail of bullets punched against the studio glass. They were attempting to liquidate the idea of Arc and not the person.

When he came out of the bathroom, he checked the screen. His three arrivals were grouped together. Whatever their separate existences, their isolated dimensions, they had discovered each other. He had them as a triptych. Ballard, Bowie, Warhol. They stood together casually, as though isolated by the camera lens, Ballard standing right profile on, listening to Warhol speak, who seemed in turn to be on the uptake from a remark dropped by Bowie. The girl was still approaching in the background, delayed by having encountered a mirrored cactus projecting from the sand, its spines impaling thousands of exotic butterflies, its central column rotating towards its own miniature satelliting sun.

Arc had achieved his temporal objective. He slung a satchel over his shoulder and, armed with his camera, stepped into the elevator. The night porter must have been murdered a long time ago. The automatic had been casually discarded on the desk-top. A brain-flash told Arc that if he had carried out the killing, it didn't matter. There was no link between his past and future. What awaited him was so apocalyptically amazing that death was a thing of no significance. He knew he would meet them all again somewhere in the light-years.

As he stepped out of the foyer's revolving doors, he could hear music. Dissonant guitars travelled down the air waves. The sound was building for the singer's intro. And the sky was suddenly blue, a transparent cerulean with a few oblong white clouds going over. Arc checked his camera to make sure it was loaded. This time there was no mistaking the helicopter, switching direction and swinging towards him on a lowered descent. Arc could see the pilot at the controls, the co-pilot scanning the white sands. It was like a film. They were watching him. They stood off directly above him in an alarmingly clear sky. Arc kept on filming the helicopter, which went off on a wide circle into the vacant day.

A PETER OWEN PAPERBACK